Promise of Magic
House of Xannon 3

Copyright © 2014 Melinda VanLone.

All rights reserved.

Published by: WrittenHouse Publishing, Rockville, MD

ISBN-13: 978-0-9887455-4-4

ISBN-10: 0988745542

Cover Illustration: Carrie Osborne
Cover design and book layout: Book Cover Corner, bookcovercorner.com

VanLone, Melinda.

Promise of Magic / Melinda VanLone

Visit the author website: melindavan.com

To my mother,
who walked through fire to save her son.

And to all the mothers who would make the same choice.

PROMISE OF MAGIC

HOUSE OF XANNON BOOK 3

Melinda VanLone

WrittenHouse Publishing
Tallahassee, Florida

1

Tarian Xannon lay curled in a fetal position on the bed and clutched her stomach as another jolt of pain rocketed through her. She sucked in air, wincing. The invasion from the inside couldn't be over soon enough as far as she was concerned. She'd never felt so out of control of her body. *I'm only five months. Surely it's not supposed to hurt like this.*

She took several deep breaths until the pain died away, snuggled further into the pillows, and stared at the ceiling. The covers had been kicked to the floor since the Pacific Ocean breeze did nothing to cool her internal temperature. Neither did the fans or the magical cooling her sister added in the room. *I swear, I'm burning from the inside out.*

Deep. Breath. Look at the ceiling. Focus on the happy leaves and ridiculously charming scene. I'm a kid in my room without a care in the world. She snorted. Yeah, right. When she was a child, the ceiling mural had been her escape whenever things were annoying or hurtful. If she was angry, she found comfort in the flowing, leafy tendrils. If she was sad, the happy little fairies cheered her up. Now that she was pregnant, surely the mural would take pity on her uncomfortable, out-of-sorts mood. At the very least it should take her mind off the kicking, squirming, soccer match going on inside her stomach.

Her eyes watered as another jolt wracked her body.

The ceiling mocked her. Green leaves twined around trees and grass, with the hint of a pond peeking through and tiny, blinking eyes that glowed when the lights were low. They almost looked like stars. She'd spent hours making patterns out of them, but today they formed curse words.

Another kick brought her right up off the pillows. She clutched her stomach and grimaced. "Dammit, kid, knock it off." Her voice sounded thin in the still night. *Great. Now I'm talking to an empty room. Perfect.*

Nobody had mentioned kicks from a tiny baby would hurt this much. The healers told her it would be little flutters. Her sister had explained it as butterfly kisses.

"Butterfly kisses my ass," Tarian muttered.

So much for resting. Everyone kept insisting she take it easy. But every time she tried all she got for her trouble was bruised ribs and worry. Better to stay busy. Better to feel useful. *Better to get some sort of control over my own damn body functions.*

Tarian rose and pulled on jeans, wrinkling her nose at the broad, elastic waistband. She'd never worried much about fashion but these were the ugliest things she'd ever seen. The stretchy material at the top accommodated her growing waistline but not the growing fear of motherhood. If anything, it pointed out how very real the pregnancy was, and how very out of sorts her body had become.

She reached for the black men's T-shirt wadded up at the foot of the bed and buried her nose in it. It smelled like spice, nature, and man. One particular man. She took another whiff. *Daric.* It was one of the few good things about this whole pregnancy gig. Her enhanced sense of smell made everything so intense. Sometimes that wasn't a good thing, but with her nose in one of Daric's shirts, it was.

Tarian slid the shirt on over a bra that encased breasts that couldn't possibly be hers. It reached her mid-thigh, and nicely hid the horrible jeans. She stared at herself in the mirror, noticing hair stuck out from rolling around in the bed and a belly that looked like she'd swallowed a beach ball.

She snorted. "If that's a beach ball, then I'm the net in a very twisted volleyball tournament."

A tiny foot showed itself along the side of her stomach. She stretched out the fabric of the shirt, and watched the foot in the mirror with fascination, fear, and repulsion. *It's just not normal. There's an alien growing in my stomach.*

Pregnancy makes you stronger, not weaker.

The words, spoken by a daemon who'd washed up on Xannon beach, chided her. *Macari couldn't have been over sixteen, what does she know?*

The shock of finding a daemon in their private, warded domain had been overridden by the dolphin's insistence that Tarian and her unborn child would need the girl someday. They'd told her the daemon girl carried something vital that must be protected.

It'd been vital all right. *Fire Artifact.* One of only four artifacts in existence. *Talk about rare.* Despite the strange circumstances and the mystery surrounding Macari's mission, Tarian had liked the daemon girl. Macari was a blend of summer breeze and mountain sunshine. Though she'd obviously been abused during her time on the human plane, she hadn't let it dampen her determination or spirit.

There's a lot to be said for someone who can come through trauma with her soul and spirit intact.

Macari had been sent to spy on Tarian and her unborn child. She'd figured out that much. *But why?* Macari left before Tarian could learn any details. The young daemon had been tortured, and her bonding with the Fire Artifact obviously hadn't been smooth. Tarian hadn't wanted to detain her for questioning. *I doubt I could have stopped her from leaving. She was pure Air, more power than anything I've sensed before. She stepped onto our beach like the shields didn't exist. Like the wards and protections were nothing but vapor.*

It'd given Alex and Frankie fits. Since Macari's visit, they'd spent every day working on stronger shields. But without an air daemon to use for a test, nobody knew if the new wards would do anything at all.

Tarian rubbed the foot shoved against her stomach. The foot pushed against her hand, and a pulse of magic tickled the hair on the back of her arm. *The baby sure has a lot of raw, undirected power.* Baby. The word drifted through her, surreal, like it belonged to someone else.

The foot moved away and then kicked, sending another jolt through her lower body. Tarian hissed, then turned her back on the mirror. If she couldn't sit still, she might as well find something useful to do.

"Thanks for nothing," she told the ceiling, then opened her door and stepped out into the hallway.

2

As Tarian left the bedroom, armed guards snapped to attention and watched her with a mixture of expectation and fear.

"Keeper." One of them saluted, snapping his heels together in a military style click.

She groaned out loud as she slammed the door, and stomped past them without making eye contact. Their disapproval echoed in the clomp-clomp-clomp of boots that followed her down the hallway. *I wonder if they'd leave me alone if I moved into Mother's rooms?*

So far, she'd refused. It just didn't feel right to make herself at home in the place that her mother had lived all her life. Moving into those rooms meant truly stepping into her mother's shoes and she just didn't feel ready.

Alex, not only her advisor and longest childhood friend but also one of the fathers to her child, assigned these guards to shadow her every move. They were meant to protect both her and her unborn child. *The future depends on you, chica.*

Right. What he means is, in case you decide to sneak out. She snorted. *He's hoping to drive me to Mother's rooms by sheer force of numbers.* There looked to be over two dozen Sentinels, all armed and ready for battle, placed up and down the hallway with a few more pacing the length of it. She knew there were still more outside, patrolling the outer walls. *Talk about overkill.*

Having a baby seemed to suddenly give everyone permission to tell her what to do, what to eat, and where to go, while simultaneously taking the rest of her free will and stuffing it in a bag shoved into her belly labeled "Do not open for nine months." As if she suddenly couldn't function, or defend herself, just because she was growing another person.

Ridiculous. Tarian felt more powerful than she ever had in her entire life. Between surges from the baby and her own intensified energy, she felt like she could take on just about anything and anyone. The healers had explained pregnancy hormones increased magical energy, though they'd never seen this much of a surge before.

It's the baby. She's somehow adding to it.

If Tarian could study her own aura, she was sure she'd see power radiating off her in waves. *Macari was right. I don't even have to focus to make a portal anymore. If I had to fight someone right now, I'd win. No question. As long as I don't have to kick. Damn belly is in the way.*

Tarian flexed a hand and pulled a bit of power, letting it flow out and into a ball of blue light in front of her. The ball kept pace with her, lighting the floor brighter than anything she'd ever produced. It didn't drain her in the slightest.

She paused mid-stride, closed her eyes and felt for her sister's signal. It leapt immediately to the forefront of her mind. *Good. She's still awake. In the archives, of course.* Tarian turned down the next hallway, trying her best to ignore the crunching of boots on the floor behind her.

Four more months of this?

She reached the archives and pushed the door open. As she expected, Calliope sat at the center table, surrounded by books and shrouded in a pool of light from table lamps. With one hand Calliope pointed at the book lying open in front of her. With the other she held onto the paw of one of the Archivists. The gargoyle, which looked more like a cross between a monkey and a dog, scrunched his face, as though upset about something.

Curious, Tarian crossed the room, pulled up a chair, and let out an audible grunt and a fart as she sat down.

Great.

Calliope turned toward her but held up a finger. *It must be some discussion they're having.* Tarian looked at the open book. The *Book of Daemon.* Of course. Her sister had been studying it non-stop ever since Tarian had made her deal with the archivists.

"You may study the Book of Daemon as long as the Caraigg remain captive." That was the deal.

It would take a lifetime to really understand the book. *Hope she managed to learn something useful.*

Her promise to the Caraigg bound her in ways the Archivists didn't seem to appreciate, but the time had come to fulfill it. The baby was so strong, so early. The Caraigg had promised to protect them all, and Tarian had a feeling she was going to need their services. She wanted them in place before the baby was born. Not to mention, it just felt right. There was no logical reason to delay. No matter what the Archivists said. They kept trying to offer her ways out of her Agreement.

I don't want out. I owe the Caraigg. I promised. Simple as that.

They'd saved her, when they didn't have to, in exchange for her promise to free them when she was able. She would not disrespect the Caraigg by leaving them to rot in that horrible place. They guarded a Stulos, one of the pillars keeping the planes of existence separate so that daemon could not mingle with humans. The column of power sucked all the heat and magic from the surroundings, effectively trapping anyone with magic and at the same time fueling itself.

The Caraigg, Earth Ancients, should be among the strongest magical beings. Instead, the Stulos continuously siphoned their power away as some sort of punishment for something they never explained. They'd lived in suspended animation in that cave for thousands of years. *It's not life. It's existence. A miserable one.* Whatever they'd done, she was sure they'd more than paid the price for it.

She shivered, despite the raging furnace her body had become thanks to the baby. The infant kicked her in response. Tarian grunted, then rubbed her belly.

"You aren't calm, and it's making her fussy." Calliope's soft voice interrupted her thoughts and made her jump.

"She's being a pain in the...stomach. It's nothing to do with me."

Calliope reached over and placed both hands on Tarian's stomach. "She's not the only one who's fussy." Calliope closed her eyes and began to hum. Warmth spread from her sister's hands through her stomach, to the baby, to Tarian's very core. Peace flowed with it until both she and the child relaxed.

"Thanks." She let her eyes close and relished the calm that overtook her stomach. "I think she's sleeping now."

"You should be doing the same. Why aren't you?"

"She was kicking me."

Calliope arched an eyebrow. "That's it?"

Tarian rubbed her stomach. "It felt like an entire soccer team." She carefully avoided making eye contact with her sister. Calliope always knew when she was holding something back. The truth was she didn't exactly know why she'd sought out her sister's company, and not knowing bothered her more than she'd admit.

"She only has two feet." Calliope snorted, then turned serious. "Does it seem odd to you? She seems so...advanced."

"I don't know. What's normal for a baby her age?" Tarian avoided eye contact. *She's definitely not normal. She's a frankenbaby made up of piece parts from two yummy men and one arrogant daemon. Never mind who her mother is. She's anything but normal.*

Calliope leaned back, the worried furrow between her eyes deeper than it had been, but said nothing.

Tarian shrugged, then pointed at the book. "You ready? You did say you'd have the rest of the spell translated today, right?"

"I think so. I'm waiting for Ms. V. to contact me."

Tarian grunted. "What's the holdup?"

"No holdup. She's just checking a couple of the more

difficult lines. We need to get this right the first time, Tari. A lot's at stake."

"You don't have to tell me." Tarian rubbed her stomach again then snatched her hands away and pressed them firmly into the table. She couldn't seem to keep her hands off her extended belly. It was really annoying. "How long? Think I have time for a swim?"

Calliope shook her head, a grin tickling the corners of her mouth. She took a breath as if to speak, then paused as she obviously sorted through her words. "It's the middle of the night, Tari. Go swim if it'll help calm you. We won't hear anything for a few hours. I'm sure Mrs. V is sleeping. She's not exactly young anymore."

"Bet she'd be pissed off to hear you say it."

Calliope giggled. "She'd agree with me."

Tarian's lips twitched. Mrs. V had been their tutor for most of their childhood. She had a soft Irish accent and a twinkle in her eyes most of the time, finding humor in nearly every situation. "She probably would. Since I'm up anyway, tell me what you know so far."

Calliope sighed. "If it'll help ease your mind I can give you a bit of background. The Stulos that holds the Caraigg captive is, I think, the element Earth. It's one of four. They hold the daemon plane separate from the human one, with the Between in the middle as a buffer. That part is in all the books, even the old histories."

Tarian nodded, relaxing into the chair. Her sister's voice soothed the restlessness she'd felt laying in bed with nothing but her own thoughts and a kicking baby.

Calliope tapped the open book. "This tells us that the only way to free the guardians of a Stulos is to destroy the Stulos itself."

Tarian frowned. "So what happens when I do that? Apart from freeing the Caraigg."

Calliope glanced at the Archivists waiting in a patient row near the stacks of books. "The end of the world?"

"Seriously?" Tarian snorted. "I doubt that. What would

be the point of freedom if the world ended? The Caraigg surely don't wish that. I didn't get evil intent from them. Trust me, it would've been hard to hide something like that, with our minds connected."

"Well, the Archivists seem to think so. But really, I don't think the removal of one Stulos is enough. It'd be like taking out a table leg…the table would still stand, it'd just be wobbly."

Tarian pictured that in her mind. "There's still the Between, too. So, what will it really do?"

Calliope shrugged. "It doesn't say. It's never been attempted, Tari. Though…"

Tarian tilted her head, encouraging her sister to continue.

Calliope flipped several pages. She stopped on a page etched with a beautifully embossed drawing. "I don't think the split was meant to last forever. Not really. The elements…they aren't meant to be apart like this. They're meant to be in balance. At least, I think that's what this image means."

Tarian leaned forward to study the picture. Symbols for Earth, Air, Fire, Water, joined in the middle by yet another symbol she didn't recognize that twined its way around the others to create a unified whole, surrounded by stars.

"I get that. Makes sense. So if the split wasn't meant to be permanent, why are the Stulos still there?"

"Probably because nobody has ever tried to remove them. Nobody ever had a need, before."

"They had a need. But nobody was listening." Tarian grunted as she leaned back in her chair. "Trust me. Nobody wants to be stuck in that cave. Nobody."

Calliope bit her lip as she stared at the drawing. Tarian followed her gaze. "What?"

"Nothing. I just get the feeling…there's more to the story. Something between the lines. Or even, some*one*."

"Like who?"

Calliope flipped a few more pages. "History is very clear on the fact that the planes were split. But not why. There's no record of exactly how it was done, or who did it. And...I get the feeling that the why and the who are very important. Especially for someone wanting to break a Stulos."

Calliope turned to face Tarian, her eyes filled with concern. "It's not a small thing we're doing. And I don't think we can know exactly what the consequences will be."

Tarian took Calliope's hands in her own and squeezed. "Like you said, the table will still stand. And we'll have the Caraigg as allies. Plus the dolphins. That's water, and earth. Plus us. It'll be okay."

"Maybe."

Tarian smiled encouragingly at her sister. "What's the worst that could happen?"

"Don't ask. The Archivists keep filling my head with scenarios."

"Then ask a different question."

"Like?"

"What's the *best* that could happen? Because that's what I'm hoping for. Freeing Ancients from captivity. That has to be a good thing. It feels...right." At the still worried expression wrinkling Calliope's forehead, Tarian continued. "Calli, I promised."

"I know." Calliope squeezed Tarian's hands before releasing them to brush back her hair and offer a small smile. "If you're going to try to break a Stulos, you need to get some rest."

Tarian sighed. "Fine. I'll float for a bit and see if I can get back to sleep. You should probably get some sleep too. You know I can't do this without you."

Calliope made a non-committal noise and glanced down at Tarian's bulging belly. "I asked the Archivists about the baby. She feels so strong. Not like the other babies I've felt before."

Tarian pushed herself up off the chair with a grunt, leading with her stomach. "You haven't been around that many babies."

"There's plenty in the daycare. A lot of the Sentinels have to bring their kids when they do a long shift. I help out." The indignant look on Calliope's face reminded Tarian that her little sister had a life all her own. They weren't at each other's side 24/7 anymore. "She feels different. I can't explain it."

"Well, she *is* different." Tarian lowered her voice. "You know she is."

"Don't you wonder what the outcome will be?" Calliope's forehead formed an eleven in between her eyebrows again. "Mixing pure air daemon essence with our own? Especially if it's true you already have daemon blood as it is. That'd make her…"

"I know, Calli." Tarian held up a hand to stop her sister. "There's nothing I can do about it now. It's done. I can only move forward."

"But if we knew what it meant, you might be able to plan."

"Plan what, exactly?"

Calliope shrugged. "Anyway, you should think about how you're going to announce it."

"Announce what?" Tarian frowned.

Calliope stared at her. "Her parentage is not going to be a secret forever."

"Why not? Have you told someone?"

"Of course not." Calliope pointed to the Archivist near her. "But they already know. They can hear her just as loudly as I can. Which means the Caraigg probably already know, because of the hive mind thing. Or will, when you release them. If I can feel her, and Daric can feel her, what's to stop someone else from feeling her too? There's bound to be questions. You can't keep something like this a secret. The second she's born, everyone will know she's different."

A wave of dread, which she quickly tried to quash, washed over Tarian. The baby mercifully remained asleep.

Calliope pressed her lips together. "Her talent is unique. I can't get a grasp on it but it's unlike anything I've ever felt. She isn't just strong, Tari. She *projects*. Even at five months. What'll she be capable of when she gets her full strength?"

Tarian shuddered. What indeed? *I won't be the strongest anymore. She will.*

Tarian put her hand on her stomach again. If the baby

were born with so much excess energy, how would they ever teach her to control it before something was destroyed in a fit of baby tantrum?

"She needs a name."

Calliope furrowed her eyebrows in confusion. "What?"

"The baby. She needs a name. I keep calling her 'baby' in my head and that's just not right. If nothing else, I can give her a really great name."

Calliope sighed. "That's what brought you here. You aren't worried about collapsing a Stulos or freeing the Caraigg. You're worried about whether you'll be a good mother." She stood and put her hands on Tarian's arms. "Tari, you're going to be a great mom. Stop worrying."

"Then you stop worrying about how fast she's growing."

Calliope frowned. A cloud passed over her face and quickly cleared. Her sister smiled then, an expression that looked more worried than happy.

"See? I thought so. This whole being a responsible adult thing really sucks. I liked it better when I chased down criminals all day. At least I knew what to expect."

Calliope gave her arms a comforting squeeze. "Go see the dolphins. They'll help soothe you to sleep."

"Maybe." Tarian smiled at her sister then waddled toward the door. When she glanced back, Calliope had already bent her head back over the *Book of Daemon*. It looked like her sister was trying to copy the entire book before it was yanked out of her hands. Tarian felt a stab of guilt at the thought. *My fault. She'll lose access to the book of her dreams when I keep my promise.*

3

Tarian left the Archives and marched out of the house with the footsteps of a dozen Sentinels trailing behind her. Since Macari had popped out of nowhere right in the middle of the beach they hadn't even let her lounge on the sand alone, much less swim. Before Macari, they'd hidden their presence in the rocks and never ventured into the water. She'd felt them, their energy signatures reaching her from around the rocks like the tentacles of an octopus. After Macari's visit, the Sentinels weren't bothering to hide. She tried her best to ignore them but how was she supposed to relax with so many clustered around her, standing at attention while she lounged? *Makes me feel lazy. And trapped.* The ocean, however, remained a sanctuary because none of them could keep up with her when she swam. At least pregnancy wasn't a factor in the water.

Outside, the fresh air and ocean waves soothed her mood a bit. She stood on the beach for a few minutes, absorbing the stillness and moonlight. In the far distance, the lights of Honolulu danced. The sight of something so normal helped to settle her nerves a fraction. Regular people, going about their lives doing regular types of things.

Sometimes it sure would be nice to be one of them.

Tarian shook her head and shoved that thought firmly away. Despite the stab of envy brought on by the thought of a less complicated life, she wouldn't give up magic for anything in the world.

Well, very few things.

Tarian rubbed her stomach again. *I'd give up just about anything to make sure she has a good life.* Surprised at the sentiment, she rolled her eyes. *These hormones are turning me into a drama queen.*

She needed to be in the water. Water was the only place she felt like herself these days. A dolphin call, lonely in the night air, caught her attention and brought a smile.

Roger.

Her oldest friend. The Ancient and his entire pod had been with her through every part of her life so far. Now that she was pregnant, they'd remained even closer to shore than normal, eager to share the journey to motherhood with her. *That, or they're aquatic Sentinels. The baby couldn't have a better set of guardians.*

Tarian tucked her thumbs into the band of her jeans to pull them down, then hesitated. Glancing behind, she saw Sentinels lined up and down the beach. They carefully scanned in all directions, alert for any possible threat, though she caught a few sneaking a startled glance in her direction.

I miss my privacy.

She sighed, then pushed the jeans off anyway. Her shirt was plenty long, and the maternity underwear covered far more than any bikini. She could go fetch a bathing suit but the thought of trying to get it on irritated her.

They'll get over it.

She shrugged, reaching under the T-shirt to undo the megabra she wore. Slipping each strap off her shoulders and through her shirtsleeves, she dropped it to sand with the jeans and waded into the water.

"Keeper?" One of the Sentinels had joined her while she stripped. He coughed and politely looked out to sea instead of studying her legs.

"It's just a quick swim. With the pod." Tarian pointed. "See?

I'll be perfectly safe."

"We can't follow you there, Keeper. We can't do our jobs." The man still refused to look at her.

"You're welcome to try. I'm slow these days, you could probably keep up." She grinned and waded into the lapping waves. "Don't look so put out. I'll be right back. Roger won't let anything happen to me."

Ignoring further protests, she stepped deeper into the oncoming waves. When she'd made it far enough, she dove in, shirt billowing out around her. Water took her hair and massaged it. The sea welcomed her, and through the waves her friends did as well, with clicks and dolphin shouts and a few tumbles in the air.

A burst of pure joy flooded through her. Startled, she realized it wasn't just her own jubilation at being free for a minute or two, but the baby's as well. The girl loved the water. Even though she wasn't exactly swimming in it herself.

Or I suppose she is, sort of. There in her little cocoon.

Tarian rubbed her stomach and grinned. *I love it too, baby girl.*

She rolled onto her back, letting the waves lift her up, then down, in an undulating rhythm that soothed and comforted. The guards on shore stared after her in consternation.

Beside her, Roger poked his nose at her, making contact with her hand. Through the brief touch he sent an image: Tarian, surrounded by dolphins, a feeling of joy and hope linking them into one unit.

Tarian hooked an arm around his fin and let Roger escort her below the waves. It was second nature to slip a shield around herself, to provide air and keep the water out of her lungs. Roger extended a shield as well, his natural aura adding a layer of protection around her that he usually didn't extend. *It's the baby. He's buffering her.*

Below, several more of the pod waited to greet her. They circled and nudged, each extending a welcome to her and the baby. Each touch filled her with a bit of raw power, a gift. They wanted to make sure she was healthy, that the baby was strong.

No worries there. She's stronger than she has a right to be.

Worry at what that might mean interrupted the happy bonding moment. As if sensing her mood change, the dolphins slowed and formed a circle around her, with an opening to one side as though in anticipation of a visitor.

Curious, Tarian waited, her hair and shirt floating out away from her in the waves. They'd gone deep enough that the overhead moonlight was lost. The only light was a natural glow from a few sea creatures and luminescent plants. The dark pressed in on her. She trusted the dolphins. They'd never let harm come to her. But the impending sense of *something* ate away at her nerves. She fought the urge to create a ball of light to chase away the shadows. Based in fire, it wouldn't work well under water, and would be considered an insult.

Instead, she hugged her stomach and waited.

Through the gap, a dark figure emerged. As it undulated closer, she realized what, and who, it was.

The Old Woman.

She gasped, even though here she made no real sound.

She'd seen the Ancient only once, on her naming day. The oldest dolphin in existence, rumor was she guarded some treasure deep below and never came up to the surface.

Yet here she is.

Tarian waited, filled with awe. Memories of childhood games involving threats to tell the Old Woman filled her head. She'd assumed, as she reached adulthood and went on with her life, that the Old Woman was dead. Ancients didn't really live forever. They weren't gods. They just existed on a different timeline. She hadn't seen any evidence of the Old Woman at her mother's funeral, but hadn't expected to.

Didn't even think about it.

The notion that she'd ignored someone so important made her uncomfortable, as though she'd done something wrong. She shifted in the water, brushing the T-shirt down with both hands in an attempt to look dignified.

When the giant Ancient reached her, Tarian bowed her head in greeting and extended a hand palm up. If the creature wanted to talk with her, she'd put her nose there. Tarian could only hear them if they physically touched. Dolphin minds communicated mostly with pictures and emotions, woven into ethereal music reminiscent of sea sounds.

The Old Woman bobbed her head, moving slowly past Tarian's outstretched hand, to place her nose gently along Tarian's stomach.

For a moment, all Tarian sensed was a greeting. A pleased, proud expression that made her smile. Directed at her first, then at the baby.

One word filtered through the emotion.

Hope.

An image followed. The Old Woman, circling a glowing, nearly transparent column of water extending from an outcropping of rock. The place didn't look familiar. The glow alternated from blue to green, like the sea, and undulated from bright to dark and back again.

Around it, several dolphins circled, endlessly.

Tired. Weak.

If she hadn't been floating in water, Tarian knew she'd be crying. The despair, no, not quite the right word…exhaustion…so palpable. It tore her heart.

How can I help? Tarian asked in her mind.

For an answer, the Old Woman merely nudged her gently, and with the nudge pushed a wave of pure water-based power through Tarian, her energy surging even higher than it had already from the pregnancy hormones. The effect was heady, euphoric. The baby jiggled and kicked. She absorbed the energy and responded with delight, despite the ripple of worry Tarian felt at what should be an overload of power. *No baby should be able to handle this much energy.*

The Old Woman sent an image then, of the Dolphin Throne. The medallion hovered above the chair it usually occupied, glowing as it revolved before descending. It slammed into her, embedding itself in her chest. Tarian felt the strength of the ocean cascading over her, and a deep burn as the medallion wiggled its way into her flesh. She slapped her hand over the spot, wincing. But when she lifted the shirt to look, nothing was there. The burning sensation slowly faded, but the image remained in her mind.

Promise. Urgent.

The Old Woman nodded, then slowly turned and floated away. The others circled Tarian once more, though now they urged her to the surface. Visions of the beach, wind in the trees, and herself gasping for air filled her mind. The message was clear. *Right. Time to go.*

How long was I down here?

As they slowly ascended, she realized how far they'd gone. It shouldn't be possible without special equipment, and certainly not something a pregnant woman should attempt. And yet she felt fine, the baby wiggled and kicked as always, and the dolphins clearly did not feel she was in danger.

When her head broke the waves, sun bathed her face and shoulders. She gazed at the bright sky, stunned. On the shore, a large group of Sentinels stared at her. Alex stood in front of them, his arms crossed over his chest tapping his foot. Several Sentinels pointed when they saw her. A few shouts reached her ears but she couldn't tell what they said. The look on Alex's face said it all.

She'd been gone the entire night.

4

"What the hell were you thinking?" Alex huffed next to her while she dried off. He'd brought a towel and a change of clothes for her. The Sentinels formed a wall so that she could change in relative privacy. *A changing booth, made of men.* She giggled with the thought.

What the hell! I don't giggle.

"I was thinking it'd be nice to go for a swim." Another giggle escaped unbidden. She slapped a hand over her mouth to stop any more.

Alex narrowed his eyes as he held out a fresh shirt. "You been drinking, *chica?*"

She laughed. "No." She took off the sodden shirt that clung to overlarge breasts and belly like a slug, then slipped the dry one Alex offered over her head and let it fall around her. "I think I'm stoned."

"You smoke something?" Alex's voice rose a few octaves.

Tarian laughed again. She couldn't help it. And it definitely wasn't normal. "How would I smoke under water, Alex? Really."

Tarian snatched the dry jeans out of his hands and giggled as a fresh pair of panties tumbled to the sand. She left them there and simply slipped the jeans on instead. *No way sand is crawling into my lady bits. I'd never get it out, not with this stomach in the way.*

The thought nearly doubled her over with laughter. Tears streamed down her face. As she tried to collect herself she noticed several of the Sentinels exchanging glances, and Alex's face contorted in a frown of worry.

"I'm fine." She took a few deep breaths, struggling to regain her composure. Inside her, the baby squiggled. Tarian grabbed her stomach. It felt hot to the touch, and power radiated outward like wildfire.

"Tari," Alex said softly.

Tarian shook her head. "Not here. Inside. I need to see Calli."

Alex barked a few orders to the Sentinels and the group parted to let them through. She heard a few whispers, quickly hushed.

They'll be talking about this for months.

It was all she could do to put one foot in front of the other. Her legs felt like she'd been running a marathon, and her arms dangled like she'd deadlifted a thousand pounds and now couldn't lift a finger. She felt heavy. Spent. Her stomach, stretched like an overfilled balloon. Her back and neck screamed.

What did the Old Woman do to me? Too much power. I'm holding too much. Why'd she do this?

"Focus on your breathing, Tari."

She eyed Alex. "Since when are you into yoga?"

Alex's lips twitched. "They say that to all pregnant ladies. Seriously, you ain't breathing. Take a deep breath."

She obeyed, then for good measure took a few more deep, cleansing breaths as they walked. Most of the Sentinels dropped out of the procession when they reached the receiving hall. She hesitated, quickly checking for Calliope's signature. She found it almost before she thought of it.

Holy crap. Strong. I could find anyone right now. Startled, she checked for Daric, just to test the theory. She found his signature easily. He was in Boston with his mother, Ms. V. She could feel him as though his arms were around her, and just make out the room full of books he stood in.

She stumbled, and Alex's grip on her arm tightened. "You need a healer."

"I need Calli." Tarian clenched her teeth, and resolutely

marched forward.

Alex escorted her with his hand on her elbow.

Tarian glanced at his face. If he furrowed his eyebrows any more they'd stick like that. She poked him on the shoulder, like she used to do. He rewarded her with a ghost of a smile, but otherwise remained deadly serious.

They reached the archive door. Alex put a hand on the door to stop her from opening it. She turned to give him a questioning look. Energy, exhaustion, jubilation, and worry warred inside her for attention.

Alex narrowed his eyes as he studied her. "What's going on, *chica*?"

"I'm not sure." Tarian licked her lips. "The baby was restless, and I thought a quick swim might calm both of us down."

Alex drummed his fingers on the door. "And?"

"It did. In a manner of speaking." Tarian rubbed her stomach with her free hand. She could feel energy pulsing from her body in waves. It made the hair on her arms and the back of her neck tingle, and giggles threaten to erupt again. *How can he not feel this?*

"You look like you got a fever. You need a healer." Alex's jaw set.

"I need my sister, Alex." Tarian gripped the door handle in an effort to still the onset of laughter. A few deep breaths, and the feeling subsided, though the waves of energy continued.

"That was way more than a quick swim, *chica*. You were gone for hours. You freaked out the Sentinels." Alex leaned toward her, and put a hand on her forehead. "You feel hot."

She removed his hand. "I need to sit down, Alex."

Before he could interrogate her any further she brushed his hand away and opened the door.

Calliope started at the sound and jumped to her feet. Confusion and surprised clashed on her face.

"Tari? You...what happened?" Calliope rushed toward her, at the same time Alex pulled her toward a chair.

"Really, both of you back off." Tarian tore her arm away from Alex. "I'm not an invalid. I just need to sit down."

"Tari...have you looked in a mirror?" Calliope pushed her into the chair, and put her hands on the sides of Tarian's face. "You look like you've been running a marathon. Your face is flushed, you radiate heat, and I can feel magic pulsing off you. What happened?"

"The dolphins." Tarian swallowed, her mouth suddenly dry. "I went for a swim like you told me."

"I told you that last night, Tari. I've been to bed and back since then."

"So I heard." Tarian swallowed again. Her mouth was full of cotton. "The Old Woman came to visit. I guess she messed up the time."

Alex's eyebrows shot up. He sat slowly in the chair next to her. "Really? Why didn't you say?"

"I didn't want everyone in the House hearing it." Tarian stared out at the room, not really seeing it, reliving the moments. Or hours, she supposed. "It felt like minutes, mere minutes. She even said a couple of words. She wanted to meet the baby, I think. And she gave me this." Tarian waved a hand in the air. "Extra energy."

"Why?"

She hesitated. *You know exactly why. Tell them.*

Alex pushed Tarian's chair around so she faced him. "What was that? I saw something in your eyes. You're hiding something."

Tarian grimaced. "It's disturbing how well you know me."

"That's why I'm your Advisor *chica*. And that's what friends are. People who know us better than we know ourselves." Alex leaned forward. "What were the words?"

"Hope. Weak. Tired. Promise. Urgent."

"In that order?" Alex frowned.

Calliope pulled her chair over and sat down. "I didn't think they could talk like us. Don't they usually talk to you in pictures and music, like they do me?"

"Usually. And emotions. But The Old Woman's not exactly a normal Ancient, is she? I guess living that many years would give you more than normal abilities." Tarian closed her eyes. The image the Ancient had given her still vibrated in her thoughts. "She showed me a column of Water, guarded by dolphins. No idea where. But the emotions…made me think it's dying. Or broken in some way. Or…maybe *she* is dying. Something's definitely wrong."

"She showed you that with which word?" Alex squeezed her thigh.

Tarian opened her eyes. "Tired."

Alex nodded. "Okay. What about the other two?"

"When she greeted the baby, she said 'hope.' Which makes sense. Any new life represents hope, doesn't it?"

Alex sat back, his eyes staring into the distance. "Yeah, but. She's never come like this before, has she? She visit you or Calli as a baby?"

Tarian shrugged. "Not that I remember. She came on my naming day, but she didn't speak to me. She just…hovered. She didn't come for the funeral." Tarian swallowed the sudden lump. A twinge of pain along the side of her stomach made her shift uncomfortably in her seat. *The baby must be kicking a nerve.* Except she could feel the baby's foot and it was nowhere near the pain.

"She didn't come on my name day. I've never seen her," Calliope offered.

Alex tapped a foot. "So why now? What's changed?"

Tarian looked down at her stomach and surreptitiously rubbed the area now shooting her with tiny jolts of pain. "Aside from the obvious?"

"It's more than that, *chica*. She came to make an impression."

"Well she certainly did that."

"Tari? You okay?" Calliope reached over and stopped Tarian's hand where it rubbed the pain. Through her sister's touch, Tarian felt a wave of energy. It ricocheted off the overload inside her and rebounded outward. Calliope's eyes widened, the whites showing.

"Tari! How long has this been going on?"

Tarian gritted her teeth. "Which part?"

"The pain, Tari. How long?"

Alex stopped pacing and stared at her. "What's going on?"

"Just since I sat down."

Calliope bit her lip. "It's too soon. Way too soon."

"What for?" Alex shouted.

Tarian winced. "It's nothing. Probably something I ate."

Calliope shook her head. "You know it's not. You're on serious overload, Tari. I don't know how you're containing that much power, and it's…it might push you into labor. You have to dispel it."

"I've been trying. It's not going anywhere." Tarian gritted her teeth as another wave of pain coursed through her. "Can't we stop this?"

"Your body rejected me, Tari." Calliope knelt in front of her. "I can't take that much power. We'd need a group."

"Or we could just use it." Tarian huffed out a breath. "She gave this to me for a reason. She wouldn't hurt the baby."

"Then why'd she do it, Tari? Use it how?"

Tarian looked up at her sister. "I think the Old Woman's reminding me that I have a promise to keep. That I should stop dragging my feet. For whatever reason, my promise to the Caraigg is important to her too. I think she gave me a way to make it happen. And I think it has to happen now." Tarian put a hand over the center of her chest. The burn had dissipated, but she'd never forget how it felt. "She pointed out that I already have the thing I need. I just have to…make it…portable."

"What?" Calliope frowned, and glanced back at the books on her table. "We know you need a powerful artifact. At least one. But obviously we can't use the one we know about. Carrying a heavy throne that's been anchored to the floor for thousands of years into a cave seems problematic. You mentioned that air daemon, Macari, has another, but she's gone home. We don't have a way to contact her. Daric's still researching the other two."

"I think there's a way to separate the medallion from the chair. That's what the Old Woman showed me. That might be why I have all this energy." Tarian rubbed her arms. Her whole body shivered as if she were cold. But she wasn't.

Calliope watched her, seemingly lost in thought.

Alex paced the length of the room. His footsteps echoed like a metronome, keeping beat to an unheard song. "Why? What difference will freeing the Caraigg make to the Water Ancients?"

"She didn't say. But maybe if I free the Caraigg, I free her too? Whatever the reason, I need to do it. Now. Right now." She gasped as another pain took her. "I need to get to the Dolphin Throne."

"You need to get to a healer." Alex growled.

Calliope held up a hand to stop Alex from dragging Tarian away. "She's having false contractions from the overload, Alex. A healer won't help. She needs to get the excess energy out of her body."

Alex took Tarian's arm and helped her to the door. "Why can't she offload the way she usually does?"

"I usually use water. I don't think that'll help with this."

Calliope opened the door and the three of them hurried through it and down the hall. Tarian barely noticed where they were. She focused on breathing. *Why? Why did she do this?*

She believed the Old Woman had good intentions. But that didn't stop her body from pushing her around. As they entered the receiving hall, a hand of light shot out from the Dolphin Throne and rushed toward her. She'd expected it, since the throne reacted to any threat to the Keeper or the Scion, and this could be a threat to both.

The force hit her as she crossed the rune in the center of the floor. Power wrapped around and took her knees out from under her. Tarian collapsed, Alex and Calliope dragged down with her in a heap. They all tumbled, but Tarian was caught in a web of light and energy from the throne itself as it met the overload of power inside her.

Energy rushed out of her and lifted her off the floor. Dolphin song vibrated through the room. Her ears filled with the sound of waves. She tasted the salt. It was as though she were back in the ocean, with the tapestries on the walls undulating like ocean waves and power rippling all around.

Her chest burned. This time, it felt more immediate. Real. Tarian gasped, but couldn't move her hands. She was caught, suspended, revolving slowly in air as energy from the Dolphin Throne comingled with the power from the Old Woman and became something more. The full weight of Water crashed around her just as waves crashed against rocks, loud and deadly. It seared her chest, twisted her insides. The baby, cocooned inside her, twisted too. Tarian felt her embrace the energy and absorb it. It was an odd sensation, like her uterus was a sponge that soaked up extra power.

Like the Stulos. The thought ran through her mind. *Oh, Light. Please don't let her be born now. She won't survive.*

Somewhere in the center of the hurricane, a calm thought emerged. *Safe.* She felt herself embraced by warm, caring arms. Contentment surged through, even as her chest burned. Tarian wanted to cry, with the pain and the relief of that one word. *Safe.*

It was a promise. The baby would be safe. She knew it. Somehow. Even with this strange assault on her body.

A thousand years later Tarian drifted in a sea of calm, her chest a hot mess of hurt, but the overload on her system was gone. She opened her eyes to find herself lying on the floor, the central rune throbbing beneath her. Dolphin clicks faded into the background, and the ocean receded.

Heat bit at her chest. Her hand flew up to swat away the fly or whatever it was. Instead of a bug, she hit something hard against her skin. She looked down and discovered a faint glow shining through a newly torn hole in her shirt. Pulling the material away from her chest she found the wooden dolphin medallion, in miniature, embedded into her skin between two absurdly large breasts, like a three dimensional tattoo.

She touched it gently. It stung as a fresh tattoo would, but already the pain faded as though it had never been. The medallion didn't move, now one with her skin. She suppressed the panic that wrapped around her heart at the thought of a foreign object embedded in her skin. *How is this possible?*

The medallion throbbed in perfect synchronization with her heart. The power it exuded coursed through her veins and surrounded her just as it had when she sat on the Dolphin Throne. The overload she'd suffered moments before vanished, or concentrated in the medallion itself. Her stomach no longer jolted with pain.

"I suppose this solves one problem." *And causes others. How is the baby supposed to inherit something that's stuck in my chest?* Tarian rubbed at the medallion as she stared at the Dolphin Throne. The top of the chair, which once supported the dolphin symbol, looked like any other chair now. Ornately carved, but just a chair. No glow emanated from it. No sense of power.

She held it in her body now.

Tarian shuddered and looked around at Calliope. Both Alex and Calliope lay unconscious on the floor next to her.

"Well that's a first." Tarian told the quiet room. "Usually I'm the one passing out."

5

Tarian crawled over to Calliope and shook her shoulders. "Wake up, Calli."

Calliope moaned, and blinked her eyes opened. "What hit me?"

"Dolphins." Tarian grinned. She turned to shake Alex but he was already sitting up.

"Holy hell. You okay?" He reached toward her, as if to assure himself she was really there.

Tarian grabbed his hand and squeezed. "I'm fine. I feel great, actually." She managed to get to her feet, though she stumbled a bit, off balance from the front weight of the baby. Alex helped Calliope to her feet in slow motion.

Everything seemed brighter. Crisper. Sounds accentuated. Colors vibrant. And the scents...Calliope's floral signature and Alex's earthy, soil-after-rain scent assaulted her nose and made her giggle.

"Oh. This is amazing." Tarian turned and studied the room with wonder. It was as though she'd been nearsighted, and now had perfect vision.

"Tari..." Alex pointed at her. "You're glowing."

Tarian looked down at the faint glow of the medallion. *If it keeps glowing like that I'll attract attention wherever I go.*

Alex gaped. "*Madre de dios, chica*! What the hell happened? What the hell is that?" He pointed at the medallion as though it were a snake about to bite.

Calliope looked at the throne, then back at Tarian. "Oh…oh my…that…I didn't know…." Calliope took a deep breath. "How?"

Tarian shook her head. "No clue. I didn't do it, they did." She rubbed the sore spot. "I guess it solves the transportation problem though."

Alex poked at the medallion suspiciously. Tarian hit his hand away. "Stop that. It's freaking me out as it is. Don't make it worse. Calli, what else do I need to do to keep my promise?" Tarian rubbed the medallion. It didn't burn anymore. It was just slightly raised, like a scar that pulsed in time to her heartbeat. *This'll take some getting used to.*

Calliope rubbed the side of her head, and winced. "Power. A lot of it."

"Got it." Tarian grinned, ruefully rubbing the shirt.

"More than one person to join in the weaving. From what we've translated, you need at least three women." Calliope paused and stared at Tarian's stomach. "Though, the way things are, two of us might work. Plus the artifact as a focus."

"Wait a minute." Alex stomped his foot. "You ain't gonna do this by yourselves. You can't do this, Tari. *Keeper.* We can't keep you safe."

Tarian stepped up to the former Dolphin Throne and sat. *It's just a piece of wood now.* She marveled at the thought. *But comforting anyway. Still a symbol of power, if not an actual one.* "I can. And I will. I have to, Alex. The Old Woman is dying. Don't you get it?"

Alex shook his head. "I don't get that. And I don't feel any extra power from you."

Calliope cleared her throat. "I think that's because it's Water, Alex, and you're Earth and Air." Calliope joined Tarian at the table, and put a soft hand on her forehead. She frowned, and moved her hands down to Tarian's stomach.

"The baby…"

Tarian studied her sister's face. "What, Calli? What about her?"

"Are you feeling any more pains down here?" Calliope patted Tarian's stomach.

"No. They left after I got this." She patted the medallion briefly. "She feels fine. I feel bloated, but fine."

"She's…" Calliope frowned again and focused. Tingles of energy invaded Tarian's stomach, but this time Calliope wasn't rejected. Instead, it felt as though her extra energy soaked into Tarian's skin and absorbed. "Are you doing that?"

Tarian shook her head. "No."

"Then she is. She's absorbing power, Tari. That has to be her talent. And it's advanced, way advanced for an unborn." Calliope took a deep breath and sent another little pulse of energy, which caused the baby to wiggle. "She's holding it all. I don't know how, but she is."

The medallion pulsed, making Tarian fidget. "I think I do."

"How can we teach her to let it go, if she's not born yet?" Calliope sat back on her heels.

"I'm getting the healer." Alex turned abruptly and strode for the door. "You stay put."

Tarian watched him leave. When the door clicked shut behind him, she spoke in a hurried whisper. "I know how, but he won't like the answer. We need to go to the cave, Calli. Right now, before Alex comes back." Tarian stood. Her arms and legs were so heavy, it was as though she moved through chest-deep water, and her stomach weighed a ton. Like she'd suddenly gained fifty pounds. "The Old Woman was right. This is urgent. The Stulos absorbs power. It'll take any extra we give it. It should pull from the baby too."

Calliope stood, her lips twisting. "You might be right. But…"

"But what, Calli?"

"What if it does more than that? Or what if we can't destroy the Stulos? The book said three women. We're only two. We'll be trapped there, and nobody will know where we went." Calliope wrung her hands.

"We can do this. The Old Woman wouldn't have overloaded

me if she wasn't sure I could make this happen." Tarian sighed, impatient. "She's our third, don't you see? She's gifted me with part of her power, just for this. She wouldn't risk me or the baby. Look, you already know the process. You've translated all the warnings. You have all the information, Calli. We have the power we need. We're ready. We can do this." Tarian kept her voice confident, ignoring the little voice of doubt creeping up from behind her to poke her in the ribs. Her heart skipped along, revving up with the thought of the task at hand.

Tarian took her sister's hands, and dragged her over to the rune on the floor in the center of the room. It served as a permanent power circle, embedded in the House, with her own magic as a conduit. It didn't get any better than that, not even one drawn from her own blood. It would work. Then she focused on the spell she'd accidentally learned. The one that had banished her, instead of the Laghairtine she'd been trying to capture. The event which had started this whole mess. She swallowed, and started the ritual.

As she finished the words, intention crystal clear in her mind and a vision of the cave filled with Caraigg behind her eyes, Alex ran back into the room with healer Chloe close behind him. They stopped, a stupefied expression on both of their faces. It was the last thing Tarian saw as everything dissolved into black mist.

6

Dust tickled Tarian's nose and she sneezed, a sure sign they'd arrived at the intended destination. The darkness of the cave wrapped around her like a blanket, disrupted only by the glinting eyes of the Caraigg. Calliope stood beside her, a dark mass against a slightly lighter blob of indistinct, bumpy rock walls.

Tarian waited for the Caraigg to approach. The medallion continued to glow, emitting enough light to cast long shadows over the rock and Calliope's face. It made the Caraigg look like evil gremlins.

"Okay, let me talk to them first. Then we'll get to it."

Calliope rubbed her arms vigorously, then pointed. "Is that it?"

Tarian glanced in the direction indicated and nodded, forgetting Calli probably couldn't see her in the dark. "If not, we've really screwed up."

"Wow. It doesn't look anything like I pictured. I thought it would be more imposing, somehow. Bigger."

Tarian eyed the Stulos. If she didn't know better, she'd have thought it was just another jagged stone erupting from the cave floor, about the height of her shoulder, and three feet in diameter. Except for the red glow, of course, and the intense cold. And the way it stole power from everyone around it. "It's plenty big. It's not the size that's important, it's what you do with it."

Calliope snorted but said nothing. Tarian sat on one of the

large outcroppings of rock. The Caraigg crowded in around them, blinking.

Calliope joined her on the rock. "Do you think I could listen in?"

Tarian glanced at her sister. "I have no idea. Why?"

"I've never met them." Her sister looked at them curiously. "They look like the Archivists but not exactly. See that one? He has thicker wrinkles and his skin seems harder."

"It would have to be, wouldn't it? Living down here in this cold. I'll take one hand, you take the other, and maybe you can listen in that way."

Tarian gestured for one of the Caraigg to come forward. Furious blinking rippled through the crowd before one moved toward her. It huddled in front of her, and held out both hands. Calliope took one, and Tarian the other.

Keeper has returned. Keeper has blessing of Water. Keeper arrives to keep her promise? The question embedded in the tones that rippled through her mind was clear, but behind it was something more. Reverence. Appreciation. Gratitude. They were truly happy she was here, and ready to keep the deal they'd made.

She spoke out loud, since she wasn't sure Calliope would hear her internal dialogue. "I'm here to keep my side of the Agreement. Are you ready to keep yours?"

We are ready. Assent followed after assent as voice after voice added to a cacophony of excitement and hope. Jubilation lifted the voices to a nearly unbearable level in her head. They stood on the brink of happiness and seemed almost afraid it would be ripped away.

"First, I need to tell you that the baby is…" Tarian gulped. "The baby needs help. She's absorbing more energy than she should. Will the Stulos take the excess from her as it does from us?"

Thoughts swirled in her head. She caught images of the baby, flashes of concern. Debate. She couldn't track it all. Finally…

Outcome uncertain. Scion unique. Full talent not apparent. Stulos absorbs, but once destroyed Stulos will release. We are allies, by

promise and honor. We stand for House of Xannon. We will protect.
Tarian turned to her sister. "Get all that?"

"Yes, I did." The awe on Calliope's face was evident. "There's so many. They talk different. Even in their heads they sound different than the Archivists. More…I don't know, more northern?"

They moved forward. We have not. They were WE, once. Sadness filled their tone now. *Now WE will be they.*

"Not true. You'll be more than them. You won't be tied to the archives." Tarian glanced at Calliope. "Right?"

"Right. They are tied to you and to the bloodline, but not the house itself. Which will be a good thing, if you want them able to move around to get information from different parts of the world."

Tarian turned back to the daemon. "You know the steps?"

Agreement resounded through her head as they sifted through Calliope's mental picture of the procedure. The Caraigg moved toward the fire, slowly at first and gaining speed as more of them poured into the center of the cave. Tarian felt their eagerness to get started.

"If they're ready, I suppose I am." Tarian released the hand of her contact, and he too turned and joined his fellows heading toward the Stulos.

She put a hand over the dolphin medallion. So much power, embedded in the wood now buried in her own skin. If she thought about how the medallion was attached, she'd try to rip it out by her fingernails. *It's like having a bullet wedged inside, or one of those earrings that makes a giant hole in your ear. It's not natural. Or normal. What would it take to remove it? What kind of hole would it leave behind?* She shuddered. The need to pry it out as the foreign object it was rolled through her, and her hand tensed. Then she took a long, slow breath. She couldn't afford to panic. Instead, she patted the medallion and sent a tiny bit of her own energy at it, as she would the chair. It answered with a surge of power and a distant dolphin call. "Okay, let's do this thing. The faster the better. Alex is probably freaked out. Who knows how many people he's called in to search for us."

"I bet I know exactly how many." Calliope shivered and rubbed her arms. "It's so cold in here."

Tarian stopped. "What'd you mean?"

Calliope grinned. "We were talking about coming here before we left. He saw us leave, he'll know you banished us here. And he knows who can call us out. Everybody does."

Tarian groaned. "Daric. And he won't be happy about it." She turned and hurried toward the Stulos. If Calliope was right, they had maybe five or ten minutes. *If time passes the same way here as it does at home.*

She led the way to the center of the cave, shivering as she went. Cold, so very, very cold. The water they sloshed through didn't help. By the time they got to the island that held the Stulos, they were both soaked in briny freezing water from the knees down and covered in goose bumps. Calliope's teeth chattered, making a clacking noise that reverberated up the walls and intensified until it sounded like an army of chittering bats.

By the time they reached the island, the feeling of anticipation in the air was nearly as unbearable as the cold. Tarian examined the space they had to work with. *Tight, but doable.* "Am I supposed to draw a circle?"

"No. It won't work. The Stulos would just pull the power from it and dilute your attempt. This is supposed to be direct. We need to combine and bond, and then use the Artifact to basically reverse the flow. Remember? Like we did with the Laghairtine." Calliope choked on the last word.

Tarian pressed her lips together and nodded.

Calliope pointed at the Caraigg. "They should form a circle around us and the Stulos. I don't think they have to be touching but it wouldn't hurt. They should be ready, because I think this will affect them the most, though none of the texts were very clear on what happens when a Stulos is released. I think that much power has to go somewhere, and most of it is theirs, after all." Calliope walked closer to the Stulos, and stood a few feet away from it.

"We'll have to touch it, eventually. After we've joined. The instructions said, *Two be tied, Earth and Water, round by three, Fire and Air, balance combine or chaos disperse, Spirit unite to end the divide.*"

"What exactly does that mean?"

"I think it means the Stulos goes in the center, with those who are trying to break it next to it. Then whoever the keeper of the Stulos is circles both, then someone…you…bonds with the artifact, which feeds and opens the Stulos. I was never able to find out why Fire and Air, Earth and Water, in those specific pairings. I know there are four Stulos, but…there wasn't time…"

The book. "I'm sorry, Calli. I know you love studying that book."

Calliope shrugged. "It wasn't ours to keep. I took a lot of notes. They should keep me busy for years. Anyway." Calliope met her gaze. "How is the baby?"

Tarian checked in with her stomach. "Quiet. And…still overloaded. But it's dampened. I can't feel *my* magic, but I feel the dolphins and I feel her. Odd."

"I don't feel anything at all." Calliope shuddered. "Except cold."

The closer Tarian stepped to the Stulos, the hotter the medallion burned. She couldn't stand this much longer. She covered the medallion with one hand, and with the other reached for Calliope's.

The Caraigg assembled into a tight circle around them, facing inward toward the Stulos. So many of them in such a small space meant bodies overlapped into one giant fur ball. The glow from the Stulos cast eerie shadows on their faces, like rocks. They waited, still as statues, for Tarian to fulfill her promise. She swallowed, desperate for some sort of moisture to ease the dryness in her mouth.

She shook her shoulders and head, trying to loosen the tension in her muscles, then stood straighter.

"Ready?" Tarian glanced at Calliope.

"As I'll ever be," Calliope answered.

7

Tarian pushed on the dolphin medallion, tightened her grip on Calliope's hand, and focused on locating her own power. She filled her thoughts with the energy she was meant to invoke here, in the place with no magic. At first she felt nothing. The Stulos sucked every magical bit of energy. *This must be what it feels like to be a normal human with no magic.* The loss made her sad for them. *It feels like someone stole a giant chunk of my soul. Like the best part of me is missing.*

A burst of heat from the medallion pushed at her hand and singed the tiny hairs on the back. The medallion, sensing the threat or the need, rushed a surge of potency through her body. It fed into the Stulos, as fast as the medallion could dish it out. Her chest on fire, Tarian kept going, trying to maintain a connection to the energy flowing from it, and at the same time trying to pull Calliope in on it. It'd been so easy before, but now they fought against a powerful artifact that absorbed magic. Now it was like trying to keep a grip on a giant icicle. It kept slipping through her fingers.

Calliope squeezed her hand, but Tarian felt no energy from her. *I need her energy or this won't work.* Now that the medallion was dishing out, she could feel her own power rising but still so very far away. Nearly untouchable and yet...a tiny spark flickered in the back of her mind and heart. A kernel of her power, kept deep within. Like an ember that needed to be fanned into a flame. She closed her eyes and fumbled for it. Tiny hairs along her arms tickled.

She could almost touch it. Just there…tantalizingly out of reach.

Nearly. Have. It.

There!

She connected to the stream of power and pulled with all her might, her body straining against the force coming from the Stulos. As her power grew, a dolphin call intensified, surrounding them with the sound of ocean waves, the smell of the sea, and dolphin cries. An Ancient thought rose.

Synergy.

The Old Woman! She's here, somehow.

Beside her, Calliope screamed, a guttural sound as though she dead lifted a thousand pounds, and suddenly her energy poured into Tarian. Tarian stumbled, clutching Calliope's hand to steady herself as a wave of unvarnished, undirected power from Calliope swirled. The baby kicked, squiggled, squirmed, and absorbed Calliope's gift, and with it the dolphin stream as well. Alarmed, Tarian first tried to break her connection to the energy flow but Calliope was too strong, their sisterly bond too powerful.

"Tari. Don't fight! Take it!" Calliope shouted.

Synergy. Right.

Tarian took a shuddered breath and let go of her ego, her sense of self, to merge with Calliope. Tentative at first, as a cat might sneak up on a mouse, and then…*Crack.*

Acceptance.

Admittance.

Hope.

Tarian fused the strands until they became one thick rope of energy, a visible spectrum of blue, red and white light that extended from Tarian's chest to the Stulos. At the same time, the Stulos tried to siphon it away, but now Tarian controlled more than the Stulos could take at one time. The excess raced around the rock form and up, encircling the Stulos.

Tarian's skin burned, like the flesh was melting off her bones. She couldn't see anything except the red glowing rock in front of her. She knew the Caraigg surrounded them, but couldn't feel or hear or see them. Everything froze. The air was heavy, pregnant with an anticipation that wasn't human. A longing that wasn't her own, or even the Caraigg's. Someone, somewhere, waited, poised on the brink of a chasm so vast she couldn't fathom it. Even the dolphin cry stopped, as though someone turned off all sound.

Tarian pulled a long shuddering breath. Her head erupted into a thousand tiny stars. Her body shook like a junkie going through withdrawal.

"Tari, now!" Calliope's voice, strained but strong. *"Touch."*

Tarian reached toward the Stulos, her fingers stretched out in a desperate attempt to keep her feet where they were so her knees wouldn't buckle. But she couldn't quite reach, couldn't quite get her hand on the Stulos.

She shuffled forward, inch by painful inch. Power increased until the light of it burned so bright everything turned to blinding white shades of nothing. The smell of burnt cloth and hair filled the air. *One more step. Just…one…more.* Tarian leaned forward, and at last placed her hand against the Stulos.

Time sped up and passed her by, taking with it a rush of air and water energy. They whipped her face with her hair, sent loose stones flying, and drenched them in stagnant, cold pond water. A loud crash reverberated, and the ground shook. The Stulos trembled and groaned. A crack appeared along the side and stretched with a loud clap.

Tarian's stomach seized as the crack extended. Pain stronger than anything she'd ever known gripped her, and her knees gave way. She fell to the ground hard, one hand holding the Stulos for support, her other hand holding onto Calliope with every ounce of strength she could muster. She willed the pain to stop. Another jolt wracked her as a piece of the rock fell away beneath her hand. She screamed. Felt her sister pull on her arm.

"Don't…break…I'm…fine." *Too much power. Too much.*

The Stulos bulged. Piece after piece broke loose and crashed around them. As the ground shook and pain wracked Tarian's body, something else took hold. A tug, a summons.

Shit, no! Don't summon me! Daric, don't. She thought the words, desperate. If he ripped her out of this place, with so much chaos and the overload of power…disaster.

The summons circled her, black mist shrouding everything and threatening to take her away. But something held it back. All the power, the energy in the air, but it wasn't that. Something in the core of her took in the summons and instead of answering it, pushed it toward the Stulos instead.

The baby.

Tarian gasped at another round of painful cramps from her abdomen. *Stop. End. Have…to…finish.* She pictured the Stulos breaking, the power flooding out, the summons broken, the baby protected from it all. She had to believe it. Magic formed from intention, and she intended this to end with her child intact.

"Reverse." Calliope's voice drifted through the haze.

Tarian forced her eyes open to focus on the rock in front of her. Earth as dense as anything she'd ever seen, more power than she'd ever experienced. The feeling of *old* that surrounded it. The sense of longing as if the stone itself wanted freedom from the long and arduous task it had been set. She grabbed onto the longing and let the stream of energy pour into it, into the Stulos, then twisted it as she'd done once before. Another twist, and the flow of power into the Stulos reversed. Three streams of colored light became one solid column of white.

A thousand voices sounded in her head. High ones, low ones, her sister's voice, dolphin cries and emotion, all around and through her. The energy bound them into something greater than mere humans and Ancients. They were timeless. Eternal. It was almost like she felt when she made love with Daric, but…different. More intense and at the same time more encompassing. Less personal. More global. As though the universe spoke through her, and she through it. The awe of it. Tears spilled onto her cheeks.

Another cramp gripped her body and she swayed on her knees, gripping the rock as it crumbled, trying to maintain her balance as the ground shifted and her body twisted. *Not now. Too soon. Not now. Too soon.* She couldn't be…the baby couldn't be…

The voices rose in her head. Everyone joined in as the power flowed around and through, around and through, until she, the Caraigg, her sister, the baby, and the dolphins were all one with it. The crack in the Stulos widened, a giant lesion extending from the floor all the way up until she couldn't see the end. Cold retreated, heat entered. A loud snap. The Stulos shattered into a million pieces that hung suspended in air for a flash of eternity before rushing outward to the edges of the cavern.

A dolphin cry sounded, triumphant, exalted, as the world exploded in a rain of cold fire, magic power, dust, ash and lava.

8

Tarian flew back with the force of the explosion, her body catapulted through the air as though thrown by a giant's hand. She landed against the side of the cave and slumped down, a cramp taking her stomach in a vise grip and squeezing. She whimpered as she curled into as much of a fetal position as she could manage. *Not now, not now.*

Intense heat replaced the cold. Why was it so hot? *Did it work? The baby!*

Your side of the Agreement has been fulfilled. The words whispered through her mind, or were they in the air around her? She wasn't sure.

It begins.

The deep voice, triumphant as it echoed through her mind, startled her. It wasn't the Caraigg. It sounded rich and foreign.

What begins? Who...are...

Tarian moaned as a contraction ripped through her.

"Tarian!" Calliope sounded frantic, and far away.

"Here!" She tried to force air behind the words, to scream, but nothing came out but a cough. She gave up and lay still.

A cool hand touched her forehead. Motherly, soft hands. "Mother?"

"Tari, can you stand? We need to move. The cave is erupting."

The words came from so far away. *Erupting?* But the Stulos

was gone. It had to be, her Agreement was fulfilled. *What's erupting?* She opened her eyes in between cramps and looked around.

She'd landed on a rock near the edge of the cave. The rock now stood surrounded by molten red liquid. The intense heat was nothing compared to the dust in the air. She coughed, lost her breath and coughed again.

Calliope put her arms around Tarian's shoulders and pulled. "Stand up, you have to stand up. You have to walk through a portal. I can't carry you."

Tarian screamed when the next wave of pain hit her. She willed the cramps to stop, but they didn't. There was no time for her body to collapse, no time. *Move. Dammit, move!* She was going to die here if they didn't move.

From behind, hard hands around her waist. *Caraigg.*

Keeper must leave.

"Help me get her through the portal," Calliope shouted at the cave.

Hands supported Tarian, and she leaned into them. They lifted her onto some sort of hard table as something scorched her face and hair. The smell of fire beat at her.

"Just shove her through, I'll catch her." Calliope yelled over the tumult of falling rocks.

Catch me? Am I falling? Confused, Tarian tried to focus, to see. The air, full of dust and smoke and acrid ash, made her choke. In front of her, a portal wavered like a mirage in the desert, the welcoming sight of the entry alcove within. *Home.* A painful fit of coughing overtook her, even as she dissolved into the familiar nothingness of a travel portal.

She rolled out of the travel portal and onto cold stone, panting, gasping through another round of cramps.

No no no. Not now. Too soon.

Tarian fought against it, her stomach muscles straining from effort, legs taut, arms clutching her stomach as if she could hold everything in place. The scent of burnt flesh, cloth, hair filled her nose and made her cough even as another wave wracked her body.

"No no no no no no." The one word, a mantra. A beacon to focus on. She couldn't gather her thoughts, or any intention to use power. *Can't use any magic to stop this. Can't do anything.*

As the contraction lessened, she managed to open her eyes, the need to know where she was and what was happening around her taking center stage for a brief moment. She saw Calliope, crawling on hands and knees toward her. Black and white marble. And feet. A lot of feet. Angry male voices filled her ears.

She closed her eyes against it all. Sweat poured down her face and splashed onto the marble floor.

The entry. I'm having a baby, in the entryway. On the floor. Too soon. Way too soon.

The realization pounded like a drum, loud and insistent. Disbelief was a cymbal, crashing in her head. And somewhere in the midst of it, satisfaction and pride blossomed. She'd done it. She'd released the Caraigg. *I kept my promise.*

Hands on her stomach, her arms, tugging at her clothes. Something soft under her head.

"Don't move her. Alex, get Chloe." Calliope's voice commanded and tolerated no argument.

Little sister's not so little anymore.

As the contraction seized her body and twisted, Calliope thrust soothing energy into her stomach. It met the pain head on. Blocked it. Contained it. The baby kicked. Calliope hummed, the melody filling the space. Tarian found herself humming with her, though she couldn't name the tune.

Somewhere inside her, the baby squirmed, delighted at the noise.

She really is happy. She loves music. I can feel it.

In the middle of baby-joy, a clear impression burned into Tarian's conscious. A need. A desire. *Out.*

"No no no no. Not out. In. Stay in." Tarian groaned, the words little more than a whisper. She internalized the thought, hoping the baby would understand. *"Safe. It's safe there. Stay there. You aren't ready."*

Confused longing. Tarian wept with the strength of just how much the baby wanted to be born.

"It's too soon." She gasped the words, her breath cut off by a strong kick. Too strong.

"Not yet sweetie, not yet." Calliope sing-songed. "Mommy needs you to be still. Mommy needs you to be quiet. Baby needs to stay with Mommy."

"Keeper?" Healer Chloe rushed into the entry, and immediately went to her knees next to Tarian. Her hands joined Calliope's on Tarian's stomach. She began muttering nonsensical words as she wove a cooling band of comfort that eased the cramps and stopped the contractions. Every muscle in Tarian's body went limp. She took a deep breath and held it, trying to relax into it even further.

That's it, sweetie. Stay with me. I want you to stay with me. Just relax. We both need to rest. Sleep, child. Plenty of time for exploring later. Plenty of time. It's all right. Everything's all right.

The baby stopped kicking, stopped wiggling. Confusion. Longing. And something more. Fatigue.

"She's tired." Tarian bit her lip, hard, and tasted blood. Her entire body felt sore, like she'd just fought five rounds in the Arena. "Keep at it."

Minutes ticked by as Chloe and Calliope muttered and hummed, pouring the magical version of a sedative into Tarian's body. Tarian closed her eyes, as exhausted as the baby. Gentle hands pushed her hair back and wiped her forehead. The scent of spice filled her nose.

Daric.

She managed a small smile. "You make a good pillow."

Daric's soft chuckle reassured her. She was positive a lecture was coming from the men in her life, one that she probably deserved. But she also knew they'd both stand by her and support her. *They are both good men.*

Eventually, Calliope and Chloe both removed their hands and sat back. Tarian opened her eyes and studied their faces. Calliope's clothes draped in tattered burnt strips. Both looked like they'd just finished a marathon, with flushed cheeks and short breath.

"I think we convinced her to stick around for a while longer." Calliope took a deep breath. "But I'm not sure how long."

Healer Chloe stood and wiped her forehead. "If I had a guess, three or four weeks. Maybe less. She's big enough now."

Tarian frowned. "She can't be. I'm only five months."

Chloe shrugged. Her purple spiked hair wiggled with the movement. "Doesn't seem to make a difference to her. I know when a baby's near term, and I'm telling you she's near term."

Alex shifted his feet and ran a hand through already tousled hair. "Thanks for coming so quick, Chloe. Can we move her now?"

"The Keeper is fine. She's not sick, she's pregnant. Though I'd say she needs a good long sleep and a lot of food. Whatever caused the contractions overloaded both of their systems, though Tarian's more than the baby's." Chloe patted Alex's arm in a reassuring way. "Food. Sleep. Male ire kept to a minimum. They'll both be fine." Chloe turned toward the hallway. "I'll have some food sent to her bedroom," she called over her shoulder as she left.

Tarian watched Alex as he rubbed his hair with frustrated fingers. Anger, fear, concern, and affection all warred on his face. She looked up at Daric, unsurprised to find the same expression.

"Help me up?"

Daric pressed his lips together, but she caught an amused crinkle to his eyes. He pushed her up, then stood to help her to her feet. Alex lifted Calliope. The four of them stood for a moment just looking at each other. Alex coughed, and his eyes traveled down the length of her body.

"You might want to change clothes, *chica*."

Tarian looked down. Half of her overlarge shirt was gone, the remnants draped in blackened tatters around her stomach. The jeans fared better, but the bottoms were ripped and burned, with a hole on one thigh, and, from the sudden breeze, one in the rear.

"Good idea." She took a step, pleased to feel her legs mostly steady beneath her. "Might as well all come with me. I know you won't let this go without an explanation. And Calli needs food too."

"You mean you want support in case Alex and I go nuts." Daric kept his voice mild, amused. But underneath she sensed his worry and frustration with her. His arm was tense, his body stiff.

"I'm gonna need more than an explanation." Alex grumbled. "I want a promise you won't do that again."

Calliope snorted, but said nothing.

"No deal." Tarian crossed her arms over her chest and rested them on her large stomach. *I swear my stomach is bigger than it was this morning. She can't have grown that much that fast, can she?*

She stifled a groan. *Three or four weeks. Could it be possible?*

Inside her, the baby stretched, and a tiny foot pushed into the flesh of her stomach. "Calli, do you think Chloe is right?"

Calliope stretched her hands over Tarian's stomach while the two men looked on. Calliope hummed a bit, then looked up. "Yeah. I think she is. Something happened to the baby in the cave. The overload maybe? It didn't burn her out, it…helped her grow. I don't understand it. She feels healthy. Her signature is so strong."

"*Chica*, what happened? What'd you do?" Alex stood next to Daric, forming an inquisition of two that would have withstood any stubborn female argument.

Tarian sighed, looking at them. She loved them both, in different ways. But it got so frustrating being coddled because she was gestating. "I kept my promise. Simple as that."

"So you were successful? The Caraigg are free?" Daric glanced around the entry. "Where are they?"

Tarian frowned. "I don't know." She hated to admit it. "I was distracted." She thought back. Between the early labor pain and the explosion, she couldn't remember exactly what had happened other than the trip through the portal. And the voice. *It begins. Who was that? Definitely not the Caraigg. Or anybody else I know.*

"They helped me get her through the portal." Calliope

offered. "I didn't see them after that."

Daric tilted his head. "You had a deal. They provide information. How can they do that if they aren't here?"

"They'll keep their side. They won't want to go back into that cave." Tarian kept her voice confident, but a seed of doubt formed in the back of her mind. *Why didn't they follow us here? There was so much she didn't know about Agreements and how they worked.*

"Was there any sort of timeline, if they don't keep their part of the bargain?"

Tarian bit her lip and said nothing. Daric flashed her a knowing look.

"The Old Woman wouldn't have wanted me to free them if she thought they'd betray me. They won't." Tarian stuck out her chin. "What else was I supposed to do? She left me with the medallion embedded in my chest and an overload on the baby. I had to act fast. I'm sure she had her reasons."

"Maybe you should find out what they were." Daric's voice was low, but she heard the words anyway.

The implication being that she should have found out before she acted, not after. *He's right. Dammit, I hate it when he's right.*

She opened her mouth to tell them she'd go find out the answer right now. She'd go to the ocean, and ask the pod to take her to the Old Woman. Before she could say anything, a portal opened in the center of the entry. The air wiggled and squirmed as the image formed. In it, she saw nothing but darkness. No discernible scene or room to indicate who might be arriving.

Tarian tensed. Beside her, Alex pulled his weapon and stood with shoulders squared and feet planted. Calliope gathered focus, and Daric tightened his grip on her arm, moving her slightly behind him.

Alex whistled, and Sentinels from the hallway ran into the room as two beings stepped through the portal. When they emerged, Tarian felt her jaw drop.

She'd never met them, never seen them before in person, yet she knew exactly who, or rather what, they were. *They don't travel.*

They never travel. Do they?

The two stood side by side, with passive expressions, as though all the time in the world passed them by and they were just fine with that. They were both short, about Tarian's height, and wore brown robes like a monk, but the resemblance to human ended there. Their eyes blinked and their chests moved in rhythm with each other. She couldn't tell if they were male or female. Their eyes were white, with no pupils to break up the expanse. Brown, red, gray, green, black, blond streaked their hair…she lost track of the colors there were so many. It made an interesting effect, and combined with something that glistened or glowed within the colors they appeared almost ethereal. They bowed slightly, and spread their hands in unison in a welcome gesture. Their mouths never moved. Not to take a breath, which they didn't seem to need, nor to speak.

On instinct, Tarian bowed her head in return, shocked. "Dulra. Welcome." She breathed the words, awed by the presence of creatures she'd only known through legends. *What is the Balance Court doing here?*

They each stretched an outside arm out in a universal sign of greeting, while the one next to each twin dangled by their side. Their movement fluid, as if they were conjoined, though she could see a clear space between them. Power rushed out from them and surrounded Tarian, and she felt her own join it without any will of her own. It grew exponentially. The full expanse of it took her breath away. It lay, waiting, ready. Something that shouldn't be possible, given the amount she'd just expended in the cave.

"Tarian A'marie Maitea Xannon, of the House of Xannon, Keeper of the Water Artifact, you are summoned to the Balance Court." The words resounded though their lips never moved. Their outstretched hands came together and clapped, the sound like a thunderbolt in the stone entry. It reverberated off the walls, somehow becoming more than just sound. It formed a ball of light that rushed toward Tarian. Before she could move, breathe, cry out, or react in any way, it hit her, cascading over her head like an ocean wave. She'd been summoned, and every particle of her being cried out to answer it.

The Dulra stepped back into the portal and disappeared into it as though they'd never been.

"Did you feel that?" Calliope asked, but she obviously knew the answer as she clutched her own chest. The remnants of the summoning drifted in the air.

"I have to go." All Tarian could think about was getting to the Balance Court. She had to. Fast. Her feet turned toward the portal that hovered a few feet away.

"You can't." Alex moved in front of her, and put his hands on her shoulders.

"Tari," Daric put a hand on one of her arms, holding her back.

"I have to go."

"You can't."

She looked at both of them in turn. "I have to. They commanded. I'm bound. I feel it. I've been summoned." Tarian swallowed, her mouth suddenly dry. "I have to go."

"You're allowed an escort," Calliope said quickly from behind them. "I'll go with you."

"No. If something happens, you need to be here." Tarian didn't want to spell out what she meant. If for some reason she didn't make it back, Calliope should be in the house, to take over. To be Keeper. The artifact would seek out the next in the Xannon line. Better that Calliope was here, surrounded by protection, if it did. She couldn't risk her sister and the Scion in the same move. She wouldn't.

"I got this, *chica*. What's the plan?" Alex crossed his arms, evidently convinced she wouldn't go without him.

Daric moved to stand next to him. "You're allowed to take two with you, for a group of three."

The two of them stood between her and the portal like a solid male wall, impeding her progress to the Balance Court. She had to go. *Now.*

"Fine. Let's go." She glanced back at Calliope, who shifted from one foot to the other as she twirled a piece of hair hanging limp by the side of her face. "Take care of things, while we're gone. Get Frankie to set up extra security, just in case. Try to find the Caraigg for me."

She gave her sister a quick hug before surrendering to the summons and stepping into the waiting portal, with Alex and Daric right at her heels.

9

Tarian, Alex, and Daric emerged from the travel portal to find the Dulra pair waiting for them. The compulsion that had forced Tarian through the portal vanished as her feet touched the floor. A sigh of relief escaped her lips, which she quickly stifled. Alex remained at strict attention, his eyes darting to every corner of the small room. Daric kept a protective hand on her upper arm, as though escorting her to a dinner party.

They stood in what looked like a hall meant just for travel. The small space held no furniture of any kind, but the walls were carved into seasons. One depicted leafy trees; the next featured leaves that appeared to be falling in slow motion. On the other side, a carving of trees and landscape in snow. Finally, flowers raised their heads to the sun. Nature, she supposed, in cycle. She glanced up at the ceiling. A starry night sky winked at her. Beautiful, and so real she felt like she could reach out and touch it.

Tarian glanced at Alex and Daric. Now that they were here, both looked like men about to face an enemy. Confidence streamed from both faces, though Alex looked ready to fight while Daric looked like he was about to do something sneaky.

"Keeper, please follow." Her greeters spoke in unison, again without moving their lips, then led the way out of the small room. They sounded a bit like the Archivists, except the voices drifted through the air, rather than inside her head, and they sounded more like fine sand than gravel.

She followed the pair, with Daric at her side and Alex slightly in front. The room opened into a round hallway so large the entire House of Xannon would fit inside it. Twice. The walls were so far away they descended into darkness. In the center a bright fire roared, throwing multi-colored sparks of every hue. The white marble floor refracted the colors into a perfect rainbow. Her stomach churned as she examined the kaleidoscope. It took a moment to realize it was the baby turning her stomach, rather than the colors. The girl had now taken up gymnastics, instead of soccer, with the ultimate goal of crawling out through her mother's kidneys. Tarian tried to send soothing thoughts, but the baby refused to calm down. *She doesn't like it here.* Tarian rubbed her stomach, hoping to ease both of their fears. The medallion throbbed to the quick beat of her heart.

As they neared the central flame, the force issuing from it eased over her skin and the medallion. Her shoulders tensed, and a soft glow radiated from the medallion. *A protective response?* It didn't feel like anything she'd dealt with before. The power wasn't any single element that she could detect. It fluctuated between pulling from her and pushing to her. The effect was like trying to hold herself upright in storm-churned ocean waves. The baby squirmed and kicked harder. More Balance Court members stood around the fire in pairs, each with rainbow colored hair and white eyes with no pupils. A ripple went through the crowd as they bowed their heads toward her in greeting, then straightened.

A regal statue of a woman stood to one side of the flame with her hands folded in front of her, a serene expression on her face. She wore white robes, and her nearly white hair braided and circled around her head like a crown. Tarian fixated on the woman's eyes. Strikingly green, like the color of deep emeralds, they looked as though they absorbed everything in the room, digested it, then spit it back out. Tarian studied her signature, finding it difficult with all the other sensations in the room. A hint of mint, with a splash of ice. *Air daemon. Powerful. Pole up her ass.*

Tarian mentally catalogued the signature and moved on to the hooded figure standing next to the woman. Nearly as tall, face and hair obscured with a white hood flowing into a cape that reached the ground. An odd tingle of something *other*. Signature…

Macari.

Startled, Tarian stared at her. Macari didn't look up, seeming to study her feet rather than the room at large. Her body hidden under the cloak so well that Tarian couldn't get a read on the girl's emotional state, nor her purpose here. Tarian looked back at the statue and realized who the woman must be. *First Mother of the Benata. No wonder she looks like she sat on something sharp.*

Tarian gave Daric's arm a squeeze while she gave Alex a stare and a subtle nod of her head toward the pair on the other side of the room. Alex's arms flexed as he tensed, alert to possible danger, but otherwise he looked confused. He couldn't scent a signature like Tarian, so he wouldn't know it was Macari under those robes. She leaned close enough to his ear to whisper the name, which got his full attention focused on the hooded girl.

She resumed her examination of the room. On the other side of the flame, closer to Tarian, stood a tall, dark man in a black suit with black tie. Rugged chin, flashing vivid blue eyes, relaxed sardonic posture and the scent of fresh, mountain air.

Ruarc!

Her face immediately flamed with heat. *What the hell is he doing here?*

Uncomfortable warmth surged in her groin as her body remembered their last encounter. She shifted, acutely aware of Alex and Daric standing beside her. *All three fathers in the same room. Awkward. This is why I wasn't supposed to know who the Potentials were. So when I faced them later I didn't have to feel this.*

Tarian quickly surveyed the rest of the space, what she could see of it. All others present were Balance, each pair standing shoulder to shoulder with another pair, forming a wide circle around the flame, the daemon, and her little group.

Tarian had never thought of the Dulra as anything other than good. They were allies. A backbone of magic in a world that didn't even believe in such things, and a link to Tarian's very nature. Though she'd never met any in person, her mother had instructed her in the basic workings of the Court. She'd painted them as benevolent, arbiters of justice, fair and impartial. *Why am I here? And why are the daemon here?*

Tarian cleared her throat, preparing to ask the question out loud, but the fire flared and words filled the air before she could utter a sound.

"Our voices unite with common purpose. Balance, spirit, the ties that bind are disrupted. Paths have crossed, ways have parted. We are called to fulfill our purpose, to maintain balance within and without."

A pair of Dulra stepped forward, each with one arm stretched out wide. The hair on Tarian's arms stood on end, and warmth moved through her like liquid fire. Fire crackled in her ears, and the baby kicked so hard Tarian nearly doubled over from the assault. In the next breath she forgot all about the baby as the recent moments of her life replayed in her head, from the Laghairtine attack to the breaking of the Stulos and everything in between.

Her own personal movie, high speed, sound not included. When it was done, she stood breathless, fear pounding in her chest, baby kicking in her stomach. Daric gripped her arm so hard her fingers tingled. Alex clenched his fists, working his jaw as if preparing for a bar fight. Across from her, the First Mother's eyes glinted, but her body maintained poise. On the other side, Ruarc remained passive, his hands looped into pockets as though he stood at a party, not an interrogation.

The Dulra began to move. At first they swayed, then they began to pace in a circle. An outer ring went one way while an inner ring moved in the opposite direction. It looked like a giant gear at work, though Tarian noticed that one pair here and there switched rings, either in or out.

A pair broke from the rings and entered the middle. They

stood next to the fire, each immersing a hand in the flame. The rings stopped moving and all turned to face the two in the center. As she watched, the hair on one turned to white. The hair on the other turned red. The fire flared in the middle, shooting red flames high in the air. The baby kicked again, so hard she was sure her ribs had been bruised. Tarian rubbed her belly in soothing circles, but it didn't help. Her own agitation made it worse. Daric squeezed her arm in support.

The pair of Dulra near the flame turned toward her. Lips closed. White eyes now glowing red. She watched, fascinated, as their hair turned slowly red until both looked as though they were on fire.

"What's begun must be finished, what's been done cannot be undone. Earth, Water, Air, Fire, combine, renew, reforge. Balance must be restored, before the turn resolves."

"Honor to the Balance Court." The First Mother spread her hands wide, as if beseeching or begging. "How will balance be restored? Who has destroyed it? Is the one responsible present?"

None of the Dulra moved or shifted. Yet Tarian felt their focus turn to the First Mother. "Fear is unwise. Blame is unnecessary. Cause and effect are not equal."

First Mother pressed her lips together before she faced Tarian and held out a boney finger pointed directly at her. "She has done this. She's created an abomination. The only way to achieve balance is to restore the Stulos, using the aberration as the catalyst."

First Mother glanced at Ruarc, throwing him the dirtiest look Tarian had ever seen anyone deliver. "Their progeny is the result of a misguided Agreement, which should be unraveled by the Court. Thus will balance be restored."

Tarian sorted through the words and the tone, trying to make sense of it. Across the way she saw Macari shift, but otherwise the girl kept her face obscured. *First Mother wants me to, what, have an abortion? Sacrifice my child to build a Stulos? Surely not. Benata don't take life.*

A tiny voice in the back of her mind whispered. *Wouldn't*

they? For the good of society? The good of the many and all that.

Ruarc cleared his throat. "Agreements between others are not the concern of the Benata. Nor is it the right of the Benata to pass sentence on imagined offense."

"Imagined?" First Mother stepped forward, directing her ire at Ruarc. "Is it my imagination that the Keeper of one of the most powerful artifacts in history is with child, a child who controls power she should never have obtained? A power that resulted in the destruction of a Stulos mere moments ago? Is it my imagination that the world trembles from the resulting imbalance?"

First Mother turned to glare at Tarian, her eyes full of ice as her mouth spewed venom. "Is it my *imagination* that the power required to create the Stulos now exists only in the hands of an unborn infant? The world is in danger of collapse because of you and your misuse of power."

Tarian glanced to Ruarc then back at First Mother. It wasn't clear who "you" was in this scenario. *She means me, the baby, or Ruarc? Or all of us?*

Tarian raised an eyebrow and returned the Benata leader's cold stare. "Overreact much?"

Macari shifted, as if she giggled underneath the heavy robe. Tarian grinned.

"Misuse? Such as a daemon, walking the Winds, traveling to the human plane?" Ruarc smiled at Tarian, though his words were clearly for First Mother. His eyes flashed. "It seems Benata are not above keeping secrets."

First Mother spun in place to point her glare back at Ruarc. "The Benata do what is best for society. Always. The Mayfanata, and it seems humans, don't seem to value society at all."

Ruarc's eyes narrowed. "I do wonder, First Mother, if your ire is for the good of society, or for the good of one particular individual. Perhaps you'd care to enlighten us as to how the First Daughter obtained the ability to walk the Wind? Such talent hasn't been seen since before the split."

The way he spoke, Tarian suspected he already knew the

answer to his question.

First Mother stiffened, her hands clasped tightly in front of her, the knuckles white. "That is not why Court has been called. That is not why we stand here, suffering the effects of imbalance. That is not why the very fabric of society collapses while we stand here, doing nothing to stop it."

Ruarc raised one eyebrow. "I was under the impression that the planes remain separated, the Between remains strong and guarded by Lasair, and that both Courts are solid and whole. Am I misinformed? Has Benata City suffered some ill effect, which the rest of us have been spared?"

"You have crossed into Benata domain?" First Mother raised her chin, her eyes flashed. "You violate Agreement?"

Ruarc continued to smile, unperturbed. He flicked at a dust fleck on his jacket. "All is written on the Wind, for those who can *read*."

Tarian watched them as she would a tennis match, her head shifting back and forth, noting how neither would step further toward each other. Both carefully kept the flame in the center between them. This was an old argument then, and had more to do with history than the breaking of one Stulos. Ruarc had sidetracked First Mother from her original question, but why?

Tarian glanced at Daric. He frowned, and shook his head. He didn't get it either.

First Mother huffed, the sound out of keeping with her regal stance. "This is your doing, Ruarc. I sense it. I feel it. I know it. I call upon the Balance Court to pass sentence on the one responsible. And to announce the correct path to balance, as is their purpose by ancient Agreement, bonded at the beginning of time."

10

First Mother's words rang out as though she spoke words of immense meaning, but all Tarian could tell was that she was trying to point a finger at some imagined hurt she wanted the Court to fix. Like a lawyer would ask of a judge.

Judge.

She opened her mouth to offer her opinion on how ridiculous the woman sounded, but Daric's hand on her arm squeezed a warning. She shut her mouth.

"You should be careful what you ask for, First Mother of the Benata." Daric inclined his head as though apologizing, though his words were anything but apologetic. "Sometimes it's hard to see the forest for the trees."

"You will not speak. *You* were not summoned." First Mother stared at him, cold, defiant. "You have no power or presence in this Court."

Tarian cleared her throat. "But I was, and I do. Shouldn't there be a judge pounding on a gavel right about now?"

Alex snorted.

She felt the weight of the Balance Court shift, subtly, toward her. It subdued the smile on Alex's face, and made her heart skip a beat. The baby kicked, hard, and she grunted.

The words, when they came this time, were soft. She had the feeling from the way everyone stood completely still that she alone heard them. *We invite you to journey forward, Keeper. Balance must be restored. Earth. Water. Air. Fire. Each pillar lost overloads the next. Either the missing must be replaced, or the others must be removed. Remember the order. Destruction and creation, each in turn. Fire must have air to burn. Water must share Earth to grow.*

I don't understand. She thought over the words, confused. Remember the order. Destruction. Creations. *You want me to remove the other Stulos? Or restore the missing one. Which? Why?*

Imbalance, long ago, leaves traces, creates more. That which is already in motion must continue, or collapse. Continuation is preferred for Balance. We charge you, Keeper Tarian, with continuing the journey, with righting an ancient wrong, with calling forth a new age, for the hope of all. The keys, safely hidden, shall be returned. The catalyst will be born, and the world unite. If the Keepers assist. We call upon you and yours, Keeper Tarian A'Marie, first key discovered, first key utilized. Do you agree?

Tarian looked around, but nobody else moved. Nobody breathed, or even blinked. Time seemed suspended. Even the flame ceased its relentless crackling.

She spoke, not liking the surreal way it made her feel to stand here surrounded by living people who acted like mannequins in a dress store window. "The Balance Court wants to make an Agreement…with *me*?"

Do you agree?

Tarian hesitated. "Agreements haven't worked out so well for me so far."

We have no power over will, thought, or mind. You agree with First Mother? That the child should be sacrificed and existence returned? Earth Ancients imprisoned?

"Of course not." Tarian frowned. "But there's no way I can fully understand what I'm agreeing to. Nor the penalty if I fail."

If you fail, the end will result. Those present in the world will disperse, to join chaos. Spirit will begin again, magic will begin anew. The world will be reborn. Balance will abide, in either direction.

"You're saying if I can't restore balance, it's the end of the world?"

Every end is a beginning.

"But someone else's beginning. Not ours. Right?"

Silence greeted her, hanging heavy around her ears and shoulders like iron earrings.

"What about the baby?" She whispered the words, barely able to finish her thought.

Balance is not an end, it is a journey begun at the dawn of time. If successful, the Scion will be needed, to right the ancient wrong. To restore the ancient break. To heal the ancient pain. We seek Agreement with the Keeper, in order to aid the Scion. In order to aid Balance. In order to restore to the world that which was lost. The alternative is to begin anew.

Tarian thought over the words. Breaking one Stulos had taken everything she and Calliope had to give, in addition to the Dolphin Medallion, and it had nearly sent her into early labor. What would breaking the others take? Could she even do it?

What if I can't?

She turned to Daric, but he stood frozen, eyes not blinking, chest not moving. Alex was the same. She couldn't ask advice. She couldn't leave, couldn't learn more. The decision had to be made right here, right now, with apparently the weight of the world hanging in the balance.

Balance. Is there really any such thing? All this is because I kept a promise?

She rejected the idea. She might have broken one Stulos, but the reason it existed in the first place had nothing to do with her. She was just another in a long line of people dealing with the consequences of someone else's actions.

I wonder what really caused all this. Or who.

Not that it mattered. What mattered was the deal in front of her. If she agreed to try, it was a promise she'd have to follow through on, because if she didn't destroy the remaining Stulos, the world would reset. Her child would never be born. Never live.

Never experience…anything.

Tarian gulped back the sudden lump in her throat. If she *did* manage to break the other Stulos, then the world would continue. Changed in ways she couldn't foresee maybe, but her daughter would have a chance. They'd *all* have a chance. And the Dulra would be here to help, she assumed. Though they were impartial, the meaning of balance swayed with the ocean tides and the Balance Court was the moon.

"What if I do nothing?" Tarian wondered out loud.

The Dulra answered in soft whispers. *Then we fail. By Agreement, all Ancients depart these planes. Without magic, the world will die.*

Tarian blinked. It wouldn't renew with other people. It would die completely. *Who had the power to make that kind of Agreement? Never mind, I don't want to know.*

"So you're saying I can go back, if I do as First Mother suggests." Tarian swallowed at the idea. First Mother seemed to think sacrificing the baby was the only way to restore a Stulos. *Not acceptable.*

Tarian studied the stationary woman. Even frozen, her eyes shot ice daggers. *What the hell happened to you, to make you this bitter?*

"Or Option B, I can continue on destroying the rest of the Stulos, which will unite the planes? That sum it up?"

Or do nothing. The voices sounded strangely matter of fact. Not nearly as ominous as they should.

"If I do this. If I agree…" She stopped. *Who am I kidding? Of course I'll do it. I started this, I should finish it.*

As she thought about it, a sensation passed over her of something warm, like she stood near a fireplace on a cold day. She shivered as the feeling settled around her body. Something, or someone, hovered in the room, unseen. Someone pulled strings, influencing things. She could almost sense a signature, not quite there, but *present* anyway. Whoever or whatever it was, it had its own agenda. *What is driving all this?*

As she thought the words, the feeling departed. Whoever it was backed off once they realized she'd sensed them.

I don't know enough. Not nearly enough. Moments like these, when she needed advice, reopened the gaping wound cased by her mother's death. Just the simple act of trying to discuss an issue with her, gone forever, hurt.

What would you do, Mother? Take on the world? Hope you understood enough to make it work?

In her mind, she could see her mother's serene face, and hear her calm voice with perhaps a twinge of amusement. *"The real question isn't 'what would I do.' The real question, daughter, is what would you do. You were never one to take a mother's advice at face value."*

Tarian thought about it, her lips twitching in a half smile. *Whatever I have to do, to protect the baby, to make things right. For everybody.*

She nodded to herself. Looked up at the ring of Balance Court. "I'll destroy the remaining three Stulos if you'll help my child, when the time comes for her to right your ancient wrong."

Agreed.

Several things happened at once. The fire crackled, First Mother drew in a breath to continue arguing with Ruarc, Macari stumbled, the baby kicked, Daric squeezed her arm, and the Balance Court spoke.

Agreement has been reached.

The fire flared. The medallion in Tarian's chest ushered a surge of power toward it. The way Macari grabbed at her stomach, Tarian assumed that she not only continued to carry the Fire Artifact in her navel, but she felt the same surge. *Or maybe, she made an Agreement too?*

To her right, Tarian noticed Ruarc studying her. She returned his stare. More than anyone else in the room, he seemed to understand exactly what had happened and who had been at the center of it. And he seemed to be very, very curious about the Agreement.

Not a chance, bud. Not without getting something in return. She offered him a wink and turned away. When she glanced back to see his reaction, he'd vanished.

The Dulra disappeared into the darkness of the outer reaches of the room in pairs, with no other words uttered. Tarian watched them go, baffled, until only two pair remained, one pair near her, and one near First Mother. *All this was to get an Agreement with me? Why bring everyone else?*

Daric leaned close and whispered, "Whatever the Agreement is, she doesn't like it."

The woman's eyes shot daggers in Tarian's direction. Her scent was stronger now, though she didn't gather focus or power. Still, Tarian felt strongly it would be better if they left. Tarian shrugged at her, cast one more curious look at Macari.

Macari shifted, causing her hood to drop enough to expose her face. She stared at Tarian with an expression that suggested a desperate need to communicate something. Intense, wide eyes, stiff body language. She kept her body turned away from First Mother. *I wish I knew why you were here. It means something. I just don't know what.*

Then she remembered something the Dulra had said. *The keys will be returned.* And here two of them stood. Two Keepers, of Water and Fire. Tarian nodded once, her gaze flicked down to the girl's navel and back up, and saw Macari relax slightly.

She's made a deal of some sort.

Not wanting to betray any of her thoughts by an errant facial expression, Tarian turned her back on the First Mother. "Let's get out of here."

Alex lagged behind, keeping himself between her and First Mother. Though overt displays of power weren't possible here in the Balance Court, she wouldn't put it past the woman to launch her body into a physical attack. *Like to see her try, actually. Even pregnant, I could kick her ass.*

They made it to the travel portal without incident. It wavered in the air, expectant, the house of Xannon entryway visible within. She glanced back, but the larger room was now blocked. As she stepped to the portal, she noticed the ceiling, which had been a starry night when they entered, was now a blazing blue.

They emerged on the other side to find Calliope sitting on the floor in front of the portal, a book on her lap, and an Archivist on each side of her.

No, a Caraigg. Tarian mentally corrected herself. They looked a bit more pale, as though chipped from granite rather than a darker stone. And the Archivists never left the archives except under extraordinary circumstances. They were bound to it, or to the Keeper. And since she'd been at the Balance Court, they should have remained in the archives. The Caraigg, however, were not bound to any one location or person, but to the family.

"Tari!" Calliope set the book aside and scrambled to her feet. "It's been three days. I was just about to come in after you." Calliope looked at them all in turn. "Is everything okay? Are you okay? Did they…what did they do? What did they want? Is the baby all right?" Calliope's words tumbled so fast Tarian could barely keep up with them.

"Everything's fine, Calli."

Alex rounded on her. "Everything is *not* fine, *chica*. Don't lie, I can tell whatever that Agreement was, you're in the middle of it. It can't be good. And the First Mother looked ready to kill you *and* the baby. And you keep sucking in air like you're in pain when you think we don't notice."

"I think that's just my stomach growling." Tarian patted his arm. "Let's eat, and we can explain everything to Calli. You're right, I've made an Agreement. And I'm going to need help with this one. A lot of help."

11

Tarian leaned back from the table, letting her belly protrude out in front of her like a round, hard table all its own. She rested her hands on it, noting how her boobs spilled over. *I look like a beached whale.*

"I don't like it. You can't do it, *chica*. No way." Alex shoved his empty plate away from him. "You can't be going off like that. Not now."

She waited for him to finish his tirade. He'd been so protective lately. The bigger her stomach, the worse he got. She raised her eyebrows, but bit her tongue. Her mother's trick of letting the silence spin out was a good one. It kept her from saying something stupid, and it let the other person come to their senses. Sometimes.

"She doesn't have a choice, Alex." Calliope stood and started collecting plates. "It's done. It's an Agreement. More than that, it's a promise." Calliope flashed a quick smile toward Tarian and then took the stack of plates to the sink on the other side of the room.

"You tell her." Alex pointed at Daric. "She's out her mind."

Daric's lips twitched. "You really think us arguing with her is going to change her mind? She's the most stubborn person I know."

Tarian rubbed the small foot that pushed against her lower abdomen, and waited.

Calliope rejoined them at the table with a pitcher of iced water with lemons. "If we can accept the fact that she will at least *try* to keep her promise, then the real issue is one of logistics. Specifically, how do we break the other three Stulos? We only know where one other one is, and I'm not sure the same steps work on all four. And we don't have the *Book of Daemon* to rely on now."

Tarian shifted uncomfortably. The *Book of Daemon* had, of course, reverted back to the nearest daemons when she'd kept her promise to the Caraigg and broken the Earth Stulos.

"You didn't get any notes on the other three?"

Calliope paused in pouring a glass of water, her eyes gazing at the ceiling as she tried to remember. "Some. Probably not everything."

Daric took the glass Calliope offered and set it down untouched in front of him. "We can all help research. What kind of timeline we looking at?"

Tarian blinked at the glass. It jiggled, the water inside bouncing like someone poked it. She looked around and saw all the other glasses doing the same.

Alex frowned at the table. "You feel that? The ground shifted."

Tarian nodded as a distant rumble like a far away thunderstorm filled the room, followed by another gentle shake of the floor.

Tarian gripped the table. "Like they said, there's imbalance. I broke the Earth Stulos. This must be a reaction to that."

"Will they all react that way?" Calliope grimaced. "This could get pretty rough before we finish if all the elements react like this. Earthquakes, for Earth. What will Water do? And Air?"

Tarian bit her lip. She shuddered at the thought of Fire, unleashed. "We need to get through the rest as fast as possible, bring balance before everything falls apart. They said before the turn ends. But we don't measure time the same way, obviously."

Calliope set the pitcher down. "I'll go gather the books with Stulos references. You might ask *them* while I'm gone." She pointed to the corner where a Caraigg crouched, observing and blinking slowly with wide-open eyes.

As Calliope left the room, Tarian shifted her body so she could face the quietly waiting Caraigg. They'd greeted each other, but nothing more than that because everyone insisted Tarian eat before she did anything else. With everything that had happened in the past few days, her body was beyond empty. Food had definitely been the right move. A little sleep would be great too, but at the moment she didn't see that happening. Every now and then a rumble or shake of the ground reminded her of everything at stake, and how important it was to accomplish her mission. *Destroy the Stulos. All of them.*

She held out a hand to the Caraigg and it leapt forward, bouncing across the floor until it reached her feet and placed a paw-like hand in hers.

We serve, Keeper. The lone voice, rather than the entire network, piqued her curiosity. Usually she had to make them all stop talking at once.

Others are occupied. Distance prevents instant thought. Relays are possible.

"What can you tell me about breaking the other Stulos?"

Caraigg guarded Earth. Keeper has kept her promise, and freed Caraigg. Other Stulos require other guardians. Other guardians must be freed.

"Any idea who the guardians are?"

Keeper knows Water. Opposite Earth. Water guarded by Water Ancients most wise. Keeper has seen; Keeper knows.

Tarian nodded. She remembered her vision, the Old Woman obviously at the core of guarding the Water Stulos deep within the ocean not far from the House of Xannon. They'd already realized that water had to be the next to go, according to the order set forth by the Balance Court.

"What about Fire and Air?"

Two pin below, two pin above. Between to guard and block.

Tarian grunted.

"What? What'd they say?" Alex tapped the table. "I hate this. I can't hear anything."

"They say the other two Stulos are on the daemon plane."

"How the hell we s'pposed to get to the daemon plane,

chica?" Alex leaned back, his arms crossed, muttering in Spanish.

"Well, at least Water will be easy. It's right here. Basically."

"Only you would look at this situation and call it easy." Alex glared at her. "I'm not so sure it's something the Keeper should be doing. We can send a team, keep you away from the danger."

"I'm the one who made the Agreement, Alex. It has to be me. The Balance Court spelled it out, and why." She took a deep breath, glanced at Daric, then let it out slowly. *I have to tell them the whole thing.* "There's more to the story than just the Agreement. It wasn't just the First Mother who threatened the baby's life. The Balance Court told me if I can't break the other three Stulos, they'd explode or collapse on their own. The only way to restore balance then is to reset everything. Everyone. Back to the beginning."

Tarian swallowed to dampen her nerves. It didn't help. "We'd all be wiped out. All of us. Everywhere. And they also said..." She paused, took a long breath. Looked away from the fear she now saw on Alex's face. "They said that the baby would be needed, after we break the Stulos, to heal an ancient wound. So even when I break the other three Stulos, there's still more that has to be done. And not by us. She has to do it." Tarian rubbed her stomach, where the baby wiggled and squirmed, awakened by Tarian's own fear. "If we don't do our part, she won't...it won't... none of this will matter."

She looked back at Alex's now dead eyes as he absorbed the impact of what she said. Beside her, Daric sat stiff, leaning forward, attentive. She felt the tension from both of them mingle with her own. So much riding on the outcome of what they did here, and so much riding on the shoulders of an unborn infant. The idea was beyond laughable.

"So the choice is rebuild one missing Stulos by sacrificing my child's energy to it, or option B. Save the world, hoping that my daughter can finish what I start. Hoping that, somehow, it all works out. Hoping that she gets to have a life. So no matter how impossible it looks, I have to try. You see that, right?"

Daric squeezed her shoulder, a confidence she didn't feel radiating from his eyes. "*We* have to try."

Alex dropped his arms. His eyes shone with tears, and he swallowed hard. "We'll make it happen, *chica*."

Daric pushed his chair back and stood. "Time to get started. We need to start researching."

Alex and Tarian stood, but Alex held back. "*Chica*, I got some reports to give and something to show you. Just you." Alex glanced at Daric. "No offense."

Daric dipped his head slightly and stood. "I'll join Calli in the archives. Tari, you might think about changing clothes. Those look a little worse for wear."

Tarian grimaced as she surveyed her now ratty T shirt and ugly jeans. "I should wear a bathing suit, since I'll be getting wet. But none of them fit anymore."

Daric squeezed her shoulders. He gave her a quick kiss on the cheek, nodded at Alex, and left the kitchen.

"So what's up?"

Alex stared at his hands, flexing fingers in rhythmic motion. "You avoided the elephant in the room, *chica*. The threat from the First Mother. And Macari."

"I don't see First Mother really being an issue right now. It's not like she can cross the Between."

"Macari can."

Tarian considered it. "True. And I have a feeling she just might come for a visit. But you met her, Alex. Did she seem like a threat to you?"

Alex shook his head slowly. His eyes softened, his hands relaxed. "She *seemed* okay. Like one of us."

She grinned. "She was good at that, wasn't she? Her talent with emotions probably helps her gain trust. Something First Mother obviously doesn't have. You liked her, didn't you?"

Alex shrugged, refusing to meet her eyes.

"I'm sure the Balance Court will make sure we can do this without interference from her. They made the deal, remember?

There's nothing First Mother can do about it."

Alex frowned. "That don't change free will, *chica*. They can't stop someone from acting. They can only punish, after. That's their job."

"You *really* think Macari's a threat?"

Alex pointed out the door. "She strolled right onto our beach without anything stopping her, *chica*. What's to stop her doing it again? Or any other daemon."

"You." Tarian let the word hang in the air. "You're better with Earth than anyone I've ever known, Alex. And Frankie knows more about security than anybody alive, magical or otherwise. You protect this house, and the people in it. I know you and Frankie have been cooking up ideas for safe rooms, and special defenses. And she didn't land inside the house, Alex. She landed on the beach, a place we've never had maximum security."

"She could have landed inside."

"Doubt it."

"Admit it, *chica*, it's a possibility."

Tarian raised her eyebrows, something she did to end arguments since they'd been kids.

Alex snorted, but let the argument drop. "Speaking of special defense, I got something to show you." He stood, and circled the table, holding a hand to help her launch her body back upright.

The Caraigg at Tarian's feet scrambled out of the way. She hesitated, then told the creature to follow them. Alex raised an eyebrow but didn't comment.

Gotta trust them sometime. They can't be my information network if I don't.

Alex led her out of the kitchen and down the hallway toward the healer quarters and her mother's private office. "Tell me this isn't an excuse to get me moved into my mother's bedroom."

Alex's lips twitched. "Trust me."

"I'm not ready, Alex."

"You don't gotta be. This is something new. Patience, *chica*. This is something you gotta see."

When they reached the outer office her mother had used for official meetings, Tarian was itching to move on to the archives. She'd rather be anywhere but these rooms. The memories were just too uncomfortable. Even though her mother had died in the receiving hall, it didn't hit her gut like her mother's private rooms did. Tarian could still feel her presence, smell her signature on everything. She swallowed the sudden lump in her throat and willed the tears to back the hell off.

Alex paused in the center of the room and then held out both hands. "Notice anything?"

12

Tarian glanced around her mother's workspace. Desk, chair, bookcases crammed with books and objects of various magical intensity. Floor, black stone like the rest of the house. Security monitors on the desk and wall next to it which showed the main parts of the house and beach. All seemed like it always was. Her mother didn't have the technology issues Tarian had, so it wasn't surprising to find two state-of-the-art computers. The bookcases held mementos her mother had collected over the years. Bits and pieces of events and people, creating a history that Tarian didn't know. *No way to know, now.*

"I don't get it. What am I supposed to notice?" Even the two chairs for visitors looked as they always had.

"Told Frankie you wouldn't see it." Alex looked positively smug. He crossed his arms over his chest and waited.

"Challenge accepted." Tarian moved resolutely further into the room. She opened her senses to allow the magical ambiance to sink in, looking for anything out of the ordinary. Any signature not her mother's. She felt a residue of Frankie somewhere, and Alex of course. But with him standing next to her it was impossible to tell if he'd tampered with anything.

She crossed to the bookcase on the far wall and let her hand drift over the books there. History. Genealogy. A few romance books. *Romance?*

Tarian picked up a book, distracted by the thought that her

mother, her *mother*, read romance books. She'd have denied it, vehemently, except that her mother's signature was all over the book. She'd held it, she'd turned each page. She'd enjoyed it. *My mother read romances.*

Dumbfounded, she slid the book back on the shelf. As she did so, her hand touched the wood, and the tingle of passive magic traveled up her arm. Startled, she snatched her hand back. The bookcase wavered, wiggled, and turned translucent. She could see it, but she could see *through* it too, into a dark space beyond. She couldn't make out any details. She turned back to Alex.

"Safe room?"

Alex grinned, obviously proud. "Nah. Better than that. Go on. It's keyed to you, me, Frankie, and Calli. And the baby. Maybe. Nobody else can open it. Not even daemon. I don't think." A brief cloud crossed his face. "Guess we could check it, now you've freed the Caraigg. Once you open the door, anybody with you can follow. Remember to close it, once you're through."

Tarian held her hands out in front of her and walked through the bookcase, not quite trusting she wouldn't just slam her face into solid wood. The bookcase and the wall beyond parted for her as though it was air. It felt like passing through a cold curtain of icicles, but lasted just a brief moment. Soon she was on the other side, standing in a dark space, her head almost touching the ceiling. Soft blue lights sparked at her feet, lighting the way.

"A tunnel?" Tarian took a few more steps, to allow Alex and the Caraigg to join her. Once they passed through, Alex brushed his hand against a small glowing stone on the left and the wall behind them solidified. It looked like solid, black stone. No bookcase, no office. No way back.

Alex gestured. "Go on. See where it goes."

Tarian took a careful step, keeping her hands out to the sides to hold onto the walls. The floor was ultrasmooth, and the way lit up as she walked so she didn't worry too much about stumbling. "It's a good thing I'm not claustrophobic."

"Yeah, I know. Bit tight. But we got limited space to work

with, plus…well you'll see in a sec."

Around her, the walls pressed in a bit, which she shook off as an optical illusion. Power tickled her skin. Every inch of the surrounding rock was embedded with power, and exuded Alex's own signature. He'd used his special talent with stone to carve this secret pathway. "So nobody can get through either end?"

"Like I said, you, me, Frankie and Calli. We dunno about the baby yet. We can test that when she's born, fix it if she can't. Frankie put special wires around all sides that he thinks will keep out daemon of all sorts, unless invited. Anybody here has to come with one of us. No exceptions. The entry key is that one shelf, not the others. I put it high, just in case."

Tarian frowned. "In case what?"

"In case a baby touches it." Alex laughed. "You remember Calli? Little fingers like to explore, *chica*."

"What's to stop her from climbing the shelves?" Tarian couldn't help the chuckle. "Calli did that too."

"Nothing. But the other side has safeguards. This whole tunnel is a safe room. A place to hide or withstand attacks. And here…" Alex touched her shoulder, to stop her forward progress. "Don't run into the wall."

It looked like the tunnel simply continued on forever. Tarian took a cautious step forward, then another, then a third. Her toe scraped something solid. She put out a hand and felt solid wall, though it looked like air. "Dead end?"

"Frankie liked it, just in case someone snuck in with ya. Somebody don't know, they'll slam into it. And if they ain't one of us, a stasis shield binds them to the wall until released. Now turn right, and search near the top."

She did as instructed, her hand encountering several rough stones protruding from the curved wall. After feeling around each one, nothing happened, she looked a question back at Alex.

"Both hands, on the third from the left. And wait."

She had a hard time reaching them, her stomach pushing into the wall as she tried to get both hands on the indicated stone.

Once she had them both there, she had a hard time talking. "How long?"

"Just a sec. It has to be calibrated. You only gotta do this once."

After a long pause, Tarian felt it. Power spilled from the stones and into her hands, up her arm, and down her spine, traveled back out again. A distant click, a whir, and a hole in the rock appeared.

"Wow." Tarian stepped through, having to duck her head slightly to get in. Inside, a small room lit by blue bulbs of power, a daybed, a table with two chairs, and an entire wall of monitors showing every inch of the House and surrounding beach. "It's a secret command center."

"Complete with food, supplies and a toilet, of sorts." Alex indicated an inset on the far side of the small space. "You could live down here if you had to. At least for a week or two. We'll have to get Calli in here to calibrate for her. That ain't all."

He pointed at the door. "Try the other side now." He bounced a bit on his toes, as if this were the part he really wanted to show her.

She slipped past him, feeling the warmth of him along her back, and into the tunnel. The other wall looked just as much of a dead end as everything else. "So do I twitch another rock, or what?"

"Nah. This part only works for you. Maybe Calli." Alex moved to her side and tapped the wall. "Frankie didn't like putting you down here without a back way out, but neither of us wanted an open back door somebody could maybe breach. So this was our workaround. Don't touch it, you probably don't wanna use it yet."

"Use what?" She couldn't see or feel anything unusual about the wall.

"We're way below the ocean surface here, and the only way out is through water. You get in a fix and need to get out, you put both hands on this wall and pulse it with water energy." Alex demonstrated by placing both palms against the rough stone. "It works like a portal, but instead of stepping through it'll suck you out and dump you straight into the ocean. Deep. You'll be on

your own then, but we both figured it was the place you knew
best. Nobody can swim like you, and ain't nobody gonna survive
a dump into the ocean like that without gear. Except you. And it
don't work in reverse."

Alex stepped away and gestured at the tunnel behind them.
"Plus, this whole thing is on the patrol path for the Ancients.
Figured a nice safety net, if it comes to that. So." Alex patted the
wall. "Back door. Just be ready to get wet."

The enormity of what they'd built filled Tarian with gratitude
and love. Her friends worried so much for her safety they'd built
her a bunker and a back door only she could operate. "I don't
know what to say. This is...this is brilliant, Alex. Really." She
turned to him, saw the pride and worry at war on his face, and
threw her arms around him. "This is the best present. Ever."

Alex folded her in a bear hug, so tight the baby protested by
kicking back. She laughed, and reached up to plant a giant kiss on
his cheek. "You really know how to impress girls. She likes it too."

Alex rubbed her arms, a giant grin on his face. "Just tryin' to
keep my girls safe."

The look in his eyes warmed her deep in her core, his obvious love for her spilling out in that look. On impulse she leaned
into him, her face pushing close to his, their eyes locked, her
lips a breath away from his. His hands on her arms stilled. For
a moment they stood, unspoken words and feelings swirling
between them. Longing on his part, guilt on hers.

If she moved her head slightly, she could kiss him. She knew
he'd take her in his arms, and return the kiss with his entire soul.
Down here, in this safe place, nobody would know but them.
He'd saved her so many times she'd lost count. He was one of the
fathers of her baby in a situation so complicated she couldn't even
fathom it anymore. She owed him so much. And she loved him.

But not the way he wants. Not the way he needs.

She watched the warm light dim in his eyes, felt the moment
slide down over them and drift away into the stone. Alex squeezed
her arms. "Time to get back. You got research to do."

Alex turned away, and started walking back through the tunnel, back the way they'd come. Tarian stood watching him, her heart aching. The baby shifted, as though she knew her mother had just broken a man's heart. Again.

"I'm sorry, Alex." She whispered. With a sigh, she followed him.

When they emerged from the hidey hole, Alex offered her a small smile. "To get back out, you just gotta send a small pulse. Small, *chica*. Not heavy. I know how you are."

"Got it." She watched the bookshelf reform, aware of the tension radiating off Alex but unsure what to do about it.

Alex stepped back and surveyed the result. Finally he nodded. "Could use a few more touches but mostly it's done. Frankie is working on the beach net. I should check in with him." Alex hesitated.

Tarian held out a hand to him, but he just shook his head slightly and left the room. She let him go, sadness and frustration melding. A distant rumble sounded as the floor shook slightly. Various objects on the bookshelf rattled. The baby squirmed, and tiny shoots of pain filled Tarian's abdomen. She rubbed it, trying to calm her mood so the baby would relax. *It's going to take a lot more than a belly rub to soothe this ache.*

She caught a glimpse of herself in the mirror on the wall beside the door. She looked abused, like she'd been in a wrestling match with an extremely dirty pig. Her belly protruded through holes in the shirt. *Some Keeper I make.* Shaking her head, she turned her back on the reflection and left the room.

13

When Tarian opened the door to the archives, she found Calliope and Daric arguing over a pile of books, pieces of paper and cloth scattered around, Archivists hunched looking resentful in corners, and a cup of PJ's coffee waiting for her.

They both looked up when she opened the door, words dying on their lips. "Whatever the argument was, I don't wanna know. Give me the coffee." She crossed to the beacon of hope and took it in her hands, letting the warmth seep into her. She inhaled deeply, the aroma sinking into her nose and pores like the rich, life-altering treat it was. *Oh, sweet heaven.*

Daric laughed at her blissful expression as he pulled out a chair for her.

Tarian savored the coffee for a moment before she dove into the problem. "Do we know anything more about the other three Stulos?"

Calliope sat down, pushing books out of the way. "Most of this is more legend than fact."

Daric tapped one of the books. "We have a good, educated guess though."

"Guessing isn't good enough." Calliope thrust her chin out. "This is dangerous, and it's going to get worse."

"Well, I do have more going for me this time." Tarian held up her hand and started ticking off her points on her fingers. "I know what to expect. How it feels. I know the guardians, and I know they welcome my presence. And with them I have the ability to actually reach the thing, something most couldn't do. Plus, I'm sure I'll have their help, since the Old Woman is the one who pushed for this in the first place."

Calliope leaned back in her chair, stretching. "The problem is Water, since it's the second to be broken, requires more effort. Definitely three women. Plus an artifact or two. Each Stulos will become progressively harder to collapse, a precaution taken against natural disasters and malicious intent."

Tarian sat back, warm cup rested on her stomach, and thought about it. *Three women. Me. Calliope. And who?*

"What kind of women?"

Calliope yawned. "It's all about power and the ability to merge it together. You and I have practice now, so it'll be easier. Whoever the third is will need to be able to join us. Not an easy thing. Especially underwater. I'd say it should be someone water based, so at least they'd be less worried about the environment."

Tarian frowned. "I don't know anyone full water."

"It has to be women?" Daric sat back. "Why can't we take a team of Sentinels down there?"

"Because a team of Sentinels would probably drown." Tarian put the coffee reluctantly on the table. Her stomach churned and somehow it didn't taste as good as it usually did. "And the only ones that can even get near that portion of ocean are those taken there by the Ancients. They wouldn't let me bring a horde down there, even if I *could* bond with them enough to harness all our power. Less is more for that sort of thing. Plus, it requires complete and absolute trust."

"So take me." Daric said. "You trust me. Right?"

"She can't. I told you. It has to be women." Calliope interrupted. "It says so specifically in several places. Your genetics are wrong."

Tarian grinned. "So this is what the argument was about?"

Calliope blew out a quick breath that moved her hair. "He

doesn't get it. He thinks he can muscle his way through this, but he can't. This is all magic, all mental. No muscle."

Calliope thrust her chin out at Daric, daring him to argue again. He smirked but only waved his hand for her to continue. "Once we get past the Water Stulos, it'll get even harder." Calliope picked up a book so ancient it looked like it might dissolve to dust with the slightest provocation. "This says Air is not whole, and until it is, it can't be broken."

Tarian glanced at Daric. "What does that mean? How can it support the planes if it's not even whole?"

Calliope pointed at the piece of cloth. "And that seems to indicate that Fire is going to be almost impossible to reach, without help. It's on the daemon side, and the guardians are difficult at best. They have a natural ability to thwart most attempts to locate them. Not to mention breaking that Stulos appears to require..." Calliope trailed off, shifting on her feet. She turned and put the cloth down. Arranged the books. Anything but look at Tarian.

"What, Calli? What's it say?" Tarian leaned forward to look at the books, but without reading each one she had no hope of figuring out what was upsetting her sister.

"I can't be sure. It's very difficult to read." Calliope continued to shuffle books. "We might need to ask the Archivists. They won't like it, but they are bound by Agreement to answer. Or maybe you can ask the Caraigg. We definitely need more information before we attempt...anything."

"You have to tell her, Calli. This isn't the time for secrets," Daric said, his voice quiet.

"Tell me what? Attempt what?" Tarian kept her tone light, soft. Calliope hated divulging things that she hadn't fully researched, especially if they were dangerous things. "Calli, what's wrong?"

Calliope shifted. "Nothing specific. It's more what's *not* here, than what is."

Tarian put a soft hand on her sister's shoulder. "What's not there?"

Calliope turned to face her, eyes full of worry. "What happens next."

"Next?"

"When all four Stulos are destroyed, what happens next? There's nothing on the outcome, nothing detailing the consequences, either to the people doing the destruction or to the world as a whole. Nothing at all." Calliope pulled on her hair. "And the information surrounding the last Stulos is sketchy at best. We just don't know enough."

"And?" Tarian urged her to continue, sensing there was still something more to Calliope's concern than a lack of information.

"And we don't have time to get it. The timing speeds up with each Stulos you collapse. Think of it like a table, with one leg missing. It's still standing, but it's not stable. And when you take off the opposite leg..."

"It's all wobbly and easy to knock over." Tarian finished.

"And when the third leg goes..." Daric supplied. "The thing crashes."

Calliope shook her head. "Not exactly, because the Between is still there. The cushion will support the structure for a short time. Very short. If the fourth one isn't broken in time...the only thing we know for sure is what the Balance Court told you."

Tarian drew in a deep breath. "Reset."

They all looked at each other. The words and full impact sank in, the weight of what they were trying to do resting on Tarian's shoulders like an anvil. Daric ran his hands through his hair, making it stand on end in a way Tarian found incredibly sexy. Calliope sniffed, her eyes wide and bright with unshed tears. Tarian took in deep breath, letting it out slowly. The baby squirmed a bit, then was still again.

"They wouldn't have asked me to do this if it couldn't be done. And they promised things for the future." Tarian rubbed her stomach. "They promised to help her when she needed it. To me, that says we'll still be here to *need* help. We can't let fear stop us from doing the right thing, Calli."

"That's what I said." Daric nodded his agreement.

"I'm not saying we should." Calliope huffed. "What I'm saying is, without more to go on, we're blind. It's like trying to fight with your hands tied, blindfolded, and both feet in shackles."

"It's not as bad as that." Tarian put a comforting hand on Calliope's knee. "We have each other. And we're a pretty damn good team. We have the Old Woman and all the Water Ancients. Think about that, Calli. Water Ancients. The wisest, most powerful beings in existence. And they're on *our* side. We can get their guidance before we go any further. We'll ask them, before we break the Stulos. We'll make sure we're doing it right."

Calliope bit her lip. "We still need a third. And I can't think of anyone either."

"We'll figure it out." Tarian sat back, her hands resting on her stomach. "Plus, I have a feeling we may have a friend we didn't realize we had."

Daric raised an eyebrow.

"Macari. She has the Fire Artifact. And she didn't seem too happy with her mother. She'll help us."

Tarian spoke with the confidence she probably shouldn't be feeling. Still the nagging voice of doubt poked at her.

What have I dragged us into? What will the final price be, for keeping a promise? Can this promise even be kept? Have I been set up to fail? Is there any way to succeed at all? Will the baby ever experience life?

A loud screech filled the air, shattering the contemplation. Calliope squeaked, Tarian jumped. Daric leapt to his feet. All of the Archivists jumped up to the top shelves, hissing. Tarian stood, readying herself for a fight. Whatever the sound was, it demanded attention.

The door to the archives burst open and Alex ran in. "We've been breached. Tari, the tunnel!"

Daric ran around the table to grab Tarian's hand and pull her to the door.

Calliope jumped up, shouting "What tunnel?" with her hands over her ears.

Alex pushed her to the door. "Run. Follow Tari."

As they entered the hallway, Alex sprinted past them. "Keep going, don't come out until we sound an all clear."

"What the hell is the screeching?" Tarian panted, trying to stabilize her overly large stomach with both hands as she ran.

"Frankie's early warning system." Alex called over his shoulder before leaving them behind as he rounded the corner into the rotunda.

Daric sped up, putting himself between her and Calliope and whatever waited for them in the rotunda. As they rounded the corner and the rotunda came into full view, Tarian slowed, assessing the situation. The room, filled with Sentinels, seemed otherwise calm. But the screeching continued, and she felt the medallion burn as though it sensed a threat. She covered it with one hand, letting out a little cry of pain as the heat penetrated her fingers.

"Tari?"

Tarian shook her head. "I don't get anything specific."

Daric narrowed his eyes. "Wherever Alex was sending you, how fast can you get there?"

Tarian frowned. "I'm not helpless. I can help defend my house."

Calliope tugged on one arm but Tarian refused to move. "This is *my* house."

Daric stopped, giving her a look that would drill holes in mountains. "Your duty is to protect the Scion, above anything else. Our duty is to protect *you*. Let us do our job, Tari. Get somewhere safe."

Frustrated, Tarian felt the power within her growing, the medallion anxious to be released. Daric, feeling it, growled. "Tari, it'll be harder with you here. Remember last time. How many died, trying to protect the Scion? How will you keep your promises if you're dead?"

Calliope gasped. Tarian's heart froze in place. *How dare he!*

Her indignation rose, and ended abruptly as the tiny voice in the back of her head told her he was right. Alex, Daric, Frankie...

they'd all lay down their lives for her. It would be doing them a disservice to treat it so casually. She could bring the whole house down on their heads. Never mind the external threat, whatever it might be. She was just as much of one from inside, in her present condition.

"We're going," She shouted, and pulled Calliope with her out of the rotunda and down the hall toward her mother's suite of rooms.

"What tunnel?" Calliope panted.

"You'll see." Tarian dragged her sister along with her, anxious to get behind the door of the safe room before whatever it was made it into the house and saw them escaping.

14

Tarian led the way as fast as she could, dodging more Sentinels as they ran to the front of the house. When they reached her mother's office, it appeared deserted. She crossed immediately to the bookcase and brushed the shelf with her fingers. Calliope gasped as it dissolved in front of them and Tarian pulled her through. She pressed her palm to the wall and sealed it behind them, then paused to breathe a sigh of relief. *Made it.*

Tarian started down the narrow passage, Calliope following behind. Once they were safely in the tunnel, the medallion calmed, the heat diminished, her pulse slowed. It felt safe here. As though nothing would ever find them, nothing could ever breach this space.

"When did this get here? How?"

"Alex. It's the secret he and Frankie were working on. Wait until you see the command center."

When they reached the nook carved out by Alex and Frankie, Calliope stopped in the doorway, stunned. Her eyes swept the room, her mouth open in amazement.

Bet I looked like that too.

Monitors covered the wall to the right, and all were active. Tarian saw every section of the house, from the beach to the kitchen. Even the archives, the receiving hall, and the arena. It provided a perspective she'd never had before. The ability to *see* everything, all at once. It made her feel voyeuristic.

Movement on the beach caught her attention. She stood in front of the monitor that scanned the area, studying the scene. Calliope joined her, and the two of them watched a large group of Sentinels, weapons drawn, circle something or someone. She couldn't see who or what because there were so many of them. She also couldn't see Alex or Daric.

"What the hell is going on?" She huffed in frustration. "I don't see any attack, do you?"

Calliope shook her head. "I can't tell anything from here. I can't read emotions through a monitor. The body language is tense though."

Some of the Sentinels shifted, and Tarian caught a glimpse of white hair. She squinted, willing the crowd to move so she could see. They stubbornly refused to cooperate.

"Wish I could hear." She'd never have thought anything was missing in this little hidey hole, but suddenly audio seemed to be a great thing to include. She'd have to ask Frankie about it.

"Wish they'd move out of the way. I can't see who's in the middle."

Almost as if they heard her, a portion of the group split, leaving an empty space near the walkway to the entrance. Through the gap, Alex, Daric and a tall, blond girl could be seen, both the girl and Alex gesticulating wildly while Daric looked on, serious but not alarmed.

Tarian let out a sound of recognition. "Macari."

"Who?" Calliope looked at her.

"The daemon. I told you about her, the one who just popped up on the beach weeks ago. The one that was attacked. Remember what Alex said about the torture? That room with the dead girls? She was the one who killed the guy. The one who unlocked the Fire Artifact. Her name is Macari."

"She's here again? How is she doing that? Did she bring the artifact with her?" Calliope gazed at the screen.

"Bet Frankie and Alex would love to know how she breaches

their defenses." Tarian turned to leave. "She definitely brought the artifact with her."

"Where are you going?"

"I'm going to go talk to her."

"Alex said not to come out until he sounded the all-clear." Calliope protested.

"She's not a threat." Tarian hesitated, thinking back to Alex's adamant refusal to agree with her on that detail.

"We don't know what she is, Tari. We don't know her. Not really. Just because she had a bad experience last time she visited doesn't make her trustworthy."

"No. But it doesn't make her untrustworthy either. I'm pretty good at reading people. My gut tells me she's okay."

Calliope glanced down at Tarian's stomach. "Is it worth the risk?"

Tarian rolled her eyes, frustrated. *This pregnancy can't end soon enough.*

Her sister was right. Alex was right. They were all right. It didn't make it any easier to live with.

"Fine." She stepped back into the room and centered herself in front of the monitor again. Alex and Macari continued to talk, both using their hands in a way that made Tarian smile. Daric shifted, but his gaze never left the scene. He studied it, his eyes raking in every detail.

The monitors couldn't convey whether magic was being used, another weakness. Tarian watched the body language of the guards, and Daric, and concluded that Macari wasn't gathering any power. But whatever she was saying, she seemed urgent to get her point across. Alex argued. Daric evaluated. The Sentinels stood ready, whatever the outcome.

When she saw Alex cross his arms, she knew. *Macari lost the argument, whatever it was.*

Daric spoke then, putting a hand on Alex's shoulder. Tarian knew that stubborn set of Alex's jaw, she'd seen it often enough. Although…as Tarian watched, tiny subtle changes in Alex's body, from the way he flexed his hands to the way his eyebrow dipped slightly showed he was conflicted. His head tilted ever so slightly to the left, another sign he was listening. As she watched, he shifted from one foot to the other, then back.

Giving in but not happy about it.

There was definitely something going on between Alex and Macari. The daemon was a natural flirt. Tarian had recognized that in the first few seconds of meeting her, when she'd first appeared on the beach weeks ago. And it appeared Alex was not immune to her charms. Tarian looked at Daric. He didn't seem to be taking the bait, but he was listening intently.

"What the hell is she saying? I wish I could read lips."

Calliope shrugged.

Beneath them, the ground rumbled and grumbled. Everything shook ever so slightly, but Tarian could tell they felt it on the beach as well because everyone froze, looked around, then Macari started gesturing even more than she had before. The flirt was gone. Her stare, intense, her body, stiff. She kept looking over her shoulder.

Finally, whatever she said won Alex over. He gestured, and Sentinels began walking up the path, Macari behind them, Alex and Daric behind her, with more Sentinels bringing up the rear. Those at the back stayed on the beach and spread out, weapons still drawn. Poised.

"What the hell?" Tarian turned to Calliope. "We should go see what's up."

"We should wait." Calliope bit her lip. "He hasn't said it's clear."

"He's on his way here, Calli. Look." Tarian pointed to another monitor, where Alex, Daric, and Macari had just appeared in the rotunda. They turned down a hallway, disappearing off that monitor to appear in another, the one in the hallway near the healer's quarters.

"Just wait, Tari. If they're really on the way here, then it'll only take another minute." Calliope poked her head out of the door, angling so that Tarian couldn't see beyond her.

A minute later she heard voices as the bookcase dissolved. Light footsteps approached. Calliope moved into the tunnel, staring with blatant curiosity.

Tarian moved over to the far side of the room, her hand sneaking up to the medallion under her shirt. It lay still, calm. A second later, Macari rounded the corner and entered the room. "Well, they certainly tried hard." Macari grinned. "You've added security since last time."

Tarian leaned against the small table, her hands gripping the edge to make sure she didn't fall off balance, and to make sure if the medallion suddenly reacted she'd be braced for it. "I told you to use the entry alcoves."

Macari bounced up and down on her toes. "Yes but you didn't show it to me. I can only travel to places I've actually seen before. Even if only in a picture. And it's not like the House of Xannon is on a map anywhere. I traveled to the one place I knew."

Tarian gestured to the daybed. "Where're Alex and Daric?"

"They went to shore up the entryway, like it'll do them any good. I don't think their defenses are going to work against what's coming."

Tarian narrowed her eyes. "What's coming?"

Calliope continued her curious stare. "Did you bring the artifact?"

Macari lifted her blouse. In her navel, something red and gold glinted in the dim light. "I have it shielded pretty tight, but I doubt I need to. It doesn't act on its own. I have to push it."

"Fire needs air?" Tarian asked.

"Exactly." Macari dropped her shirt, staring at her curiously. She flounced onto the daybed, staring around the room as if taking in every detail. Calliope sat next to her.

"I'm…"

"Calliope." Macari finished. "I know. Alex told me. And you know who I am." Macari surveyed the wall of monitors. "I love technology. It's truly amazing how people have adapted to a life with no magic energy. You can feel the power humming, can't you?"

Tarian watched her, waiting. *Why is she here? What were they arguing about? What's coming?* Curiosity burned through her, but she kept her mouth shut as she watched the daemon study the wall of monitors, focusing on Alex whenever he disappeared from one and arrived in another.

Tarian leaned against the table, her hands gripping it for support. "Macari. Why did you hide your face at the Balance Court?"

Macari's back stiffened, and she turned away from the screens to look at Tarian. "Do you mind-speak?"

"You mean like with the Archivists?"

Macari shook her head. "No. I mean, with each other. Now. Are you mind-speaking now?"

Calliope shifted. "We…"

"Sometimes." Tarian interrupted.

Macari stared at her, and after a minute shook her head. "You don't. At least, not without help."

"So?"

"So, you wouldn't understand what it's like. In the Benata, mind touch is routine, and someone very powerful can know all of your thoughts. Anything that goes through your mind is in the open for all to see." Macari bit her lip. "If you can shield, then you keep some privacy. If you can't…well."

"Oh. How horrible." Calliope grimaced. "Having everyone know everything you're thinking?"

"So you were shielding? That's why you didn't look up?" Tarian studied the daemon's face. If she were human, Tarian would have guessed her to be about sixteen and an open book. Except…the only emotion she ever displayed on her face was a sense of playfulness. *Is that a shield?*

Macari's lips quirked. "First Mother is incredibly powerful. And as her daughter, and a member of the Court, I serve her and the Benata Court. It's a binding Agreement. If she wanted to know my thoughts, I'd have to reveal them. I was summoned to the Balance Court, but I didn't want First Mother to know why. So I tried not to give her a reason to ask."

"Why do I get the feeling there's more to that story?"

Macari shrugged. "Court structures are very political. There's always more to the story. Always layers."

"You're really good at deflecting." Tarian rubbed her stomach as the baby kicked. "Let's go back to the first question."

"Why didn't I look up?" Macari tilted her head.

Tarian tapped a foot and waited.

Macari's eyes widened. "You don't trust me."

"The jury's still out. And you're not making it easy. What're you hiding?"

Suddenly Macari froze, her entire body still, her gaze focused on one of the monitors. Tarian followed her gaze. The beach, now with only a few Sentinels standing guard, sparkled as though glitter infused the air. She took a step closer to the monitor. The sparkles swirled, dipped, swayed, moved.

"What is that?"

"Stars." Macari jumped up. "So soon. I thought we'd have more time. That's…we have to leave. Now."

Tarian turned to her. "What *is* that? What have you done?"

"I didn't…" Macari stared at the screen. "Didn't think they'd…which ones did she…"

"Try finishing a sentence."

Macari pointed at the glitter and groaned. It swirled and moved up the walkway with more purpose than glitter should contain. "Those are Erckling scouts. They must have followed me. I don't know how. But it's not good. Stars." She said the word like it was the worst swear word she knew.

"Erckling?" Calliope asked, studying the scene. "You mean the fairies that carry away children in stories? I pictured them larger, somehow."

Macari turned her back to it, her words tumbling over themselves in an effort to explain. "They come in all sizes. Those are scouts. After you left the Balance Court, I returned to the Wind through the window the members had left when they summoned me. The scouts must have followed me through. But I didn't think anything could do that, or trace me through the Wind. Is there a back door to this place?"

Tarian watched the trail of glitter, fascinated, until it reached a Sentinel. The woman shot her weapon, but it had no effect. She collapsed, surrounded by the sparkling fog. Then it moved on, leaving her sprawled on the ground. "You mean a travel portal? Like Alex taught you?"

"Yes, the window. The Balance Court summoned me and I stepped through. Nobody knew it was there…" The way Macari shifted and trailed off told Tarian she'd just thought of someone who *did* know.

"And you didn't close it behind you when you returned? You left it open?"

"Close?" Macari tilted her head.

"Shit. Anybody can walk through an open portal. How could you not know that?"

Macari shrugged. "We don't travel that way."

Tarian pointed at the screen. "These Erckling. They have bigger friends?"

"Much bigger." Macari bounced on her feet. "They're used for protection, most of the time."

Calliope squeaked. "Tari, look."

The shining trail had moved beyond the beach and now swept down the hallway toward her mother's office. Along the way, Sentinels lay on the ground, either unconscious or dead, Tarian couldn't tell. *The alarms. Why aren't they going off?*

"They can't get through the door." She tried to sound confident but she distinctly remembered Alex's non-confident "I think." He hadn't tested to see if it was daemon proof down here, nor creature proof.

"They can get through anything." Macari winced. "I don't feel anything down here that would stop me or them."

A buzz, growing louder, entered the hallway and Tarian knew they'd been breached. "What stops them?" She focused power faster than she ever had. The medallion grew hot and glowed.

"Nothing. They don't stop until they do what they were sent to do."

Dread filled Tarian, from her head to the tips of her toes. Inside, the baby squirmed, kicked, and used her internal organs as a drum set. The overwhelming sense of fear from the inside thrust Tarian into full-on panic. Power circled around her, waiting for focus, for intention. Her first thought was a shield, but the entire tunnel was shielded and these creatures had waltzed in like it was nothing. Calliope put one up between them and the attackers anyway, but Tarian searched for something else.

Back door. We have to take the back door.

"There's another way out. Can these things swim?"

Macari's head whipped around. "Why?"

"Can they?" Tarian pushed past Macari, brushing her with her stomach.

"They're air daemon, just lesser. They don't like water." She said it as though the fact should be obvious.

Buzzing, like a thousand angry bees, filled the space as the creatures descended on the three of them crammed into the hallway. Though Tarian couldn't feel any wings, she felt stings, hundreds of them, on every exposed inch of her body. Each sting sank white-hot fire into her bloodstream, which traveled so fast Tarian's knees buckled before she could even throw any power at them. She couldn't focus on what to hit, there were so many. She screamed as they continued their attack. "Wall. Door. Touch." Sentences refused to form, but her anguish caught Calliope's attention.

Her sister pulled on Tarian's arms, trying to get her to her feet. Her legs felt like rubber, her arms, worse, and the baby...the initial jolt of fear and panic had been replaced. By silence.

Are you okay? No answering emotion, movement of any kind. "The baby." Tarian managed to gasp.

"Help me! Get her up." Calliope screamed.

For an answer, Macari, instead of reaching for Tarian, began to spin in place, her arms outstretched. Energy rushed from Macari, over Tarian, into the surrounding space. Words Tarian couldn't understand infiltrated the deafening, angry buzz, then silence.

Every inch of her body felt like it was on fire, but the pinches and stings had stopped. The buzz, gone. Tarian looked down the hallway. No glitter on the floor. Nothing. As though the creatures had never been.

Calliope stared down the hallway, then back at Macari, her hands still on Tarian's arm. "What'd you do?"

"Sent them home." Macari said. "They aren't the problem. The real problem is, they'll do what they were designed to do."

"What's that?"

"Report. They're scouts. And they're keyed to me. And now, Tarian." Macari grabbed Tarian's other arm, helping to lift her back onto wobbly feet.

"Kill them?" Her lips refused to form anything more than one syllable. Frustrated, Tarian shook her head to clear it, but everything was foggy. Her arms were rubber balloons with no air.

Macari shook her head. "I don't do that. It's not their fault. They were sent. They're only doing what they were told to do."

Calliope pushed Tarian against the wall, both hands on her shoulders. Warmth spread from her sister's fingers into her shoulder blades, deep into the muscle, and worked its way down. The fiery pain lessened, her arms and legs feeling more like limbs and less like rubber bands.

Macari bounced up and down on her toes. "We really need to leave. Do you have a back door or not? I can't sense anything here except a dead end."

"Gone. Right?" Tarian blinked several times, trying to clear the fog.

Macari shook her head. "Scouts never operate on their own. They soften the target for the next wave, leave a scent that can be tracked, then report back. Their big brothers will be here fast."

"Why are they following you?"

"They aren't really following *me*. They're looking for you." Macari pointed at Tarian's stomach. "Or more specifically, her."

Tarian held her stomach with both hands. The baby hadn't moved much since the attack. If at all. "Why?"

Macari shifted, and bit her lip. She seemed to be fighting with herself, then finally responded. "They've been sent to find her so the second wave can take her. As backup."

Tarian froze. Her blood turned to ice. Every instinct said to run. It also said there was more to the story.

Calliope disappeared into the command center.

Tarian stared at Macari. "Backup to who?"

Macari held her gaze. "Me. I was sent to kill her."

15

Tarian's body reacted a lot slower than she'd like. She tried to launch her power, but it felt sluggish and weak. Her mind swirled, disoriented. Then she realized it wasn't her power at all, it was her body, despite Calliope's healing. The dolphin cries grew louder. The ground rumbled, nearly throwing her off her feet.

Calliope rushed out of the command center, her face white. "Alex, Daric, the others. All out cold." Calliope swallowed, not voicing the other obvious reason for everyone lying crumpled on the ground. *They can't be dead. They can't be.*

Tarian pushed herself into the room, to see for herself. In the monitor, she saw glistening creatures that flowed like white fog. Their bodies shone in the sun as they spun in place, five or six of them, and then started up the path. They ignored the prone bodies of the Sentinels and continued into the house.

The room shook. A loud rumble, as though a thousand large trucks pushed their way through the house, filled her ears.

"Tari! We have to go. We're trapped in here."

Tarian couldn't clear her thoughts. *What's wrong with me?*

"It's too late, it'll take forever for the effects to wear off. The scouts inject a venom that keeps the victim disoriented until the drones can arrive."

"Whatdotheydo?" Tarian's words slurred. She felt drunk. The baby didn't move.

"Back door?" Macari repeated, her tone urgent.

Tarian barely made out the words, but latched onto them as a lifeline. She managed to point in what she hoped was the general direction of the hallway and the wall she needed to touch.

Macari took one arm, Calliope the other, and the three of them squeezed awkwardly through the door, into the hallway. To the left, Tarian heard a hissing, buzzing, slurping sound. The medallion burned so hot she thought her chest was surely on fire, but she couldn't focus any energy. She felt Calliope extend power around them as though she intended to shield.

"Won't work."

With the two holding her up, Tarian managed to surge forward to the wall. As she touched it, she felt the magic in it tingle on her arms. *Pulse. Need pulse.*

Gathering focus was like pulling sludge through molasses. "Calli. Pulse."

A sucking, tugging, sensation, like sliding down a drain through a long dark tunnel took her.

The first few seconds on the other side of the wall seemed more like a dream than reality. Tarian floated, encased in gentle ocean waves. Hair spilled around her, water embraced her, and the gentle song of dolphins filled her with joy. Her head still spun, but she felt less disoriented.

Instinct kicked in, her ability to manipulate the ocean water to provide air acted on automatic. Or maybe it was the medallion, which seemed to be humming. Or it might have been Roger, who circled around her in tight revolutions. His warmth and energy infiltrated her senses and helped clear her head. She turned, looking for Calliope and Macari.

She found Calliope only a foot away. Her sister wasn't as adept at breathing under water, but she seemed okay, if a little wide-eyed and panic-stricken. *I should have told her about the back door.*

A little further away, Macari struggled and thrashed in the

water. Her face was not a good color. *She can't swim. She can't use her Air under water, like those Ercklings.* Tarian started to swim toward the girl, but her body still felt sluggish, especially when faced with the drowning girl. Macari had used all of her oxygen within seconds, and didn't appear to know how to swim. Tarian held out her hands toward the girl, letting her power drift into the water. Calliope saw her, whipped around in place, and joined with Tarian to guide the energy. Together they formed a protective bubble around Macari, with Roger encircling them all in a protective shield.

More dolphins surrounded them while they worked. Their song added to the energy, soothing away the rest of the fog in Tarian's mind and body. As her head cleared, Tarian looked behind them to see if they'd been followed, but saw no rock, no wall, nothing to indicate the House of Xannon was anywhere near them. She realized she hadn't asked Alex exactly where the back door led. Looking up, the light was so far away she realized just how lethal this back door was. *Unless you're a fish.*

Roger bumped into her, sending a vivid image of greeting, happiness, concern, all wrapped into one. She held out her hand to touch his sleek side, sending a thought in return. *Danger. She can't breathe. We may be followed.*

She included images of Macari, struggling, and the creatures in the tunnel. Maybe they couldn't follow under water, but what if they could? They needed to keep moving, put some distance between them, and even better, obliterate the trail.

Macari hung suspended in the bubble, motionless except for the rhythmic rise and fall of her chest. Tarian saw the dolphins each bumping into her, along with pulses of energy. They'd make sure Macari didn't drown. *I hope.*

Roger circled back to her, his scar winking at her in the dim sea. He paused beside her, tilted toward her in clear invitation. *Let's go for a ride.*

Tarian held onto his fin, looking to make sure Calliope didn't get left behind. She'd hitched a ride with another of the pod, while the rest buffeted Macari along with them, taking off at high speed.

This far down, the water menaced, cold and dark, with odd shapes whipping by at high speeds. Tarian usually kept closer to the surface, but she felt safe enough with water ancients for an escort. Along the way, Roger sent occasional images. One, the Stulos exploding. Caraigg released, scattering in all directions. Bits of earth tumbling to the ground. A group of daemon, Macari and First Mother at the center.

Can I trust her?

The images stopped. Roger had no answer for that question.

Do you know how to break the others? Fire, and Air?

A dim image surfaced, as though Roger were relaying it from someone else. It didn't reassure her, as it held only one central object that didn't help at all. A column of fire, vibrant, red, orange, blue, in the center of black emptiness. A shadowy figure stepped into the flame and was consumed. Tarian shuddered, picturing that sort of death.

As they descended, darkness gave way to a blue and green glow. The area, illuminated by groups of small phosphorescent blobs, took on an impressionistic painted look, as though Monet had been by and given the spot a once-over with his brush.

They powered through deep water until they reached what looked like an underwater Stonehenge of sorts. Several large outcroppings of rocks extended from the ocean floor, each one covered in lichen that glowed. Within, energy radiated in the form of tendrils of light that penetrated the shadows. The dolphins took them straight to it. When they neared, Tarian felt the tingle of magic as they passed through some sort of shield. Inside the shield, the water cleared, bringing everything into sharp focus. What she saw astounded her.

A pit in the center contained the base of a cyclone of water, which extended up into darkness above. It wavered, as though pushed by ocean waves, and swirled like a waterspout in reverse. Tarian felt a pull on her power, gentle at first, then stronger and more violent as she drew closer. She backed away, easing the pressure. *Stulos! We made it.*

Tarian glanced behind her, checking for Erckling, but she couldn't see anything outside of the shield. Just vast blackness, as though this safe-haven bubble was the only thing in existence in an endless, black, starless night.

She glanced at Calliope. Her sister's skirt floated up. She'd extended her hands in an effort to keep her balance even though there were no real waves buffeting them here. Her sister's hair was in a braid, so it didn't float like Tarian's did, and her face was the picture of calm determination. *Like Mother. Tarian ignored the stab of pain in her heart that accompanied the thought.*

Dolphins escorted Macari past the Stulos toward a hollowed-out section of rock. The girl disappeared into the inky water within.

Several dolphins circled the Stulos, in constant motion just as the sea was in constant motion. The rest surrounded Tarian and Calliope, or patrolled the outer edges of the shielded area. But something was missing. Someone, more specifically.

The Old Woman?

Tarian turned in place, seeking the giant ancient. Though she saw more dolphins than she could count, more than she'd ever seen at one time and certainly more than she'd ever thought the pod contained, she didn't see the Old Woman anywhere in evidence.

The Stulos' constant tug on her energy left her feeling drained to the point she couldn't catch any signatures, not even Calliope's. Pressure pushed at her from all sides. She forced herself not to gasp. It wouldn't help since, technically speaking, she wasn't exactly breathing air.

A nudge at her elbow drew her attention to Roger. He winked, and tucked his nose up under her arm, lifting her slightly and pulling her at the same time. She let him take her, holding on and grimacing as they passed the Stulos. On the other side, it felt as though the blood sank through her body and drained out her toes, to be replaced by ice water poured over her head. Pressure intensified, in her ears, her mind, her stomach. Strangely, the baby didn't react. *She didn't like the Earth Stulos. She kicked me black and blue. Why isn't she reacting?* Worry formed a knot in Tarian's chest.

She pushed her free hand into her stomach, looking for any movement. Nothing. She tried to detect any thoughts or feelings from the baby, something that had been happening more frequently as she grew nearer to term.

Nothing.

Tarian's pulse quickened, and a rock lodged in her throat that made it impossible to swallow. Panic made her grip Roger tighter around his fin. He sent reassurance back to her, but no images or other thoughts.

They reached the blackest portion of the clearing, which turned out to be a cavern. Once inside, a gentle glow illuminated the Old Woman where she floated, power radiating from her to the Stulos like an umbilical cord. She looked strained and tired, her eyes drooping, fins hanging limp, tail pointed down. Beside her, Macari floated in the protective bubble, hands over her stomach where Tarian knew the fire artifact waited, ready to be fanned into a flame. Macari's eyes stared so wide and white they'd taken on a reflected glow of their own in the dim light of the cavern.

She's really freaked out.

Worried that Macari might start thrashing and throwing power in a panic, Tarian drifted over to the girl, keeping a reassuring expression on her face. Calliope followed behind, until the three of them floated just inches away from each other and about a foot from the Old Woman's nose.

Dolphin song rippled through the currents around them. Their clicks and squawks indicated an intense debate or discussion, though Tarian had no idea what they discussed. She'd let go of Roger when she entered the cavern, so had no connection to their collective consciousness.

Movement out of the corner of her eye made Tarian study the shadows on her right. A face bulged out from the rock. She blinked, rubbed her eyes, and stared at it. Definitely eyes. Large, round eyes. And a monkey-like face.

Caraigg? Here?

She'd forgotten about them entirely in the attack. One had been following her around, and she'd simply grown so accustomed to him he blended in with the surroundings, an afterthought. Shame filled her. She drifted over to the face, and touched it lightly with her fingertips.

Are you okay? She felt immediately stupid for asking, but couldn't think of anything else to say or any way to apologize for having forgotten him.

Apology not necessary. We watch, we wait. Keeper be wary. Danger approaches. They seek.

Tarian looked back over her shoulder. Dolphins, Macari, and Calliope were all she saw, and all that she felt was the overwhelming presence of the Stulos as it pressed in on her from all sides. Ripples in the water pushed at her, then stilled.

Scion sleeps and does not wake. Scion is in danger.

Pulse pounded. A catch in her throat. *Why? Why isn't she moving?*

Attack by Erckling targeted Scion. Water brethren cannot maintain current stream. Stulos requires more energy, or collapse. It draws from all surrounding, including Scion. Shield will fall. Erckling approach.

16

Tarian closed her eyes, willing fear to go away long enough to think. To figure this out. *There has to be some way to get rid of this poison so the Erckling can't track us.* She spun in the water, her hair flying out to tangle with a passing fish. Her shirt billowed up, exposing her stomach. Ignoring both, she swam over to Macari, pushing against the weight of the water.

She opened her mouth to demand information from Macari, then glared when nothing but bubbles formed. It was easy to forget, when using magic to do something as improbable as breathe under water, that magic didn't fix everything. It couldn't turn the ocean into dry land, or make it possible to speak in the usual way, because that required air. Real air, not magical air.

Macari glared back at her, and gesture with both hands as if to ask "where the hell have you taken me?"

She has a very expressive face. I can almost hear her saying "stars" instead of "shit."

Macari waved her arms, like a bird flapping. Tarian frowned. *What is she doing?*

Calliope drifted closer, and from the look on her face she was as confused as Tarian. Macari stopped moving her arms, and panted. The effort looked exhausting, especially when all it did was bob her up and down in place.

Finally, Macari held out a hand, and beckoned with one finger. Universal signal for "come here."

"Oh." The word came out as a large bubble that brushed Tarian's nose. She swam forward, stopping just outside Macari's protective shell. Macari held out her hand, palm facing Tarian, and with the other hand pointed at it, then Tarian. "Copy me" seemed to be the message.

Tarian held her hand out, palm facing Macari, and brought it as close to the edge of the shell as she could. Macari did the same, and they touched palms.

"Where the stars are we? What have you done? I hate the water, I hate it. I itch all over. I can't stay here. They'll take away the air and I'll die. The Shee can't come here, I can't come here, we have to get out of here. Can't you feel it?"

Tarian blinked at the onslaught, startled by the sudden voice in her head and the images that came with it of Macari drowning, frantic, being chased by giant creatures with glowing eyes.

She's afraid of the dolphins?

I'm not afraid of the Ancients. You…you…get me out of here!

You heard that? Tarian tilted her head, studying the girl. *You talk like the Caraigg?*

So do you. You were doing it before. I could hear you, but you couldn't hear me. I shouldn't have to touch you for you to hear. Why haven't humans learned to mind-link? Is water interfering? The tone equated water with the worst kind of filth imaginable.

Tarian grinned. *It won't hurt you. How do you bathe if you hate water?*

I use Air like any sane daemon. Is this really what we should be talking about? Can't you feel them? They're coming. And the earth is still shaking, and that Stulos is stealing every bit of power I have. I'm going to die here. Why did I even try to help?

With the reminder, Tarian slipped back into anger and suspicion. *You wanted to kill my baby.*

Macari shook her head vehemently, then a vision exploded into Tarian's mind, so clear it was as if she stood in the middle of it. Tall white columns surrounded her, with a fountain in the center. Two women stared at each other, neither moving their lips. Macari and First Mother. And then First Mother spoke, though no lips moved. "The child carried by Tarian Xannon must be destroyed. For the good of society. As the only daemon of the Court capable of reaching the human plane, I assign this task to you, First Daughter. Destroy the child. By whatever means necessary."

The hurt and betrayal Macari felt was evident on her face, by the lines etched across her forehead.

Tarian forced herself to listen rather than shut down at the damning death sentence the First Mother had issued. She watched as Macari protested. Saw First Mother brand the girl, and utter a banishment for failure. Felt every raw nerve as Macari absorbed the impact of a mother who cared more for a non-existent threat than for her own daughter.

Oh. Crap.

The Caraigg never sent complete scenes like this. She'd felt raw emotions, heard every word as though she stood right there.

I can see yours too, so don't think about what you don't want me to know.

Tarian stared at Macari. Processing. Thinking. Taking in the sincerity shining through her eyes and mind touch. Macari shrugged. *It's not the Benata Way, to kill an innocent.*

Ripples in the water pushed at Tarian, bringing with it another round of pressure from the Stulos. She'd made her own cushion of air for the journey but she felt it weakening, with her attention so occupied. Everything felt more unstable than when they arrived. The Old Woman grew tired, and from what Tarian could tell, she was the only one actively feeding the Stulos. A Stulos now overburdened because one leg of the table had been removed.

The fact was, if Tarian didn't destroy this Stulos soon, it would collapse on its own, taking the world with it. Unless First Mother had her way, and the baby was used to rebuild the missing Stulos in time. Every ounce of her being balked at that idea, though a bit of doubt brought on by the First Mother's argument took hold and squeezed her heart. If she sacrificed her child, the world would return to what it was. Everyone could continue their lives. The world would go on. Without the baby. The ache that brought was unbearable. *Why isn't she moving?*

The enormity of it all washed over her as the sea pressed in and fish swam by as though nothing at all unusual were happening. *How can I do this? It can't be done. Maybe I should do what she asks. Maybe that's the only way. But I promised, and if I go back on it…and the baby…*

Keeper. What do you need to break this Stulos? Macari's tone was gentle, soothing. Almost as though she patted Tarian on the back.

Emotions. She can sense my emotions.

She saw a glint in Macari's eyes. If they were above the water, the girl might be crying. Tarian struggled to stop the rising panic. *Three women, combining their power. And an artifact. Maybe two, Calli wasn't sure. And them.* She gestured at the dolphins.

Macari smiled. *Sounds like we have everything we need. The baby merely sleeps, but she'll act as a beacon for the Erckling. That's what the poison does. With all this…wet…and the shield, it will take them some time to reach us. If we break the Stulos at the right time, it might shatter their trace on her, or if we're lucky, they'll be consumed by the release of power. It's worth a try.*

A tiny kernel of hope bloomed, and Tarian latched onto it like a drowning man holds onto a rope. *You're suggesting I wait until they show up and then break the Stulos, hoping they get caught in the blast? And if they do, the baby will be safe?*

I can't promise. If they aren't caught in the blast, then they'll keep coming. We'll have to move, immediately. And keep moving. They never deviate from a mission. Ever. And they're elemental creatures, very hard to destroy. Once this Stulos breaks it'll be a ride to the end.

Tarian turned to Calliope, wishing more than anything she could speak to her sister the way she spoke to Macari.

Macari gestured, and Calliope drifted forward, mimicking their placement. Tarian felt her sister join the conversation, her thoughts a lighter, brighter tone. *Oh, I had hoped to try this some-day. But air daemon don't have to touch. Why do we have to touch?* Macari smiled. *Practice. We learn by touch when young. Letting go comes in time.*

Letting go. Tarian wondered if she could ever really do that. Let go of fear, doubt, and worry. Let go of the feeling that at the root of this mess it was she alone responsible. Frustrated, she stomped her foot, an act that did nothing but ripple water. *No time for this.*

While she'd been absorbed in her own private thoughts she realized Macari had been talking with Calliope.

We still don't know how to break Fire, and we have no idea why Air is in two pieces, nor how to break it, nor where the pieces are. We can't start the roller coaster until we know those things. We won't know where to go, Tari.

Macari interjected, her thoughts tumbling over Calliope's in Tarian's mind. *It's not the Air Stulos that's in two pieces. I've spent my entire life near that Stulos. It's whole. But the Air Artifact isn't. Is that what you mean?*

Calliope frowned and bit her lip. I don't know.

Macari continued. *The Air Artifact was split when the planes were divided. First Mother holds the main piece, but it's locked. The Mayfanata hold the key. I can't do it; Benata aren't allowed to cross into his domain. And Mayfanata do nothing that doesn't suit their purpose or benefit them personally in some way. It'll take an Agreement of some sort to get the key. The leader is bound to demand a very high price for this.*

Leader of the Mayfanata. Ruarc. Tarian's heart sank. She'd hoped to never cross his path again. To keep her daughter as far from him as possible. To pretend their joining had never happened. If she hadn't been encased in water, she'd have groaned out loud. She tried anyway and glared at the bubble as it rose and drifted off into the dark sea.

Will he know about the Fire Stulos? Calliope's thoughts, logical, wiggled through Tarian's mind.

Macari answered. *Doubtful. But, I know someone who does.*

Tarian and Calliope both looked at Macari.

Lasair.

With thought transfer, planning a course of action took on the pace of a runaway train. The merest hint of a suggestion was instantly transferred to the others. The process both fascinated and terrified Tarian. She discovered she had no skill whatsoever in blocking her thoughts, though Macari obviously did. *I need to learn that.*

Calliope looked questioningly at her, one hand waving in the water to keep her balance. *Learn what?*

How to block thoughts.

Macari grinned. *Later. Are we ready?*

Tarian thought about it. Was anyone ever ready for something like this? But she nodded anyway. *We gather the Water Ancients, like we did for the Caraigg. The three of us, all around the Stulos. I'll merge my power with Calli's first, then bring you on board. Those mental shields will have to come down, Mac. The only way this works is to let go of ego.*

So you keep saying. I'll do my best. The hesitation in Macari's tone set Tarian's nerves on edge.

When it's done, split up, and everyone meet on the beach at home. Macari will get us to the daemon side from there. Ready?

Calliope and Macari nodded at her, thinking "ready" simultaneously. Tarian broke contact then. There was nothing more to say. It'd taken precious minutes to get the plan in place. And it wasn't a very stable plan. So many ifs, so many unknowns. Even with Macari as an escort, could she and Calli even cross the Wind to get to the daemon plane? What if they couldn't? What if Ruarc wouldn't deal? What if the First Mother…

Tarian gulped, and realized she swallowed a mouthful of water. *Focus, Tari, focus. Keep the shield up.*

She solidified the small shield around herself, keeping her ability to breathe, keeping the baby safe. *The baby.*

Floating here, it was easy to forget she was pregnant.

Especially since the baby didn't move or kick. Now that the constant soccer game had stopped, she missed it. Movement meant everything was okay. This stillness...she couldn't stand it. Mounting worry was not helping the situation but she couldn't stop it.

She might go through all of this for the sake of a baby who would never be born. The thought...

No. She's okay. She'll be okay. I'll make this okay. I have to. I will.

Tarian approached the Old Woman, who had hovered in the darkness the entire time they'd been conferencing on what to do. She needed the Water Ancient's blessing, and her help, to make this happen. Now was the time to ask. She gently touched the Ancient's side, her fingers light on the slick surface of a creature so old Tarian couldn't even fathom it.

Honor to you. She thought, picturing the destruction of the Earth Stulos and the scene at Balance Court so the Old Woman would understand. *I've come to finish what I started.*

The Old Woman rolled on her side, eye blinking at Tarian. She sent an image of Tarian, Macari, and Calliope, holding hands, facing the Stulos, with dolphins surrounding them. *Ready.*

Behind the word, a feeling of gratitude, relief, and determination. Dolphin song rippled through the water, filling Tarian's heart with hope. The Old Woman turned slowly, moving away from Tarian's hand, lowering her nose to nudge Tarian's stomach. A wave of power, gentle but insistent like a mother's hand on a feverish forehead, pushed into her body, penetrated her womb and pressed into the baby. The baby moved, slightly. Enough to send Tarian's heart racing. She felt for more, but the slight wiggle was all. Tarian gestured to the others, and started to swim toward the funnel of water, hoping that the wiggle meant everything would be okay.

Dolphins circled them as they made their way to the Stulos. The water funnel helped propel Tarian forward until they reached the outer edge. Her heart pounded so hard it threatened to rip a hole in her chest. The pull on her energy increased, intensified until she struggled just to stay conscious. To hold onto her ability to breathe. Beside her, Calliope wiggled her hands frantically, fighting for her place next to the storm. Macari had the easiest time getting near the Stulos since the dolphins guided her protective bubble to it and held it in place.

Tarian waited a few seconds for the dolphins to form a circle around them, until the pressure in her head and body made it impossible to wait any more. Inside, for the first time since the attack, the baby squirmed. It felt odd. Not like before. The movement wasn't frantic. It felt more like a worm wiggled in a circle. As though she spun in place. In the midst of it, one thought wormed its way to the surface.

Out.

17

The need, so clear in her mind, startled Tarian so much she dropped her protective shield for a split second, flooding her mouth and nose with true water rather than oxygen. She gasped, and choked on the flood. Pulled her thoughts to the suddenly very real problem of breathing under water.

A bump against her elbow, a thought. *Breathe.* And a pulse of power, from Roger. She took it, weaving it with her own in a quick shield that put air back into her lungs, even though she continued to cough, sending bubbles out into the surrounding water like fish in an aquarium.

Hurry.

Tarian turned to Calliope, wondering if the thought was her own or someone else's. It didn't matter, really. She held out her hand, and took her sister's, clasping it tight, pulling them toward each other so their shoulders and hips touched. Calliope's signature drifted lazily toward Tarian. She snatched it as soon as she was able and merged it with her own. Calliope's warm glow flooded into Tarian, a complement to her own, cooler energy. Water, Air, and Fire became one band of raw, undirected energy.

The stress caused by maintaining her grip on the newly formed band of energy pushed her heart into overdrive. If she were above water, she'd be pouring sweat. Tarian touched the medallion, feeling the heat on her fingers, a heat she hadn't noticed in the cool of the water. It glowed as she called the power forward. As dolphin magic surrounded them, cramps wracked her abdomen. She held her breath through them, willing her muscles to relax.

Dolphin song rang through her mind and pulled power from the pod toward her, wrapping it around her own, around Calliope, around the baby. The baby kicked, and a jolt of pain shot around Tarian's stomach. She gasped, flooding her mouth again with water.

A wave of fire traveled from her groin up into her chest, down her legs. Her knees folded, almost to a fetal position. Calliope squeezed her hand, sending healing power into the mix of magic.

She's coming. Shit, she's coming. No time. No time. Keep going. This can't be happening.

The cramps felt as they had before, with the Earth Stulos. But she hadn't even started to push at the Stulos yet. The false contractions from the overload of power were happening before the power was called.

Oh shit. Oh shit. Oh shit. No no no. Not here, not now. Not here, baby. Please not here.

Macari waved, frantically beckoning. Tarian struggled with muscle spasms, willing them to stop. When they'd subsided to a dull ache, she reached out to touch the protective bubble surrounding Macari. At once Macari joined her, palm to palm.

They're coming. I can feel them, they're close. Hurry.

Tarian nodded, and grit her teeth through another cramp. *Open to me, let your power flow.*

Macari set her jaw, and sent a trickle of power toward Tarian. Tarian tried to take it, but it remained so locked with Macari that she couldn't. It was like trying to tug on a loose bit of twine in a mound of cloth. She couldn't quite grasp it.

Around her, dolphins clicked, their song switching from joy to worry and frantic motion. They were sounding an alarm. *Out of time.*

Open, Macari. Let it go. You have to let go.

Macari screwed up her face in concentration. She was obviously trying, but her hold on her power remained locked tight. Then the girl's eyes widened and she held up her other hand in the universal sign for stop. She took her palm away, and Tarian watched as she began to spin in place, twisting her body until she was whirling in a circle, her body flipping, her legs working to keep herself in motion. She looked like a dancer, performing an underwater ballet. Hair spilled out around her, skirt billowed, shirt opened, buttons loosening until they strained and popped. Macari threw her head back, her arms wide, and released a wave of energy so strong it threw Tarian and Calliope back in the water.

Shocked, Tarian belatedly started to pull on it. *Air. Solid Air energy, here under water.* It shattered the protective shield around Macari. Water rushed to fill the gap. Tarian pushed against the flow to reach Macari, grabbed her hand, and extended her own shield so that the girl would be able to breathe.

But it didn't matter. Macari ripped her hand away and continued to twirl, caught up in her dance. Power flowed through Tarian, toward the Stulos. Macari glowed, her body a vibrant stream of white in the dark ocean.

Tarian stared at the incredible scene of Macari, spinning in the sea, surrounded by dolphins, encased by white light. It was beyond beautiful, beyond terrifying, beyond logic. She found herself absorbing the scene as though she sat in a front of a bonfire on the beach, the waves lapping on shore next to her, not a care in the world.

Flickers of flame erupted along Macari's body, encasing her in reds and oranges. Tarian gasped. *Fire. In the ocean.* She blinked hard, twice, but the vision remained. Macari continued to whirl, encased in a white glow, with fire inching along her arms and legs.

Through the flames, a signature pushed outward with each flicker of improbable fire. Tarian automatically soaked it in, categorized it. *Burning leaves. Ozone.* A sense of longing and excitement came with it, both so intense they took her breath away. She knew without a doubt it wasn't Macari generating the sensation. It was someone connected to her.

Before she could even guess at the origin, another contraction pushed all thought out of her head. Tarian doubled over, holding her stomach, unable to do anything but wait for it to pass.

Calliope hugged her tight, providing stability and comfort. She rocked Tarian in the buffeting waves. Dolphins clicked, frantic. The Stulos pulled, threatened to swallow her whole.

No time. Please not here. Need to finish.

Out!

Not here not here not here.

Tarian shook herself as the pain receded. It had to be now, before the next wave of pain, before the Ercklings arrived, before the Stulos collapsed. *No time.*

She held out her hand, using it as a conduit. The medallion burned in her chest, power bursting forth as a fountain of raw energy, slamming into the white fire surrounding Macari, dispersing it, merging with it, forming a water and air tornado. When the two primal forces had twisted around each other she pulled it back, into herself, letting it flood her body, fill her mind, take her soul.

It raged through her, a thousand needles poking every pore, every inch of flesh. The baby, as before, grabbed it too, pulling it into herself, absorbing more and more until Tarian thought they'd both burst with the pressure.

She couldn't feel her hands, couldn't tell if she held onto Calliope. *Now. It has to be now.* With one last effort of will, Tarian twisted the jumble of potential into a giant rope of unified raw energy.

Pain exploded in her head, chest, and stomach. Wave after wave, the bits of fiery needle pokes turned into a pressing heaviness as though a million pounds of brute forced squeezed her flat.

I have to release. I have to send it. Have to break the Stulos. Have to...

Despair flooded through her. Overwhelming despair, loneliness, longing. The pain of losing something precious.

The baby.

Her body collapsed, though she knew it wasn't possible.

She was held suspended in the sea, held aloft by water, by the Ancients and by power. But inside, she knew. Her body couldn't take any more. Couldn't hold herself up. Couldn't push. Couldn't anything.

I. Can't. Too much. Too much.

Calliope grabbed both of her arms, Macari grasped her shoulders, both women so close, their faces and noses touched Tarian's. Energy coursed through her to the medallion. It flared on her chest. It became a red hot, pulsating, living thing that writhed in an undulating, serpentine fashion.

You can do this. The voices, both Calliope's and Macari's, reverberated in her skull.

I can't.

You can do this.

Tarian closed her eyes. Tried to push, tried to send the magic to the Stulos. Desperation filled her, combined with the dolphin songs, the clicks, the tumult around her.

She shook her head. Took a deep breath of magic infused air, burning her lungs with the force of it. Pulsed, as though pounding a hammer against a solid rock wall. The Stulos received the pulse, sucked it in, thirsty for more.

So much power coursed through Tarian that her vision wavered. Black spots appeared before her eyes, followed by a rainbow of colors. Her head pounded, and with each strike a hammer crashed into her eyes sending blinding flashes of white light. She retched, then swallowed salt water and choked.

Tari. Calliope's voice was soft, calm, in her head. *You're having the baby. That's all. It's going to be okay. You can do this.*

Calliope hummed, the music coming through in her mind, a comforting sound that made Tarian wish for home. The deep longing and despair inside lessened, eased a bit by the sound.

Tarian tried to wrestle the overloaded rope of power into some sort of loop she could tie to the Stulos. It waved and lapped at her, but didn't bend to her will. It liked her, and didn't want to leave.

The dolphin song shifted. *Let. Go.*

The medallion's power refused to focus. She felt for her sister, but she'd taken all Calliope had to give. Macari too.

It wasn't enough. The Stulos remained, stronger than ever.

It's not working. She sent the thought, weak, out to the sea. She had nothing left. She'd drained all the power she had, plus that of the medallion, and Calliope and Macari.

The Ancients around her continued their song. *Let go. Let go. Let go. Let go.*

Tarian gritted her teeth. She'd let go so much she had nothing left.

You Shield. Let go.

I can't.

Sparkling white shapes appeared at the edge of her vision. They didn't look large, but she felt the menace. She'd seen them, in the hallway. They wanted her baby. They wanted to kill her child. They wanted to stop her from breaking the Stulos.

We're going to die.

She closed her eyes as the next contraction roared through. Her body curled in on itself, a tight ball of spasms she could not release. She shook, strained. The need to *push*, to thrust it away from her, drove into her spine. She gave in, let go. And *pushed.*

Power from somewhere deep inside, thrust out toward the Stulos. The Stulos accepted it, grew, expanded, ready to burst. If she could just send a bit more. Just a bit more.

Tarian screamed, though no sound emerged. Hands on her shoulders, her hips. Frantic hands. Busy hands. It made no sense, those hands. What were they doing?

Push.

Pressure. Power. Dolphin cries. Song.

Longing.

Hope.

Push.

The pain ebbed, muscles relaxed, though now the ache through her abdomen remained and she couldn't seem to make her body straighten out. Utter exhaustion settled on her like a heavy blanket, weighing her down, making it impossible to move, making her *unwilling* to move. Her eyes burned. If she were on dry land, she knew tears would be pouring from her eyes. But here they were just tiny drops in an endless sea. She tried to survey the area in between convulsions. Her sister's eyes stared directly into her own, their noses almost touching. Calliope's hands on her shoulders, concern and something else in her eyes. Excitement? *Wish I could read emotions like she does.*

Macari swam into view, face white as a ghost, the whites of her eyes glowing in the dim water. She placed a hand on Calliope's, and through the contact all three women joined thoughts.

Tari, with the next pain, push. Push hard, okay? Calliope nodded her head for emphasis and half shook her. *Stop fighting it.*

Something brushed her elbow and she started, alarmed. Her ugly maternity jeans floated by, taken by the whirlpool created by the Stulos. She watched them go, wondering how they'd managed to get free of her body. Suddenly the hands made sense.

Oh. Oh shit. Oh shit. This can't be happening. This can't...

The pain took her so fast and hard that her entire body stiffened and shoved all thought out of her mind. She could only feel it and the pressure. So much pressure. *Let it go.*

Push, Tari. Push.

No no no no. Can't. Not. Ready. No no no no. Tarian shook her head in what felt like an emphatic gesture.

Push. You have to. You can do this. You can. We're here. You're not alone. Push.

Not here. Not here. Not here. She'll die. We'll die. They'll die. Not here.

Push. Now.

As the pain grabbed her again, she finally did as commanded, helpless in her body's process. She grabbed her sister's arms, and heaved, like throwing up but in reverse. The thought that she'd probably just dropped a load in the ocean crossed through her mind, giving her the insane need to giggle.

One more, Tari. One more. Big push.

She pushed with every ounce of strength she possessed, her mouth wide open, an unheard scream sent into the relentless ocean.

18

The baby slipped out of her body, leaving a void in her stomach and the sudden need to urinate. Tarian gasped in water and choked on it. Dolphins near her pressed forward, each bumping her and the baby with their noses, adding their own magic to the power surrounding her. Calliope's hands on her stomach eased the cramps. Her lungs cleared. She was able to look down, where Calliope held the baby's arm with one hand to prevent her from floating away.

The baby.

For a moment, the ocean ceased its relentless motion. All hung suspended, everything stilled as the baby opened her eyes. Vivid, blue eyes stared sleepily, while wrinkled hands and feet and pasty white skin glowed. Tarian stared at her, unable to look away. Unable to process that the person who'd lived inside her body was no longer there. Was floating beside her. Was looking *at* her in a way that said *I know you.*

Emotion she couldn't put a name to swelled. Everything, the pain, the pressure, none of it mattered.

She's here. Holy shit! *She's born!*

In those precious seconds, a connection forged so deep it ripped through Tarian's soul and wound around her heart. In this instant, she knew she'd do anything for this child. Anything. Love, stronger than anything she'd ever felt, poured through her like water on an open flame, hissing and spitting and *alive.*

The baby blinked, her face screwed up tight. Her mouth opened, and a loud sound, like a sonic boom, pulsed through the water. The power driving it, a hundred times greater than anything Tarian had been holding, pushed them all backward in the water and raced to the Stulos.

The Stulos expanded, inflated like a balloon pushed past the breaking point, and burst.

Water rushed out and away, a torrent of power and sea. It thrust them backward, along with everything in the area. They reached the edge of the shielded area and rebounded. For a second, everything hung suspended. Before anyone could react, the undirected power of the Stulos collapsed back in on itself like the backdraft of a fire. Debris, rocks, creatures, dolphins, fish…all rushed toward what used to be a Stulos on a collision course.

Tarian couldn't fight the pull, couldn't swim against the stream. All she could do was tumble helplessly toward an invisible center of gravity. *The baby!*

As they all collided with each other, the shield, which had been providing life-giving oxygen, also collapsed. Water rushed into Tarian's lungs, lungs she'd forgotten about since breathing had been so natural moments before. She choked, and everything else took a back seat to one overwhelming instinct. *Breathe.*

Tarian held her breath, but water had already seeped in. She coughed, and more water rushed into her mouth and lungs. She struggled against the water. Desperate, she kicked, moved her arms. Her stomach felt empty, drained, her body beyond exhausted. *The baby!*

Fear of dying replaced with fear for a newborn infant she hadn't even been able to hold. *The baby the baby the baby.* Panic drove her, prodded her to do something. *Anything.*

Tarian grabbed at everything around her in an effort to search for the infant. Thoughts of using her power fled in her panic. She didn't have any to use. Everything around her dimmed. Her thoughts muddied as the water filled her. *The baby.* A rush of sadness. She'd never know her. She'd never live. *All of this. For nothing.*

Something brushed her hand and automatically she grabbed at it, but her fingers refused to latch on.

The last thing she heard was a dolphin cry.

19

Tarian lay on sand, unable to move, the sheer weight of exhaustion driving her down, down, down. The thought that it was definitely sand, rather than marble, wood, or any other surface drifted past, and the *why* of it pushed at her, tickled her conscious. *Sand. Beach.*

The word beach circled her head. It felt comfortable, familiar.

Reality slowly crept back into her body, starting with unbelievable soreness in every single muscle. It was as though she'd just run a marathon while simultaneously lifting a thousand pounds and having her body smashed by one of those machines she'd seen crushing cars. Her fingernails hurt. The hair on her head hurt. Hell, the hair all over her body hurt.

I must have died. I didn't know death would be this painful, after. Shouldn't death be the absence of pain?

She couldn't open her eyes, but it didn't stop her nose from catching the salt air, nor her ears from hearing the rolling crash of waves.

I made it home?

She struggled to remember. There was pain. Sparkling, hauntingly beautiful Ercklings trying to kill the baby. Pain. Power. Pain. Pressure. Incredible pressure. More pressure than anyone could possibly bear. And the release of it. The release of magic energy so intense it ripped the fabric of reality. And it came from...

The baby!

Panic welled inside, spurred action. Action her body was unable to produce. Instead of leaping to her feet, she lay there twitching. Spasms in her legs and deep inside her stomach reminded her that she'd just given birth. She sucked in air, gasped, and choked on it. *She's here. She's born. I gave birth.*

I don't know what to call her.

The ridiculousness of the thought. A name was the least of her concerns. *Where's the baby? Did she make it? I felt something, before. Did I grab her?*

Tarian tried to open her eyes, but the light was bright and she couldn't manage it. She coughed, and rolled over on her side. Water seeped out of her mouth. She took stuttered gasps of air and choked again. Air. Sweet, beautiful air. She focused on it, relished it. Coughed. Sputtered. Coughed. Heaved. She quashed the urge to vomit, and coughed again. Less painful this time. Her lungs protested, but resumed their usual in and out rhythm.

Holy.

Shit.

Not once had she ever come this close to drowning. Water used to be a friend to her. *Not today.*

She raised her head and saw…water. Rushing toward her, then away again. She lay on a white sand beach. She coughed, then pushed herself up halfway. Her arms shook.

The beach stretched in both directions, empty, bordered by trees on her left, water on her right. Waves lapped up and down the shoreline, and in the distance a dark, menacing cloud churned deep red. It occurred to her something was incredibly wrong with this scene. The beach should be black. Not white. The rocks that should be to one side remained stubbornly absent, replaced by trees swaying in a fairly strong wind.

Where am I?

"Calli! Macari!" Tarian screamed, or tried to. The sound came out as a raspy whisper. Her throat wasn't ready to talk after the insult of nearly drowning. "The baby!" She pushed herself onto all fours but couldn't gather her feet under her to stand. "The baby!"

Wind rustled the leaves behind her. Hair plastered to the side of her face refused to budge no matter how many times she raked her fingers over it. Her shirt, now covered in sand, clung to her skin. She wanted to rip it off. She wanted to rip her hair out. Where was she, where was her baby? Her sister? Macari?

Tarian tried to stand, but her legs refused to cooperate. Frustrated, she tried again. Managed to get upright on trembling legs. Stared out at the water. "I don't see her. I don't see her." Panic seeped into her voice and mind. She panted, unable to calm her breath or racing pulse.

She spun, and began to search the immediate area for any signs of an infant too small to crawl, much less survive what they'd just been through.

Her throat throbbed, and the pounding in her chest hammered away at what little sanity she had left. "Calliope!" She shouted, the fear in her voice making the sound weak and insubstantial. It went nowhere. The sand echoed the dark storm cloud, all of it menacing and unwelcoming. She couldn't catch her breath, and found herself doubled over, heaving. Water leaked out of her ears, nose, and eyes. Calliope. Gone. Macari. Gone. Alex, Daric, dead or injured. Caraigg? Had they followed? The Old Woman, Roger…did they survive? The baby…

She gulped, swallowed the lump in her throat that refused to budge. Her hands pressed into her stomach, willing there to be movement and life within the void. She hadn't had time to even register that she was a mother, and now the baby…

Her thoughts whirled. She couldn't think of a scenario in which the baby had lived. Not in the torrent of water that rushed them all up from the ocean. Her sister and Macari, maybe. But if they had, where were they?

Thunder crashed in the distance. She glanced up to see lightening split the red clouds in two. Sheets of rain blurred the sky, or was it her own eyes that blurred? She rubbed at them. The approaching storm and pressure on her ears added to her confusion and panic. She whirled to face the tree line. There was no break in the trees, no path or way through or out of this place. Nothing but trees and sand and the dark, cloudy sky.

She grabbed her head with both hands. The baby had to be here. She had to. Tarian searched the immediate area, then moved down the shoreline, pushing one foot in front of the other, willing her body to recover. The baby would be right by the water, if she'd survived. When Tarian didn't see a tiny body lying on the beach, the tears came. Unbidden. Unwanted. And she was completely unable to stop them. She tried to run, to search further, faster. Her feet kicked up the sand. It pelted the back of her legs, and her toes squished with it. She ran until the air deserted her lungs and she dropped to her knees, heaving.

The storm churned the ocean into a frenzy, but she ignored the approaching waves. If the baby was still out in that water, she was lost. Tarian couldn't even wrap her mind around the idea. She closed her eyes against the brutality of the scene. Her arms hugged her stomach, a stomach which no longer held a life inside it.

Desperately, she tried the one thing that had never failed her. Tracking. She felt for her daughter's signature, but couldn't calm her mind enough to engage, and felt no power surge rushing to help. The medallion remained silent. Her body had nothing left to give. *Overload.* She was probably lucky to even be conscious. *It's gone. All gone. My power evaporated with the Stulos. That backlash...it took everything.*

She gulped as she remembered the collapse, the rush of water. How the baby had magnified energy until everything exploded up in a rush.

How can a newborn infant be capable...she didn't...if it overloaded me, if I'm drained, there's no way she survived it. And those creatures. They were there, I saw them. They could have...they were there to...

She couldn't finish the thought. Her knees ached from sitting at an awkward angle but she refused to budge. She took as deep a breath as she could manage, forcing air in and out, trying to calm her mind and body enough to focus. The crash of waves, familiar on the foreign sand, helped. Breathing helped. She closed her eyes and tried to meditate. Tried to drag calm and focus into her body. It didn't work, but she had to do something.

Breathe.

Focus.

Waves, in and out.

Her mind raced ahead, refusing to quiet. Scenes played out before her, each more horrible than the last. Scenes of her baby, drowning. Being ripped apart by strange creatures. Being taken and shoved into fire. Being used to create a Stulos. She gulped a breath. It came out as a sob.

In the middle of her despair, a new sensation emerged. Not power. Or if it was, it was shielded. She detected no signature, yet she sensed someone there as surely as if they stood next to her. It felt familiar, like a half-remembered character from a story. A *presence.*

She looked around wildly, seeking whoever or whatever it was. The only thing she knew for sure, it wasn't the baby. Again, she tried to focus power, call energy from the medallion.

Nothing.

She was in no condition to fight. She couldn't use magic. She took the only option available to her.

Run.

20

Tarian managed to sprint a few yards before her toe caught in the sand and she sprawled face down on the sand. It scraped up her thighs, embedded in sensitive areas still raw and sore from giving birth, branded her palms and face. Whatever she'd run from had followed. She sensed it draw closer. If she turned her body just right she might get off one or two well-placed kicks, but getting up was beyond her abilities. Drained, wrung out like a sponge, Tarian wasn't even sure she could lift her head or roll over. Too exhausted to cry. Her head pounded. Sparks of color danced behind her eyes. She winced, and pressed her hands onto her skull, willing the pain to go away. Whoever followed her drifted close. He made no sound, gave off no power signature. But still, she felt him along the back of her neck like a ghost in spooky stories. She waited. If he stopped by her feet, she could kick. If he didn't, she was done.

Beside her, he knelt. A gentle, warm hand brushed hair off her face. A delicate finger brushed tears off her cheeks. She kept her eyes closed. It wasn't Daric. Or Alex. Or even Ruarc. It didn't matter, really. Her baby was gone. Dead. Lost forever. Nothing mattered.

"You do not belong here." The voice was low, gentle, and foreign. The hand stroked her hair. "You must continue, Tarian Xannon."

That he knew her name sparked something inside. Curiosity

forced her eyes open. With enormous effort she rolled to her side enough to allow her to make eye contact with the speaker.

His eyes danced with blue, red, and orange flames. They glowed with strength and a vitality she could never even hope to match. But something behind that nagged. They contained in their depth an eternity of existence from the beginning and end of time as though he'd seen both and survived. She could think of only one being with eyes like this. The one who helped Macari cross the Between, into the human plane, and back again. The one who'd given Macari a very rare artifact. The one, she now realized, who'd been spying on her as she broke each Stulos, and who'd been an unseen presence in the Balance Court. She knew it by the force of his signature. It was laced with longing so intense it brought tears to her eyes.

She tried to speak, her voice rasped and the sound came out a squeak. Coughed. Tried again. "Lasair."

For an answer, he took her shoulders in his hands and helped her sit up. Her head spun. The colors and sounds and pain collided, made her gasp. She paused, trying to breathe, willing it all to settle the hell down. Beside her, Lasair waited. The waves rolled in and out, crashed against the sand. In the distance, lightning and thunder rolled. Wind tossed the tops of the trees and her hair. She squinted against it, and the bright light that came from nowhere.

No sun.

"How did I get here?"

"This place is not unknown to you." Lasair glanced down, his eyes taking in the state of her clothes, the shape of her body. "The child has joined the world."

"Yes." The word came out more a sob than an affirmation. "Is she here?"

Lasair shook his head. "She is not."

Tarian drew her knees in as much as she was able and hid her face on them, wrapping her arms around them in a hug that did nothing to comfort. "Does she live?"

A wave lapped close to her feet, receded. Lasair said nothing.

She listened to the waves, ignored the tickle on her toes, the itch of sand. The breeze in her hair. The anger of the storm in the distance. It didn't matter. Nothing mattered.

Lasair brushed her hair back, his hand resting on her shoulder. She shook it off. In the back of her mind the thought that angering a Fire Ancient was not a wise move taunted her. She didn't care.

"You do not belong here." Lasair put his hand back on her shoulder.

Persistent. Stubborn.

"You must continue."

"Continue what?"

"Your journey. The strain on worlds grows. Between struggles to cushion the impact. I..it will not last. The child needs you."

Tarian looked up, staring at him, incredulous. "I barely survived breaking the Water Stulos. And it destroyed my power. How can I help my child? She's probably...she couldn't have..." Tarian bit back a sob.

"You can. You must." Lasair squeezed her shoulder. "You are not without friends. You are not without power."

Tarian choked out a harsh laugh. "Power I can't feel or touch, anymore. It's gone. Overloaded. Done."

Lasair shook his head, his eyes crinkling. "The Between does not allow power. Your strength has not abandoned you. It waits. You must continue. Onward."

"Does she live?" Tarian looked for the answer in his eyes, those strange, dancing eyes. It was like watching an open flame, hypnotic, and dangerous. "You don't know, do you?"

"Possibilities are endless as the sand. Where there is chaos, there is hope."

"How did I even get here?"

Lasair stared out at the ocean, as if that answered everything. "Two Stulos create strain. Balance is a precarious thing."

Tarian searched his face. From the profile, his clenched jaw gave him a pained look. His arms strained as though he held something very heavy. *Is he Atlas? The weight of the world on his shoulders? I've never thought of the Between that way.*

"Few regard the Between. Support is only noticed by its absence." Lasair turned to face her. "As you've no doubt discovered in the past few moments."

She thought of her own support system. Daric. Alex. She didn't even know what happened to them. Calliope and Macari. Where had they ended up? Did they survive? She thought of their plans, to break the remaining Stulos. To meet back home, at the beach.

"I should go home." The words sounded flat and empty. She didn't mean them. What did it matter, really? *The baby is dead.*

Lasair shook his head. "You must journey forward."

"What's the point?" She stared out at the ocean. Water rushed the shore. Water stole her child. "She was the hope for the future. And she's gone."

"Her status is unknown."

Tarian turned on him. Anger welled in her like the next tide and crashed over her, driving words toward Lasair like physical blows. "Nobody could have survived that blast. Nobody. Certainly not an infant only minutes old. She could barely open her eyes. She was helpless." Tarian picked up a handful of sand and threw it at him. "Helpless! And I left her there. I just left her."

Tears poured down her cheeks. Tarian pushed to her feet and kicked at the sand, sending it cascading over Lasair. He watched her, more understanding in his eyes than she deserved.

"I might as well have killed her myself. Shit. Shit Shit Shit!" She turned for the ocean, the last place she'd seen her child.

Lasair's voice crackled like a stoked fire. "The breaking of another Stulos weakens the barrier. The others must be destroyed, before they collapse on the Between. Disperse the power, or it will crush existence."

Tarian watched the sea as it sent waves to wash her feet. It felt cold, cruel. Life, going on, without the baby. "It doesn't matter. Without her, it just doesn't matter. We're done anyway."

"Those who can, must act for those who cannot." She heard

Lasair stand. Felt him join her. Noticed the water lapped around his feet, rather than over them.

She turned to face him. "I failed. It's done."

Lasair took her shoulders and shook them, his eyes flashing sparks. "Those who *can* act, *must* act."

"That's not me. Not anymore." She couldn't shake the emptiness. She'd lost something precious she didn't even know she had until it was too late. *I'm always one step behind. I'm always just a little too late.*

Lasair squeezed her shoulders, so tight it crunched the bones. She let out a small yelp of pain, but didn't struggle. She welcomed it. She deserved it.

"You have responded as well as anyone would in impossible circumstances. The Erckling were repelled by the backwash of power. The tide brought you here. You *live.*" He shook her again. "You live. So you must fight. You must continue."

"Why?" She stared up into his eyes. "I'm a bull in a china shop. I destroy everything I touch."

"The child needs you."

"She's dead." Tarian thought back to her deal with the Balance Court. *Some Agreement. They failed. They said they'd be there when she needed it, and they weren't. They let her die. I let her die.*

Lasair's eyes flashed.

"The Court sees. They would not speak, if the possibility weren't great. The child lives."

"Bullshit. Complete bullshit. You know it and I know it."

"I know Balance stands at the center of past and future. I know they created an Agreement with Keeper Tarian, to aid her unborn child when the time came for her to unite the world. I know they would not create an Agreement they had no hope of fulfilling. I. Know. She. Lives." Lasair pushed Tarian away from him, his eyes open flames that reached up to lick his eyebrows.

At his words, a tiny spark of hope flared inside Tarian. "How do you know about the Agreement?"

Lasair frowned. "It is written in your thoughts, Keeper. As is the collapse so recently wrought by you and the child. Together. Water, your namesake and the child's, lifted you both. It destroyed the Erckling drones. It pushed you both up and out."

"If that's true, where is she?" Tarian gestured to the empty beach. "Why isn't she here?"

Lasair shook his head. "I see no more in your thoughts." He hesitated. His eyes swirled, the pupils enlarging until they turned black and swallowed the flames. He frowned.

"What?" Tarian tried to read his expression but had no idea what that set of his jaw meant.

His closed his eyes and drew a deep breath. His nostrils flared as he let it out. When he opened his eyes, the swirl of flame had returned.

"She lives. She is held by Macari, Keeper of Flame."

A surge of excitement and elation rushed through her. *Macari made it, and the baby!* "Macari. Where?"

"The child of Air has returned home, though it is not as hospitable as it once was for her. You must continue, Tarian. You must hurry. The child will need you."

Knowing that her daughter lived washed away the heartache and emptiness. Suddenly, Tarian's shoulders felt a thousand times lighter. Anything seemed possible. *I can do this.* "How do I get to the daemon side?"

"The Wind is open to such as you. One with a touch from both sides. One who has traveled before." Lasair glanced down at her stomach, and she reflexively smoothed down her shirt, suddenly aware she stood there basically naked. Her stomach felt deflated, empty, *void*. She gulped away the sudden lump in her throat. *Focus, Tari, focus.*

"Ruarc? That's why everything was so…" She trailed off as she thought over the scene. There had been no beach, when she met Ruarc. When she joined with him.

"The meadow lies on the daemon edge of Between."

"You saw?"

Lasair didn't answer. Which was answer enough. *Of course he saw. He probably sees everything that passes through here.*

He'd given her the answer she needed. Though creating a travel portal without any power was a major problem.

"There are other ways to travel."

She ran her hands through her hair, struggling to pull thoughts together. Travel, without a portal. Like she'd done when looking for Sucole. Like Macari usually did. "Will it work?"

"I will assist the beginning, but you must guide the end. I may not leave this place." Lasair gestured to the trees. "There are yet limits."

"And when I get there, how will I break the last two Stulos without help from my friends?"

"I can offer this. Fire must be last. It is guarded by Chaos. They will know you. To break it, power must be dispersed." He squeezed her hand again. An image slammed into her mind, a raging fire, in a bed of red hot lava. Surrounding it, a caldera rose up, forming a bowl that contained it. It looked familiar, like something she might find on one of the Hawaiian Islands. Except calderas formed when a volcano collapsed, and yet here it looked active. And very angry. The vision faded, leaving behind a sense of hopelessness. How was she ever going to get there, much less destroy it?

"Will you be there?"

"While separation exists, I may not leave this place."

"How do I destroy Fire, without you there to help?"

Lasair's eyes spun. A flame licked out the side and up his forehead. "Chaos cannot be destroyed. But it can be embraced, dispersed, released. Chaos contained is dangerous. Chaos dispersed…"

"Is still chaos."

"Creation." Lasair's eyes calmed to mere swirls. "What destroys, creates."

"Yes, but will we like the results?" She couldn't help remembering Calliope's concerns. No hint about what would happen once the planes joined. No clue what the consequences would be.

She could imagine it, though. Chaos would be a good word for it.

And would any of this save them or her child?

"Once through Between, power will return. Use it wisely." Lasair pointed at Tarian's chest. "There, as here and everywhere, power can be corrupted, intentions misunderstood. You have many friends, Keeper."

She put her hand over the medallion. It remained silent. No hint of dolphins, no hint of home. "I also have enemies."

"At times, they are one and the same." Lasair glanced back at the ocean. Rumbling thunder growled, and the ground shook. "You must continue."

Tarian bit her lip, then nodded. She still felt spent. Used. But she also felt a sense of purpose. Her daughter was out there. She had to believe that. And once she was out of the Between, she could track her. She could track anyone.

I'm coming for you. She told the ether, hoping the message would miraculously reach the baby. It was a silly hope, but that was the thing about hope. It was rarely rational.

Lasair's lips twitched.

"I'm ready when you are." She told him with a bravado she didn't quite feel.

"You must begin."

"Right." She took a deep breath. Closed her eyes. Thought back to her travel to Sucole. To the place where she'd joined with a daemon, conceived her child. The woman had repeated the same phrase over and over until Tarian wanted to scream. *You do not see.*

No, I don't. But I will.

She pictured the scene. Ruarc standing in front of her. The dreamy landscape. The grass. The joining. Every nuance of it. Though she couldn't reach her power, she acted in every other way as though she could. The ocean waves faded into the background.

Suddenly the image took on vibrant edges, every color enhanced. It swirled around her, making her dizzy, surrounding her with heat like she stood near an open fire. When her stomach turned, she fought the urge to throw up, keeping the vision of the meadow and Ruarc firmly in place. When it stopped spinning, the world right side up again, she kept her eyes closed. Focused. *The sun, the grass, the trees.* It felt so real, in her vision she reached down to touch the grass. The sun felt warm on her shoulders. A slight breeze teased her legs and hair.

What destroys, creates.

The words drifted around her head and were gone. The medallion pulsed. Dolphin clicks answered her touch. She opened her eyes, and found herself standing exactly where she'd meant to go.

21

Tarian stood at the edge of the meadow she'd occupied before. Once. At the time, it felt like a dream. But now the dream had turned very, very real. She immediately tried to focus power, but her body was too exhausted. The fact that she felt it at all flooded her with relief. *Not overloaded, then. Just tired. Food and sleep would fix this.* She snorted. As if she had time for sleep.

She glanced around, looking for fruit or something that seemed edible. Anything would work, at this point. Anything that helped her regain enough control to track.

Behind her, Tarian sensed energy. One second she stood alone, the next a silent companion radiated heat along her back. She didn't have to turn around to know Ruarc stood behind her. Having joined with him once, she'd never, ever forget his signature.

She kept her back to him, trying to gather her wits before he could see the truth in her eyes. She needed his help, and if he sensed weakness he'd pounce. Any help he might offer would come at a high price, regardless. She studied the meadow in front of her as if it were the most interesting thing in the world. As if she didn't have problems so pressing that her legs wanted to buckle under the weight of them. She was just a girl, contemplating nature.

In a T-shirt, and no pants.

"You seem…unlike yourself." Ruarc's voice, deep, full of double and triple meanings, caressed her spine right through the thin cloth of her shirt.

Tarian stared at the meadow.

"I am unused to conversing with a human's backside, even one as beautiful as yours." His voice reverberated in her ears, a whisper that filled her and excited parts of her body it didn't have a right to touch.

She stared at the trees.

"There is more disturbance in the balance. Yet the Balance Court does not summon." Ruarc moved to stand beside her. Just two people, contemplating the grass.

"You don't sound surprised." It was all she could do to remain still, instead of backing away from the reaction her body exhibited in close proximity to his. Her body remembered all too well the last time she'd stood near Ruarc. The energy exchange had rocked her core and of course, helped to produce the baby.

The baby. She gulped, the knot in her throat still threatening to choke her. She schooled herself to not to move, not to show emotion. Face neutral. Not a care in the world.

"The sign of significant Agreement could not be missed by any in Court. This game has been played out over centuries. Surprise was lost eons ago."

Confused, she ignored her stern reminders to herself to not show him anything and turned to face him. "Game?"

His eyes flicked down to her newly deflated stomach. She clutched the fabric of her shirt, wishing it stretched as tight as it used to. Suddenly she felt the scratch of every sand pebble on the beach along her butt and the back of her legs. *Talk about underdressed. I might as well be naked.*

"Keeper, it seems you are aptly named. Secrets settle within you."

"Secrets?" Her mind tried desperately to get back into the conversation.

"The child. Either the pregnancy has terminated or the Scion is born. I feel only your energy, not hers."

That makes two of us. She kept her mouth shut, but cast her eyes down to her feet. She tried to focus her power again, but it refused to cooperate. Her thoughts were too scattered.

"Where is the child, Keeper?" His voice took on an edge she'd never heard before. Usually so smooth, almost fluid, now it sounded tense and almost human.

He'd fathered her child. He'd delivered on the Agreement, hadn't tried to trick her. He deserved to know. She looked up, locking onto eyes that were so dark she felt lost in them. It was all she could do to say the words. "I don't know."

His lips tightened.

She turned away, staring back out at the meadow. Trying to formulate a strategy for how to get what she needed from this daemon for whom Agreements were games, and nothing was free.

Next to her, Ruarc stood motionless. Now that she couldn't see his face she had no idea at all what he was thinking. What he planned. But she felt the heat of his body, and his tension radiated outward creating a statement louder than words could manage. Finally, he spoke, his voice quiet. Schooled. Thoughtful.

"You seek assistance."

She didn't answer. To say yes would give him the upper hand. To say no was a lie, one he'd know instantly simply because of the way she was dressed, if nothing else.

"Use your talent, Keeper. Is the child nearby?"

You think I haven't tried? I can't focus. She screamed the words inside her head, but kept her mouth shut.

"Nothing threatens you at this moment. Relax, the flow will return." He whispered the words. She shivered. "Close your eyes. Relax your thoughts. Seek your child."

She did as he commanded. More than anything, she desperately wanted to feel her child's signature. To know that she *could* be tracked. Deep breaths, one after the other, followed by a mantra to help her meditate. To let go.

Beside her, Ruarc stirred the wind with his own power, and it soothed, comforted, enhanced. He helped her calm enough to focus. When she latched onto the center of her energy, she breathed a sigh of relief. It was still there. Still strong, if a bit chaotic. She sent it out into the air, seeking the signature which had, until recently, been embedded in her own body.

At first, she sensed nothing. Just Ruarc. And, more distant, a familiar ping. *Macari. Lasair said she held the baby.*

Suspicion reared an ugly head and twisted the simple fact of Macari's presence into a threat. *Why did she live? Did she take the baby to kill her? Like she said she'd been duty-bound to do?*

"Keeper. The child." Ruarc's admonishment was gentle, quiet, relentless.

Right.

She pulled back, and tried again. Sought out only the one power strand. After another long, timeless moment, she found it. Faint. Distant. But present, and near Macari. She couldn't stop the surge of relief and excitement, nor the words that blurted out before she could stop them. "She's here. This plane."

Tarian turned in the general direction of the strongest pull, and opened her eyes. "That way."

Ruarc stared in the direction indicated, his expression calculating. "How far?"

"Pretty far. If I were in Philly, I would say the other side of the country. California, perhaps. I'd have to triangulate to know for sure. She's near Macari."

Ruarc nodded once, sharply, as though deciding something. "Come with me."

Tarian narrowed her eyes. "Where?"

"That which you seek lies within my domain. I offer you renewal."

"At what price?"

Ruarc smiled. "Renewal is without strings. Please."

"Why?"

"The child carries daemon blood. *My* blood." He said that as though it ended all arguments. Perhaps it did.

Tarian took his hand, knowing the game was just beginning.

22

As the new location formed around her, Tarian stared in shock. It was not at all what she'd expected. She knew immediately that Ruarc had brought her to his home. The place throbbed with his signature and power. But it looked like the most sophisticated Manhattan penthouse she'd ever seen. It certainly wasn't what she'd expected from the daemon domain. Floor to ceiling windows let in a sky full of gathering storm clouds, and a white sectional sofa filled one corner of the room.

One large monitor, surrounded by smaller monitors, covered an entire wall opposite the sofa. *What are the odds he gets ESPN here?* It was a bachelor's paradise, complete with wet bar. The place felt so sophisticated, her disheveled state made her feel like a teenager caught out behind the building doing something naughty. Her hair fell in tangled knots of seawater and sand. Her shirt fell in tatters that barely concealed anything. Add to that bare feet and a fine layer of sand that covered every inch of her body and she looked like she belonged at a luau.

She surveyed the rest of the place, noting the mirrors, the marble floors, the fine wood grains that shouted "money." *Do they even use money like we do? Or did they just conjure this stuff?*

Two daemon stood on either side of an archway that led into a hallway beyond. Four more stood by the windows near her, plus one more behind the bar. All of them wore black pants, white shirts and empty expressions. They didn't even stare at her bare legs or the revealing hole in her shirt. *Very well trained.*

Ruarc kept hold of her hand and led her toward the sofas. She pulled back, resisting him. He stopped, but didn't release her hand.

"I don't have time to relax or whatever it is you think we're doing here. How are we even here? I passed through the Between. I know I did." She glanced out the window again and saw New York City aglow with early evening lights and peeks of sun through the storm clouds. She could make out Central Park, far below. After all that she'd been through it felt surreal.

"Did you expect a pit of despair? Appropriate punishment for the eternally selfish?" Ruarc's amusement was obvious from the quirk of his lips to his raised eyebrow. "Some keep their head in the clouds, refusing to see. Others prefer their feet on the ground, and the reality."

"Which is?"

"That all of creation has potential for both. And that embracing one over the other is a choice, while embracing both…"

"Is Balance?" Tarian stared at the window. "So which is this? The clouds, or the ground?" She turned to find Ruarc standing behind her, flanked by two more daemon, dressed in black pants and dark blue shirts. *Servers? How'd they know I was here?* One held what looked like a black robe, the other a tray of fruit, cheese, and protein bars, as well as a large glass of orange juice.

Ruarc gestured to the clothing. "I thought perhaps you'd like to change."

She took the robe, staring at Ruarc as she slipped it on over her head. It fell around her body in graceful folds. As she smoothed the fabric, her hands brushed against her stomach. A wave of panic enveloped her as she thought of what wasn't beneath the over-extended flesh any longer. Her insides felt like jello, all wiggly and disconnected. Like her uterus would slip out any second if she didn't keep her legs crossed. And though Calliope had obviously helped heal spent muscles in the few seconds after birth, everything still felt achy and stiff.

Oh, Calli. I hope you're okay. I hope you made it back home.

Not knowing would drive her crazy if she focused on it. Resolutely, she traced her daughter once again, comforting herself with the bond that continued to connect them.

When she noticed Ruarc staring at her hands and stomach, Tarian turned away from him to the servers and took a piece of cheese. She ate quickly, keeping the line to her daughter open. It was easier to find, now. And, Macari's remained in close proximity, at least as far as she could tell from this distance.

"If I'm to provide assistance, it would be helpful if you told me what you most need."

Tarian thought back to the terrifying moments when the Stulos had exploded.

"What are you offering?" She said the word slowly, drawing it out. *Just remember, Tari, he won't make any deal that doesn't benefit him in some way.*

Thinking back on the First Mother's protestations at Court, and everything Macari had added, Tarian knew with a sinking feeling exactly what the First Mother would be doing with her child. Admitting it hurt. Admitting she needed Ruarc's help hurt even more. Maybe Macari would be able to stop the First Mother from doing anything to the baby. Or at least delay her. But…Macari was bound by oath and First Mother was, after all, her mother. Would she really defy her for the sake of someone else's child? *There has to be punishment of some sort if Macari betrays her oath.*

The baby's life, everyone's lives, were at stake. Not knowing exactly what the two Benata women were doing was maddening. The only comfort was wrapped up in the baby's signature, still steady and strong.

"First Mother means to use the baby to create a new Stulos, to replace the one I destroyed." Tarian cleared her throat. "And I'm on a deadline, to collapse the other two before they crush us all. Think that about sums it up."

Ruarc shifted slightly. His lips tightened almost imperceptibly. It was more emotion than she'd ever seen. Obviously, he had not expected this development.

When he didn't speak, she continued. "I need to combine the pieces of the Air Artifact, so that I can destroy the Stulos. And I understand you might have one of the pieces."

Ruarc raised his eyebrows slightly.

Tarian took another piece of cheese.

"You seek this, above recovering the child?"

She kept her gaze steady, looking into his eyes for any reaction. "I mean to do both."

Ruarc leaned against the arm of the sofa, one leg draped over it in casual, ridiculously hot elegance. "First Mother believes that allowing daemon and human to mingle will be the downfall of society, of civilization. To her, allowing such would be far worse than the reset of the world that the current imbalance will cause."

"And you?"

"I prefer experience to cessation." Ruarc's eye glinted. "A game is hardly worth playing if it's called before the final score is announced."

"That's what this all is to you, a game?" Tarian crossed her arms. She clenched her teeth. *I'm a game to him? Just a one-night stand? Is that why he joined with me? For the thrill?* "All of it? Even me?"

"Most especially you, Keeper."

"Bite me." She turned away from him. *Why am I angry? I didn't even know him. He had what I needed. We used each other, end of story.*

In the back of her mind a small voice whispered *Yes, but you were left with something precious.*

She glared at the windows and the daemon guarding them. "Do you have what I need or not?"

"That depends, Keeper, on what exactly you need. Perhaps another joining?"

She whirled on him. Opened her mouth to shout a few curse words. Closed it again. *He's baiting me.*

Forcing herself to relax and breathe, when she finally spoke she was proud of her smooth, calm voice tones. "Are you suggesting I must pay for your portion of the Artifact with another joining? I was that good?" She tilted her head.

Ruarc's lips twitched. "You were and are truly fascinating. I did enjoy our moments together. But I never make the same Agreement twice."

"Do you have what I need or not?"

Ruarc's lips twitched, his eyes crinkled in genuine amusement. "I do."

"What will it take, Ruarc?" *The man is impossibly frustrating.* Tarian took the orange juice and gulped it. Sugar helped. Food helped. Her energies rebounded faster with food. Something he hadn't truly needed to provide. She wondered what even that small courtesy gained him. Her good will, she supposed.

"You seek Agreement?" He waited. Calm. As though time wasn't a precious commodity and their daughter didn't hang in the balance.

His own daughter. He'd deal even knowing she was at risk.

And aren't I doing the same thing?

Her cheeks burned. She pushed the shame aside and focused. *Just the basics, Tari. What do I actually need?*

Making a decision like this should be done over weeks. Months, even. Not minutes. Not while exhausted, drained past the breaking point. Not while her newborn child was in danger. In someone else's arms. Tarian kept the trace on her daughter open, a constant link to the baby and Macari since the two appeared to be intertwined. She opened one more track, to Calliope, and hit a wall. No hint of her sister anywhere. *She didn't make it to this plane.*

Her sister wasn't without powerful skills of her own. She had to be okay, somewhere. Tarian had to believe that.

Focus.

The way to win an Agreement, she'd discovered, was to never make the first move. "What do you offer?"

Ruarc's eyes flashed. She could almost see the calculations of various outcomes passing through his mind. Finally, he gestured with one hand, indicating she should follow him. He brushed past, letting his shoulder rub against her body, sending a tingling jolt up her arm and down her spine. The daemon exuded power without thought. She didn't doubt that he'd done it on purpose. The soft cloth of the robe caressed her, leaving warmth in places she'd rather not think about right now. She'd no doubt that was on purpose too. His every move, a seduction.

It made her want to rip the robe off and leave it in a crumpled heap, but then she'd be back to nearly naked and that didn't seem like much of an improvement.

He knew that too. Knew I'd take it. What's his game? What does he want out of all this?

It made her head hurt, trying to decipher his every motiva tion. *If that's even possible.* He appeared to change the rules of the game anytime it suited his purpose.

At the end of the hall, they reached what looked like a dead end, except what should have been wall looked more like an especially dense, very angry storm cloud. She heard thunder, and wasn't sure if it was coming from the cloud, or from the outside pretend New York skyline.

What she couldn't see, she could feel. An odd tug of power. Faded, subdued, but persistent. Power that was familiar and comfortable.

Air.

As she contemplated the depths of the storm, the medallion warmed her skin. Not quite a pulse, but definitely a reaction. Instead of draining her, however, this energy invigorated and revived.

Ruarc hovered so close behind her she could feel the heat of him along her back, and when he spoke, the warmth of his breath traveled a sweet caress along her neck and cheek. "It grows dark. Do you sense the strain?"

A chill ran through her spine, warmed her groin. The storm hypnotized her, as did his voice. The nerves on her arms begged to be touched.

"That doesn't look like a Stulos."

"Looks can be deceiving. But you are correct. It is not. It is something even more timeless."

Was that his hand on her back, caressing her? She shifted slightly, not daring to go forward, unable to retreat.

"What's in there?"

"Your deepest desires and fears, Keeper."

She swayed, taken in by the rhythm of the storm. Pure Air energy beckoned, seduced, and called to her own. *Power calls to power.* She could no longer hear dolphin calls. Water would not help her here.

With sheer force of will, she turned her back on the hypnotic storm and faced Ruarc. They were so close together their lips nearly touched. His eyes bore holes through her defenses. Her deepest secrets, laid bare on the Wind. She stood more naked now in the borrowed robe than she had in the tattered T-shirt.

"Tell me, Keeper. What is your deepest desire?" Ruarc tilted his head just enough, as a lover would when about to kiss.

Tarian swayed toward him, a snake to the charmer. All thought abandoned her, her body taking over with a deep-seated *need* to touch and be touched. Her hands reached for him.

Below, the floor shook as a loud clap of thunder sounded. It was enough to break the spell. Tarian blinked and shuffled to the side slightly. She didn't look into his eyes again. "That's cheating, Ruarc."

He smirked. "Knowing what you desire is essential, Keeper, if you're to use Air to achieve your goals."

She turned back to the stormy doorway, determined not to let him seduce her again. "How is this going to help me?"

He pressed close to her again, and she could do nothing. Another step forward and she'd fall into the doorway. A step back…she shook her head to clear the thought.

"What lies within is that which you seek. An object which will aid you in your quest, both to reach the Stulos and to destroy it."

Her pulse quickened. "The artifact?"

"A key. You will still require the lock, if you are to use the artifact."

"And how will I find the lock?"

"Know the deepest desires of the First Mother of the Benata."

Tarian thought. She didn't know the daemon at all. Only what she'd heard from Macari or witnessed with her own eyes at Court. And rumors. Stories. Pieces of history all fuzzy in detail. All she really knew was the part she'd witnessed firsthand. "She wants to re-establish the Stulos I destroyed."

Ruarc leaned in, to whisper again in her ear. "And to do that she needs…"

"The baby."

"And…"

"I don't know."

"Power calls to power, Keeper. When formed, each Stulos bore another until all four stabilized. Each, split from a unified whole. As a tree, with limbs."

A flash of understanding. "She'd need another Stulos, to recreate one."

"And before you, at my disposal, is the key to creation and destruction. Neither of you may act without that which is lodged beyond this portion of Wind."

His intentions suddenly became crystal clear. *He'd make a deal with whomever benefitted him most.*

She spun in place, so quickly Ruarc took a half step back, something she considered to be a triumph. "And what is *your* deepest desire, Ruarc of the Mayfanata?"

A loud bang, followed by rough shaking of the ground, nearly toppled both of them into the shaft. Tarian fought to keep her balance. Ruarc grabbed her arms and pulled her back from the door. "Perhaps it is you." His face, inches away from hers. His body pressed against her. Her body responded to memories of their joining with a surge of lust that shocked her.

Tarian put her hands on his chest, to keep a physical barrier between them. She just wished she could trust her body to keep his away, rather than pull him toward her. "I seriously doubt it."

Ruarc smiled, his eyes crinkled in genuine amusement. "Think you so little of your own charms, Keeper?"

"You didn't want me the last time we met. Not really." She lowered her eyes, away from his hypnotic stare. *He wanted to father a child.* A light went off somewhere, and she knew she had him. "Is there some reason you can't or won't father a child with someone here, Ruarc?"

She felt his arm muscles stiffen and knew she'd scored a small victory. She smiled, leaned in, and whispered. "Name your price."

He leaned back slightly, put a finger under her chin to tilt her head up, forcing her to meet his gaze. "Time, Keeper. I require time. I wish to know the child I've fathered. I would have equal access to her as she matures."

"Equal access? You mean split her time between me and you? Not happening." Tarian stepped away from him. "You are a mere fifth of her. You don't deserve equality."

Ruarc remained silent. He spread his hands in a gesture that clearly said "your move." He waited for a counteroffer. She pondered for a moment.

"Help me break this Stulos *and* rescue my child, and I will allow you one hour with her. Per year. Until she turns sixteen, her naming day." Tarian thought furiously. Had she put enough caveats that he wouldn't find a loophole? She added quickly, "Supervised by me."

Ruarc chuckled. "You learn quickly, Keeper. I counter. One day with her, per year, supervised. One hour with her, on her birth hour anniversary, unsupervised, until her naming day. After which the choice to continue will be hers to make. In return, I swear an oath she will remain unharmed. She will be returned to you, unscathed by anything in my power to influence."

"Unchanged in any way?"

Ruarc shook his head, a wry smile pulling his lips. "I cannot promise she will remain unchanged. Every interaction changes us."

Tarian considered. He would help her rescue the baby. Accomplish her mission, which would result in a restoration of balance and the joining of the planes. In return, she had to let her child know the daemon who had tricked his way into her life. *What's in it for him?* An hour hardly seemed worth it, but the fact that he'd included unsupervised time meant he had an agenda.

The ground shook, and the lights dimmed. Pulses of power washed over them. Tarian grabbed at the wall to steady herself. Ruarc pressed into her, holding her firm against the wall. The warmth of his body, the shaking of the building, all of it knocked her off balance.

She put her hands up to his chest, pushing him away. He didn't budge. Instead, he said, "Do you agree?"

Why did it feel like a deal with the devil? Why did it feel like she could study his offer for a hundred years and still not fully understand it? On the surface it seemed so simple. She needed the Air Artifact, and he could provide access. She had no other way to get it, and no time. And doing this would put her near the baby. Near Macari, who could help her collapse the Stulos. It all fit.

And all it would cost was time with her daughter.

Something about the entire thing didn't sit well. Was she being irrational? Perhaps Ruarc truly did just want to know his daughter. Maybe that's all it was.

Maybe not. Maybe there's something he gains by being in her life.

Whatever it was, the impact was not immediately obvious. She didn't know why, but he'd obviously wanted to father her child and wanted to be a part of the child's life. Somewhere, down the road, it would benefit him or the Mayfanata. Or he hoped it would. She'd have to deal with those consequences when they came.

"What's the penalty? How do I know you'll return her to me unharmed? Or that you won't simply take her somewhere I can't follow?"

Ruarc considered, his eyes dark, fathomless. "She is my child. Though you may not trust me, know this. I would die to protect her, as I know you would. Therefore, I offer my life as penalty. Should she be harmed, I will stand before you and await whatever punishment you desire to inflict. Locked in stasis."

She weighed that, considering the angles. It didn't seem to have a loophole. It felt solid, serious. Deadly serious. "And me? My penalty?"

Ruarc's eyes flashed. "Our situations reverse. I shall raise the child, and you shall visit as stipulated, once per year."

And be locked in stasis if she's harmed. Not that I'd ever let that happen.

The weight of this Agreement settled around them, pushing her into him, stealing her breath. His hands tightened on her shoulders. "Do you agree?"

She held up a hand. "You haven't stipulated what I get out of this Agreement. Specifically."

Ruarc gestured to the swirling doorway. "Access to the Wind, and the key to the Air Artifact. You will have what you seek, Keeper. The ability to destroy the Stulos will lay in your grasp. Our daughter awaits. The First Mother is most likely readying herself to seek out the same key. Agree, and it's yours." He spread his hands, the warmth on her arms fading. "Save the child. Break the Stulos. Return Air to the world."

He was offering her the keys to the kingdom, so to speak. And in exchange, a day with her daughter, once a year. It felt uneven, lopsided. *There's something I'm not seeing.*

But as the floor shook again Tarian knew she didn't have time to figure it out. She had to get to the baby. She had to finish what she'd started. She had to hope that in the end, it was all worth the price. All of it.

Ruarc brushed her forehead with his lips, a hot caress that lit a fire in parts of her body that didn't need to be excited so soon after giving birth. They ached. "Do you agree?"

She looked to the doorway. Behind the storm, lay the answer to her problems and a path to her daughter. "I agree."

23

The bond settled around them like a hot cord, branding them and binding them in place. The sheer enormity of the deal, which would stretch over years and lifetimes, hurt far worse than her previous deal with him. It felt momentous and life altering. With far-reaching consequences she couldn't fathom. Yet.

It doesn't matter. She's all that matters. Destroy the Stulos, so she can have that life. And deal with the rest as it comes.

Ruarc closed his eyes, his face a mask. She wished she could use the Caraigg talent of telepathy. Or read his emotions. Something that would give her a clue to what he was thinking. But all she could go by was her own instinct and intuition.

"What now?"

Ruarc opened his eyes, and smiled. "Now, Keeper, I sincerely hope for your success. Know this. The Wind can be all encompassing and seductive. Contained within is all that has been. Near the center lies the key. You go with my touch and blessing, the key will accept you. It will then seek out the rest of the object, in order to unlock it. It will guide you, if you let it."

"And where is the rest?" She rubbed her arms, trying to soothe away the goose bumps that had suddenly appeared at his ominous tone. *Why can't he just issue a plain warning? Why the riddles?*

"The object was split as the world split, each piece given to the two factions of air daemon. The main piece lies within Benata domain." Ruarc's gaze intensified. "Be warned. First Mother is not likely to relinquish the Stulos or the Artifact without force. And she'll stop at nothing to get the key. If you wish to break Air, you must do the same. Stop at nothing to obtain the artifact and make it whole."

Tarian swallowed the warning along with the last bit of moisture in her mouth. If she managed to get the key *and* travel to the Stulos, she'd still have to somehow get the artifact from First Mother, put it together with the key, then destroy the Stulos while simultaneously saving her child and keeping First Mother from killing them all. First Mother…the most powerful daemon in existence, apart from Ruarc.

"Another word of caution. The guardians, the Shee, might also be opposed. They rarely communicate directly, and I am not a Wind Walker. I cannot guarantee their loyalty."

Tarian started at the name "Wind Walker". She knew someone who *was* a Wind Walker. Macari. And Macari was currently somewhere near the baby. Maybe, just maybe, there was hope of a friend within the storm.

Everything Tarian knew about the Benata seemed to conflict with the First Mother's actions. She'd sacrifice an innocent baby, a newborn child, for fear of change? The chilling reality was the First Mother had already proven that she would. She'd commanded her own daughter to kill Tarian's unborn child. And when that didn't work, she'd sent the Ercklings to take the baby at a moment when Tarian had been most vulnerable. *What kind of person, human or daemon, does something like that? What is driving this blind hatred? No, not hate. Fear?*

Ruarc put a hand on her shoulder. His warmth seeped into her, a comforting blanket cushioning her panic. "Your power is not yet recovered. I offer exchange, for the purpose of bolstering your strength. Take some of my energy, and my signature, and then I will open the pathway to the Wind. Recover the key. It will act as a portal, directly to the artifact. If you deviate, you will be lost inside the Wind, even as the world reforms around you. The child will be lost. I cannot follow. I cannot encroach on Benata domain."

Another joining? No way to make a baby this time. Can I trust this? He wanted her to be able to fully fight, so that he could have his days with the Scion. Exactly why he wanted that time she'd have to discover later. It didn't seem very important right now, with her daughter's life dangling in the balance and the world collapsing around their ears. If she didn't succeed, her Agreement with him would be canceled anyway. She needed her full strength.

"Once again, I find I have no real choice."

"All of life is a choice, Keeper. You can pass through my gate without energy from me, and you will not be at full power as you face the First Mother. It would be unwise, but…" Ruarc spread his hands. "The choice is yours, as always."

"I accept your offer." She closed her eyes. "Just…get it over with."

She felt his energy envelope her immediately, and drank it in. This time, she didn't fight or fear it. She welcomed it. Air licked her from the top of her head to the bottom of her feet. It filled her soul with endless possibilities, a surge of joy and desire that wasn't only Ruarc's, but her own. The orgasm, when it came, filled her with more than renewed energy. It filled her with passion and determination even as it caused a deep ache within body parts that hadn't fully healed from giving birth.

She would get her daughter back. In that moment, she had no doubt. Hope ignited a flame in her heart that filled her with energy.

As the exchange faded, she was shocked, as she'd been before, to find herself standing there fully clothed. To be so intimate with someone, to share a piece of her soul, and not ever touch physically simply didn't compute with her normal way of doing things. She wondered briefly what it would be like without clothes, in the middle of the normal act, then realized she already knew. She and Daric had climbed that mountain already. The thought added to the flush she felt on her cheeks.

Ruarc caressed her palm. Tarian looked down to see that his fingers traced thin black lines in the shape of a mark that hadn't been there before. The symbol for Air.

"You seek an object which will contain the centermost portion of the symbol, roughly this size. It is white, nearly translucent, and blends with the surroundings. Touch it with your palm and it will bond to you." He released her hand and gestured to the door. "As the Wind spins, step to the center. Focus on your destination and your purpose. Do not deviate, no matter what you might see or feel. I will be unable to pull you out should you become trapped. And be warned, it is an easy thing to lose oneself in the past and forget the future."

"Got it." She focused her thoughts on the baby. She could follow the signature, which should lead her out.

"Keep our daughter safe, Keeper. I will see you both in one Earth year." Her stomach lurched at the caress in his voice.

Ruarc didn't look at her again, but turned to the storm. Energy poured from him into it. She felt it weaken, open to her. With a deep breath, she stepped into the storm and let the Wind take her.

24

As the storm closed around her, Tarian felt like it ripped her body into a million pieces. It was as if she'd been consumed by an F5 tornado, along with every other piece of debris in its wake. She tumbled, hair whipping her face unmercifully, legs and feet tangling hopelessly in the long black robes. Attacked on all sides by things she couldn't see, her eyes blurred from tears that tried desperately to combat the Wind.

A roar equal to a million trains and the pressure of the deepest ocean filled her ears. Her body stretched until she formed a starfish, tossed around like the trash on a jet stream. If there'd been water, this would have been the rapids as they tumbled over deadly rocks to form a waterfall of death. But with water, she'd be able to control it, harness it, use it. This was air, in the purest form. He'd called it the Wind, and he was right. It was that, and more. The intensity and power of it, combined with the chaos, ripped at her clothes and tore at her heart.

The baby.

Tarian struggled to maintain her focus, to keep in front of her a vision of her baby daughter and the feel of her child's signature. Through the swirling debris, a bolt of energy jolted her body, like lightning. Dolphins cried in the distance but did not reach her, offer comfort, or a way out. Her thin hold on her destination stretched taut. One wrong move and it would shatter.

She tried to pull her arms and legs in tight, but all it did was make her revolve through the chaos faster. No up, no down, no way to ground herself. Just the endless spin and roar of the Wind.

As she toppled from the force, she caught a glimpse of something, like a scene through a window. The black storm split, formed a hole large enough to stick her hand through. Within she saw her mother, standing there, serenely contemplating something off to the side that Tarian couldn't see. *Mother!*

Tarian put her hand to the image, and it sucked her forward through the morass and into another level of the Wind. Here, scenes and debris whirled even faster. Too fast to understand or capture. The scene which held her mother gone as though it never existed. More whipped past. She caught glimpses of black sand, blue sky, dirty alley, the Laghairtine as he raised a claw to attack.

It's showing me my life? She turned her head, even as she tumbled, desperate to see more. The lure of it seduced her far more than Ruarc's warmth and intimate touches. Here, an image of Alex and herself as children, tumbling in the Arena. There, Calliope as a baby. Further, an image of her mother as the ceiling fell.

Tarian gasped, taken by surprise. *Mother!*

New scenes brushed past, each more strange than the last. People she didn't know, some going about everyday life. Washing clothes. Walking on the beach. Playing with a child. Then one lingered a bit longer than the rest. A woman, black hair striped with gray, sitting on a black sand beach bordered by tumbled black rocks, ocean licking at her toes. Dolphins, chittering just offshore. The Dolphin closest bore a scar over one eye.

Roger.

She stared at the woman. *Who are you?*

As if she heard, the woman looked up, directly at Tarian, and smiled. Then the vision faded, taken by the Wind, replaced with more scenes moving so fast she couldn't make out what they contained.

Tarian mentally shook herself. She didn't have time to play with memories written on the Wind. Though she felt the pull and the fascination of it, and wanted with every breath of her body to seek out any containing her mother, still. She had something she needed to do. Something she desperately wanted, more than the ability to wallow in the past.

I need the key. I need to save the baby.

Ruarc had said to step into the center. As she twisted and turned, pushed about by the Wind, she realized she should have asked him exactly *how* such a thing was accomplished in a place with no up or down, or anything resembling something she could walk on. How did someone simply *walk* through a tornado of images from the past? The only thing she'd managed to do was get pulled along from one scene to the next, with no way of knowing if she actually advanced toward anything at all.

Walking the Wind is obviously a metaphor someone forgot to tell me about.

The only real wind skill she possessed was tracking. It was a fantastic ability, one that'd saved her ass many times. Even here, she kept a tight grip on the track she held for the baby. Like holding a very tight rope, she knew even in this chaos which way she should turn to find her child. It reassured her that somehow things would work out. As long as she could feel the baby, then the baby was alive and reasonably well. *For now.*

She could track the artifact key. Tarian stared at the symbol on her palm. *I can use this. Ruarc's signature is all over it. If he touched the key, then I can forge a link. But I'll have to drop my link to the baby to do it.* In a place like this, it would take every bit of strength she had just to form the focus necessary for a new trace. Finding something so small in such chaos would be like shifting an entire beach of sand looking for one specific grain. No way could she hold more than one trace.

Without that key, everything was over before it began. Tarian wouldn't be able to put the artifact together, to destroy the Stulos, to get her child. The world would collapse. It would all be for nothing. Without that key, she'd never get out of the Wind. She'd tumble here, forever going from scene to scene, as history passed her by.

Her heart ached. Letting go of the lifeline she held to her baby...how could she? She'd never be able to pick it up again here. She'd only held it because she'd formed the link before she stepped into the storm.

With a cry of frustration, she dropped the trace. The link to her daughter severed as though cut with a knife, tossed to the Wind, gone in a second. Tarian closed her eyes, absorbing the loss. Not just the physical loss of birth, but now the bond of magic as well. *Gone.*

The pain of losing the link to her baby, more than childbirth, more than anything she'd ever experienced, sliced through her. It took her heart, ripped it out of her chest, diced it to a million pieces and scattered them into the Wind that swirled around her.

A determination stronger than anything she'd ever felt took hold within. A sense of right, a seed of hope, the fire burst through her. The *need* to accomplish something so pure it took over the grief and pain and made it into something new. Fuel, for power.

Tarian used it, gathered her focus, and wove it into the fine strands she used to track objects. She caressed the mark on her palm, absorbed the feel of it, the power left behind by Ruarc. Then she added some of Ruarc's signature as well, with the intent to find the object closest to her that he'd touched with his own hands. When she had the trace ready, she shoved it into the Wind, keeping a tight hold on her end, letting the storm take the other.

Show me the way.

The strand tightened immediately, bolstered by the air energy around her. She turned, and when she had her body facing exactly the direction of the key, she spread her hands in front of her, and *shoved.*

Her body tumbled into the next stream, the Wind taking her for a ride. Through it, she kept her focus on the artifact piece. It was closer, but not stationary. Usually, when tracing an object, she'd simply travel from point to point until she determined exactly where she needed to be. That wasn't possible, tossed around in the storm as she was. With nothing physical to use, to stand on or get her bearings, she wasn't sure how to move forward. The only other air ability she used on a regular basis was a travel portal.

Why not?

Tarian formed an image of the artifact in her mind, as described by Ruarc. A palm-sized white object with the air symbol etched on it. When she had it as clear to her as if it lay in her hand, she opened a travel portal using her trace as a guide. When she finished, the portal wavered in the air next to her. Within, she only saw more storm. Lightning, without thunder. She used the trace as leverage and pulled herself into the portal.

Tumbling out of the other side of the travel portal was like diving head first into a whirlwind. The Wind spun faster, tighter, created by so many scenes and visions of the past that she couldn't make out anything specific. Just colors and shapes. She used her tie to the artifact to position her body in what she assumed was an upright position. The wind pulled her hair in all directions, the robe wrapped and flapped around her. But she knew, in front of her, lay the object she sought.

All she saw, however, was more Wind streams. More images, more colors. Somewhere in there was the key. *How do I reach it? How do I get to it?*

Frustrated, she pushed her hand out in front of her, palm forward, as though telling the Wind to "stop". The mark on her palm itched. She resisted the urge to scratch. It began to burn, taking the breath out of her, but she resisted the urge to rub it.

Instead, she tried to follow the power that assaulted her palm. It connected to her through Ruarc's signature in her skin, but didn't come any closer. It was a few inches away, she was sure of it, but remained invisible, and just out of reach.

The power current engulfed her. Tarian screamed, the sound barely touching the chaos of the Wind. She'd turned loose of her daughter, let go of everything, to get the key. And now she couldn't reach it. Her head throbbed and her heart broke from the strain.

That which you seek lies just out of reach. Take it, Keeper of Water, Child of Wind, Bearer of Fire. Embrace it. It is yours, if you wish it.

The words circled around her and through her. Like a soft breeze they caressed her cheeks, soothed her heart. The voice, light, a mere whisper yet heard above the roar of chaos as clearly as though she stood in complete silence. A soft signature reached her then. Power, ancient power, with the scent of jasmine.

She didn't know the owner. The power was not daemon. Nor dolphin. Nor Caraigg.

You bear the mark, you wield the power. Take the key, save the child.

In front of her, she caught a glimpse of a girl, all in white, her eyes deep with the knowledge of Ancients. Silver hair drifting around her as though she merely floated in a pool of gentle tides. The girl giggled, then dissolved. *Take the Air, walk the Wind, save the child.*

Where the girl had floated incongruously among chaotic winds, only a glow remained. Tarian blinked, trying to clear her vision. The tug of power, the same as the mark on her palm. *The artifact.*

She held her hand out, this time palm up, as though waiting for something to be placed there. Stared at the object, even though she couldn't make out its shape, even though it was nothing more than a light in the darkness around her. *I was sent by Ruarc of the Mayfanta to claim the key. It is mine by right of Agreement.*

The words felt right, and within them power stirred and grew, reached out from her palm to the glowing thing before her.

It slammed into her palm, and she closed her fingers, clenching it into a tight fist. Her hand and arm tingled as the artifact accepted her, the sensation racing up her arm to her chest where it stopped. The dolphin artifact formed a barrier.

Tarian immediately dropped her trace on the key to locate the rest of the artifact. *Come on, show me the way out of here.* She focused on her need so intently that she forgot about the Wind, the chaos. She forgot her body was tumbling through space. Forgot everything but the one burning desire...to find the other part of the artifact. To reunite the pieces. To make them whole.

When she found the thread, she seized it, a lifeline in the storm. She wrapped the strands of power around the artifact in her hand, then allowed the key to pull her forward through the Wind. She ignored the scenes that floated past.

Tarian slammed into what felt like a brick wall and tumbled down, landing on her back. One minute she was in the tumult of the Wind, the next she sprawled on grass, the roar behind her. Tarian took a few ragged breaths and then wrenched her body into an upright position. All around her, various power signatures flooded her senses, the combined scents and strengths an assault that made her wrinkle her nose in distaste. So much power, overlapping. Usually she held a shield in place against this very thing, though power of this magnitude wasn't often experienced on the earth side. She knew without looking that she was surrounded by daemon, that they were each more powerful than she ever hoped to be. And three of them were familiar.

Macari. First Mother. And...

The baby!

25

Tarian looked everywhere, frantically seeking her daughter. What she saw turned her heart cold and her stomach to rock.

First Mother held the infant, bundled in a white blanket. The baby slept, seemingly at ease with her surroundings. Macari stood next to them without expression. Behind Macari, the sky boiled with impending storms, and a nearly invisible disturbance in the air pulsated with the ebb and flow of power, the sucking of energy from all around.

The Stulos.

Tarian slowly got to her feet, gathering power. It leapt easily to her will, boosted by Ruarc and her connection to the medallion. It gave her confidence she probably shouldn't have, considering what she faced.

The ground trembled and she shifted her feet automatically. *Earthquakes. Thunderstorms. What will Air cause, when released?* Tarian's gaze swept over the assembled daemon. First Mother's face, immovable as a carved statue, an odd juxtaposition to a newborn child's peaceful sleep. *This is the first time I've truly seen my daughter. MY daughter. And she's in someone else's arms. Jealousy flared.*

On top of the baby, nestled in the folds of the blanket, lay a white glowing object. It looked like a thousand small whirlwinds danced in a sea of white around a dark indentation. There was no doubt what it was.

Air Artifact.

Tarian gripped the key tighter. She could feel its desire to reunite with the larger piece. Tarian shifted her gaze to Macari. The daemon didn't meet her eyes, instead staring at the ground in front of her, arms tense and stiff at her side. Hands clenched into fists. *Friend or enemy?*

At least a dozen more daemon flanked First Mother. Tarian noted their lack of emotion, their passive faces, confident stances, their gathered power and the way they all stared at her as though they'd already sized her abilities and found them barely worth noting.

Tarian did a little comparison of her own, and realized they were right. Their power outweighed her own. And from what she knew of the daemon in general, they were probably in mind-conference right now, speaking in rushed thoughts to each other so that Tarian couldn't hear them plan, nor know their projected attack.

Definite disadvantage.

Tarian returned her scrutiny to the First Mother.

"Why have you taken my daughter?" Tarian kept her gaze locked on the First Mother, looking for any inflection or sign that would help her know the next move.

First Mother raised her chin slightly. "This child will serve society, as do all of the Benata." The tone, dignified as a queen when speaking to her subjects. The face, a neutral mask. But the eyes…Tarian saw a world of information in the woman's eyes. They opened wide, until more white showed than pupils.

Fear. She's afraid. Deeply afraid. Terrified.

"She is *not* Benata." Tarian squared her shoulders, and placed her feet shoulder width apart, firmly planted on the shifting earth. "She is *not* yours and she will *not* serve you."

"All within Benata domain serve the Benata. Including you, *Keeper.*" First Mother glanced down at Tarian's fist. "You carry that which does not belong to you."

"You realize how ironic that statement is, right?" Tarian clutched the key tighter. "You hold *my* child in your arms. *My* child."

First Mother's arms clenched slightly. Tarian took a step forward, then paused at an almost imperceptible shake of Macari's head, a slight flinch that was gone almost before it started. Tarian stopped. *Trap?*

Tarian's fingers twitched around the artifact key as she quickly ran through her options. Rush forward, possibly hit a barrier. Be the first to throw power at First Mother, in the hopes that surprise would give her the advantage and that, somehow, it would miss hitting her child. Shoot energy at the daemon standing ready, in the hopes that by distracting them it would leave First Mother vulnerable. Somehow break the Stulos, so the resulting chaos would make First Mother drop or abandon the baby.

Nothing seemed right. Nothing sounded plausible or even possible. She looked to Macari. The girl didn't move. Shift. Blink. No indication at all what she was thinking.

I wish I could mind-speak without touch. This would be so much easier.

Macari's eyes widened slightly, and she blinked, the movement so slow it had to be deliberate.

Tarian's pulse quickened. *You can hear my thoughts?*

Macari blinked slowly, once.

Right. I knew that. Can she?

Macari blinked twice in slow motion.

Tarian's gaze flicked back to First Mother. "You would destroy an innocent child, for the good of society as you see it? What happened to the infamous Benata Way, First Mother? Isn't it the creed of the Benata that no harm should come to any life?"

First Mother's grip tightened on the baby, and her eyes narrowed. "Our Way has come to pass through thousands of years of wisdom and life, such as you cannot fathom. Your race, your existence, is in infancy. You cannot possibly hope to comprehend the consequences of your actions."

Tarian shifted to the right, so she could see Macari without shifting her gaze from First Mother. *Is there a barrier between me and First Mother?*

Macari blinked once.

First Mother raised her chin, defiant. "You have been deceived, Keeper, into believing you act for the right reasons. Your actions put all of existence at risk. Even now, the world cracks. One more step, and it will break. All will be lost. Tell me, *Keeper*, is not one soul worth sacrificing if it will save millions?"

Tarian maintained eye contact with First Mother. *Need to keep her distracted while we plan.* "Call me selfish, but perhaps millions are worth risking, for the sake of that one soul. She *matters*, First Mother. She is not a tool, a toy, or a sacrifice. She's a baby. She's hope. She's the future."

"She's the *lack* of a future." First Mother twitched her arms as if to throw the baby. Tarian tensed, her power crackling around her, ready to lash out.

Steady, Tarian. Steady. She flicked a glance to Macari.

Will the barrier stop me from reaching her?

One blink.

Will it stop an object? Like a rock?

Two blinks. And a frown.

It's specifically for me, then?

One blink.

Interesting.

Tarian swept the area lightly with power. She couldn't feel the barrier at all. *Clever trick.* She licked her cracked lips, stalling. Realizing First Mother watched her every move, she lowered her gaze slightly, as though admitting defeat.

Are you inside it?

One blink. Macari raised her eyebrows and tilted her head slightly. Tarian smiled.

"What are you afraid of, First Mother? Her strength? Or is it something deeper? More personal."

First Mother pressed her lips together, but didn't drop her gaze.

Tarian tilted her head. "Personal, then. Not just her strength, but her existence as it relates to you. You're afraid for yourself. And here I thought the Benata were all about the good of the many over the good of the one."

First Mother opened her mouth to speak, but then closed it again without uttering a word.

She's got a lot of self-control, I'll give her that.

Macari blinked once, her lips lifted in a half smile.

I'll distract her. You try to get the artifact piece. When you have it, I'll throw you the key. Ok?

Macari hesitated, her eyes wide. Tarian waited for her to blink, and when she didn't, her heart sank. Macari couldn't, or wouldn't, help her.

Or maybe there's something wrong with the approach.

Macari blinked once, quickly.

"Are you afraid of change, First Mother? Is that what bothers you? That the world will be different?" It was very difficult to keep two conversations going at once. Tarian felt First Mother's attention slipping. The woman was about to act, and Tarian had no idea how or what it might mean. She needed to control the pace. Ruthlessly she pressed on, trying to drive the woman to speak, to give up something. Anything.

"Or is it more than that? Have you done something you don't want others to know about? Are you ashamed? Will the combination of the planes make it obvious?"

First Mother's eyes widened again, briefly. *Gotcha.*

"That's it, isn't it? You're ashamed. You've done something. I wonder what it is." Tarian looked at the baby, then back to First Mother. "You've stolen a child. Somewhere deep down that bothers you. But it's more than that."

Tarian glanced at Macari. *Can you get the artifact?*

Macari hesitated again. Then finally blinked once.

Whatever had bothered her about the plan, she'd do it anyway. It was risky, but what other choice did they have?

Macari shrugged slightly as if to say "no idea."

When we get through this you have to teach me how to hear you. This is a pain in the ass.

Macari smirked. Blinked once.

Tarian returned her gaze to First Mother to find her studying the two of them intently. "It's Macari. Something about her makes you ashamed. I wonder, First Mother…how did she get the ability to visit the human plane in the first place?"

First Mother pushed her chin out in defiance. "Enough." She turned toward Macari and held out the baby. Macari took the child gently into her arms. She didn't look at Tarian.

"What the hell are you doing?" Tarian protested, knowing she couldn't just run at them. Knowing a trap would spring if she tried. She definitely didn't understand what was going on. *Are you on my side or not?*

First Mother ignored Tarian's outburst, instead raising her left hand over Macari's forehead like a priest anointing a faithful subject. "First Daughter, you are bound to serve the Benata Court, and to carry out any command issued by the First Mother. I decree, by right of station, that this child shall be used to re-create the missing Stulos. The spell is already in place. Activation will now commence. You will take the child to the Wind, and release the artifact."

Tarian watched, horrified, as the mark of Air etched itself onto Macari's forehead with each word spoken. Macari, to her credit, didn't wince or protest. She kept her eyes closed and her face neutral, as if she'd collapsed in on herself.

First Mother held out her right hand, palm up, and Tarian felt the key ripped out of her fist, tearing the flesh on her palm as it went. It landed neatly in First Mother's outstretched hand.

First Mother placed the key next to the artifact. The two pieces rose in the air, glowing and rotating. A loud snap accompanied the jolt of power as they touched. Bolts of energy shot out in all directions, striking everyone. Tarian stumbled, working hard just to remain upright in the buffeting gusts. Several daemon were knocked off their feet. Others crouched to avoid the brunt of the wind. Of everyone, only First Mother and Macari remained unaffected by the blast. They both stood tall and strong, though Macari's hair whipped her face and First Mother's robes twisted.

Tarian gaped as the artifact pieces fused together and whirled. Though she knew the key had fit in the palm of her hand, now it looked several feet bigger and resembled a storm of white, glittery dust. It swirled and snaked in on itself, thrumming with raw energy. Macari stared at it, her eyes locked on the process while her hands remained tightly around the baby.

Between the ground shaking and clouds roiling and the artifact spinning, it felt as though the world was about to fall apart. Tarian cringed back as a loud thunderclap sounded just overhead and the first drops of rain splashed onto her face.

Maybe I can grab it.

Tarian shifted her feet to act on the thought, but knew it was futile. She wore the Water Artifact. A person could only hold one artifact at a time. She'd been able to carry the key because it was only a piece of the prize. It did nothing on its own. Now that it was whole…

Tarian looked to Macari. *She can't hold it either. She has Fire.*

It struck her that for the first time three artifacts of power were in proximity to each other. *All this power is pushing the seams of reality apart. Wonder if we can combine Water and Fire to take Air?* She saw Macari's expression flinch and eyes widen in response to the thought, followed by an almost imperceptible shake of her head.

Tarian glanced to First Mother. The daemon watched the artifact turn with an air of satisfaction. *Bitch.* She couldn't stop thinking the word, and thought she saw a flicker of a grin from Macari. *We have to strike now, while she's distracted.*

Again, Macari responded with a slight headshake.

Tarian leaned forward in frustration. *Why are we waiting?*

The moment slipped by. Already the artifact, now complete and whole, shrank in size. It settled slowly back onto the baby's bundled form. Now, instead of looking like a small white whirlwind, it looked like a larger white jewel formed of swirls of stardust. A glow surrounded it and the baby as though they were encased in a bubble of power, or shielded.

The spell. It's activated.

Macari met her gaze then. Her vivid blue eyes flashed.

What are you doing?

Macari's shoulders stiffened, her lips parted. Then she closed her eyes, cutting off all communication.

First Mother raised both hands. Power streaked from them to Macari. "Go. Do as I have commanded."

Macari shuddered and took a step backward, then another. Tarian reached for her just as she stumbled and fell off the edge of the cliff, taking the baby with her.

26

Tarian's stomach sank as Macari and the baby disappeared from view, and bile rose up into her throat. She gagged on it even as she choked out a scream.

Macari rose in the air before them, supported by some sort of cushion fashioned from energy, the baby safe in her arms. Even if Tarian wanted to send some sort of assault, or break the spell, she couldn't. Wouldn't. *No way to strike without hitting the baby.*

Macari spun in place, hair pulled by the wind, dress billowing around her. They formed a blur of color as they revolved faster and faster until they both vanished.

Tarian gaped at the spot where they'd hung suspended not seconds before. The space was empty. No trace left of either one of them.

Tarian screamed, a primal shout that originated in her gut and roared through the air. She turned on First Mother, pure rage coloring everything a deep red. "You fucking bitch! Bring them back!"

Power, which had been bubbling beneath her skin waiting for direction, leapt to her blind intent to cause damage to anything and everything. Dolphin song roared in her ears as the Water Artifact burst into life within her chest.

First Mother blanched as Tarian's rage reached her. Water jets lifted the daemon off the ground and tossed her against a nearby rock. She slumped against it, stunned.

The guard leapt into action, swarming Tarian. Some were

repelled by bolts of water, but others broke through. Three of them tackled her in a group lunge that knocked her off her feet. Her back hit the ground hard, knocking the wind out of her. She gasped, furious. Pushed out with water boulders. "Get. Off. Me." The three flew back and Tarian scrambled to her feet, dangerously close to the cliff's edge.

She slammed a shield in place around her so another physical attack wouldn't be possible, then turned on the First Mother. She'd been helped to her feet, but she looked shaken and out of breath. Eyes wide, she stared past Tarian, to the sky behind her.

"I don't fall for stupid tricks." Tarian shouted at her. "Bring them back. Now."

First Mother pointed, and several other daemon followed suit. Tarian hesitated. The look on all their faces was one of disbelief, or horror. Though she'd like to believe her display of power had caused the reaction, she seriously doubted it.

Slowly Tarian shifted her position until she could get the sky behind her in peripheral view.

Even at a glance, she could see the Stulos glowed. The Wind, transparent when Tarian arrived, had turned dark, nearly black. The sky around it writhed with angry clouds and streaks of lightning. Only now did she hear the thunder crashes. She'd been so focused on the baby and First Mother, she'd tuned them out. Something was very, very wrong with the Stulos.

Keeping her focus of power in First Mother's direction, Tarian looked closer at the Stulos. Several hundred large birds circled frantically around it as though they stirred the pot. *The Shee?* Ruarc had warned her the guardians might not agree with her mission. From this distance, Tarian couldn't tell.

First Mother made a guttural sound. "What did you do? What have you done to the Stulos?"

Tarian turned to gape at the woman. "What have *I* done? What about you? You're the one who kidnapped a baby. You're the one who shoved your own daughter off a cliff, with *my child* in her arms. What the hell is wrong with you?"

First Mother started to speak. Stopped. Glanced at the daemon. Back at the Stulos.

Thunderclouds surrounded the hill they stood on. Lightning forked in all directions. The Stulos bulged, expanded. It reached for the storm, gobbling the power like a hungry dog, fighting for more. Tarian felt her life force draining with it and stumbled. She crashed down to her knees, her hands reaching out to catch herself before she tumbled off the mountain. The ground shook. Thunder growled and wind roared.

Terrified, Tarian stared at the Stulos. She no longer had eyes for the First Mother, or the other daemon. All attention focused on the Stulos. *They're in there. My baby is...* Tarian pressed at the medallion. It pulsated, increasing with the beat of her heart until she thought both would burst.

The Shee swept up and around the Stulos, their wings an odd calm in the storm. One descended close to Tarian and for the briefest flash it was no longer a bird, but a girl with white hair and the scent of jasmine. The girl held out a hand, and beckoned to Tarian, before dissolving into the Wind once more.

Tarian tried to get to her feet, but the ground shook and a crack appeared, knocking her sideways. The mountain split, a chasm forming between her and First Mother. Several daemon winked away, but whether they'd been swallowed or merely traveled away from it Tarian couldn't tell. So much power stolen, so much in the air, she couldn't tell she ended and the rest began. All she could do was try to breathe. The medallion burned against her hand, as though a fire had kindled there. It poured energy into the storm, a steady stream of blue light feeding the Stulos. Dolphins screamed. With the next clap of thunder, Tarian pitched forward onto her hands and retched. Her head split in two with pain. A kaleidoscope of colors that only came with the most intense migraines blurred her vision.

The Stulos, hungry for more, expanded. It reached for her and First Mother, fingers of darkness engulfing them into a dizzying haze of Wind.

The darkness *flexed*, like a weight lifter offering a bulging bicep for inspection. It was as if the hill and surrounding atmosphere sucked in on itself, pulling everything in, compressing, pressurizing. Like steam built up in a kettle, or a bullet waiting to explode from a gun. Everything stood still for a fraction of a second, then it all *flexed* back into place, then onward, pushing out, expanding, dragging everything in its wake as it reached the outer edges. Like a balloon filled with too much air, it exploded, shoving everything and everyone out in every direction.

Tarian screamed as she, the First Mother, the daemon remaining all raced with the Wind out, out, out. She screamed as the world shattered, and kept screaming as reality broke.

27

Tarian sat back in a rickety metal chair, warm cup of coffee in hand, and inhaled as she surveyed the street in front of her. It was early morning, and traffic was the usual mess of exhaust and horns. People in suits, heels, carrying brief cases and bags, scurried this way and that, heading to work in Center City. Most of them were probably lawyers or government workers, but some were students, or retail clerks. The ones in jeans and T-shirts were probably waitresses. It was all so normal. So relaxing. And the coffee, as always, manna from heaven in the palm of her hand.

She sighed. Frowned. She had a feeling she was forgetting something. A tickle at the edge of her memory played with her. She was supposed to be somewhere, she was sure of it. Probably another meeting her mother insisted she attend.

No. That's not it.

Mother's dead. The thought fled as soon as she had it. Tarian took a sip of coffee, and savored the slight chocolate bite to it.

Down the street, a car collided with the one in front of it with a loud crash. Horns blared, voices screamed. Nearby, people paused in what they were doing. Some ran forward. Others ran away.

What's going on?

Tarian stood to get a better view. Down the street to her left, smoke billowed out from under the hood of an old blue sedan. The car in front of it, rear end crumpled up to the back seat, wiggled in the morning sun.

Wiggled?

She narrowed her eyes, squinting at it. *Cars don't just wiggle.*

The car shimmied, then leapt into the air and revolved in place, suspended on a column of water 15 feet high. People screamed. Those standing nearest ran. The man in the car held the steering wheel, eyes wide in panic.

The thought that something was wrong poked at her, more of a nudge than a tickle this time. Waterspouts just didn't happen in the middle of Philadelphia. *Could be a water main break.*

She snorted at the how ridiculous that sounded. A water main wouldn't make the car shimmy. The metal swayed and buckled even as the car revolved. The man inside, his face a mask of pure terror.

Tarian sat back down, and took another sip. *I should help him.* She frowned at the cup. *Why?*

The *something's wrong* feeling slapped her.

What is this? Why am I here? She tried desperately to remember how and when she'd come to PJ's. It eluded her. She tried instead to remember where she'd been before.

The faintest trickle of a memory. Wind. A lot of wind.

Tarian closed her eyes, ignoring the chaos around her, willing the screams to stop so she could just *think* for a minute.

A breeze tossed her hair, brushed her legs against the silk black gown she wore.

I never wear a dress.

She opened her eyes to stare at the foreign fabric. Something about it nagged at her. *It's not mine.*

She pulled at the material with both hands, stretching it out and away from her body. It was tattered along the edges, ripped in a few places. As though she'd been in a fight. It was then she noticed how incredibly sore her muscles were. Her stomach drooped. Her nether region throbbed. Her breasts felt full and sore. They ached for something. Someone.

The baby.

A flood of adrenaline brought the memory back to her. *My baby.* She'd given birth. In the ocean. Just before…

The Stulos.

"Shit!" Tarian leapt to her feet, knocking the chair over in her haste. The Stulos. She had to break the last Stulos. Fire, all that remained. The odd scene in front of her was a direct result of magic crashing down on the earth plane.

My baby!

She panted, out of breath as panic threatened to make her hyperventilate. The image of Macari, the baby in her arms, disappearing into the Wind, and then the Stulos exploding, filled her mind. The rush of wind, the power, all of it vivid in her memory. *Nobody could survive that from inside. Nobody.*

She forced herself to realize the harsh truth. *Macari and the baby are either dead, or trapped in the Cosaerie.*

Did the path of air even exist, if the Air Stulos no longer existed? Was it a function of the Stulos, or something else entirely? She didn't know. Didn't have time to find out.

How am I here? Why am I on Earth side again?

The only tiny spark of hope lay in the idea Macari and the baby were trapped, rather than destroyed. Maybe somehow Macari had shielded her daughter and taken the baby into the Wind on purpose, to save her from the First Mother.

It was a slim hope.

Tarian gathered focus and launched a trace for her daughter. After a few minutes with no response, she tried again for Macari. Nothing. Again for the Air Artifact.

Nothing.

Pulse pounding, she tried for Calliope. Daric. Alex.

Nothing.

The scene before her spun in a dizzying array of sound and color as the realization sunk in. She couldn't track. They were dead. All dead.

Or I am.

Anger and despair warred inside her. It was like watching

herself from a long distance away. She wished for the ocean, her beach, the warm sand, anything but this.

What have I done?

A faint whisper near her ear brushed by. *Walk, Keeper.*

The briefest image of a girl with white hair breezed past.

Tarian blinked, and it was gone. Had it even been there at all? *I'm hallucinating. I'm on overload. It's too much. All too much. I've done all I can do.*

A deep, familiar voice, laced with the sounds of crackling flames. *Have you? Walk, Keeper.*

More voices. She couldn't make out the words, there were too many. They all sounded urgent, amused, depressed, angry, confused. She clapped her hands over her ears to block them, but they wouldn't go away. They pounded at her skull until she wanted to scream. Then she did scream, letting out all the frustration into a primal yell.

Reality tore, leaving a rip directly in front of her through which she could see black sand. *My beach.*

Without hesitation she stepped through the opening.

28

Tarian's toes sank into familiar black sand. Ocean waves rushed in, licked her toes, and receded like a happy puppy bounding away for play. Overhead, the sun warmed everything in a pleasant glow of afternoon peace. She turned to the right, noting the tumbled black rocks that formed her home.

No guards.

Waves rushed in again, further up the beach this time, soaking her feet up to the ankles. Tarian stepped back away from them. *The tide shouldn't be so high. Not now.*

Frowning, she started up the path to her house. The cave opening yawned at her as she approached, the mouth seeming to stretch and grow as she ascended. Inside, it was cool, dark, and completely empty.

No benches. No alcoves. No Sentinels.

Her heart raced as her mind whirled through possible reasons for the lack of anything familiar.

Walk, Keeper. A bright voice giggled.

Tarian whipped around, expecting to find the girl right behind her. But nobody stood there, and no sound but the muffled crash of the ocean. Just the hint of sea, salt, and jasmine on the breeze.

She pushed further into the house, her bare feet making a slapping sound on the rough stone floor. *It's always been smooth.*

The rotunda, devoid of any plants, benches, or people, opened in front of her like the wide-open mouth of a whale, and threatened to swallow her whole. It was as though the whole place had been abandoned. Devoid of life, of all the things that made it home. She stood in the middle of the open space and stared at the place where the door to the receiving hall should be. Instead of giant, ornately carved wood, a small black hole greeted her. Beyond it, the faintest hint of a glow.

Walk, Keeper.

She brushed the voice away, and stepped through the opening, ducking a bit to get through a short tunnel. On the other side, she stopped. Instead of a huge, open cavern with a dome roof that let in the sun and sea, instead of a marble floor with her power mark embedded in the center, instead of the tapestries that made it her favorite room in the house, a small deep cavern extended into more rock. A roughly carved floor bit at her feet. And in front of her, in the center of the small space, a fire burned, painting the walls with black soot and ash. Around the fire, Tarian counted seven people, two of whom, both men, held a woman by the arms as though she were a prisoner. All of them wore primitive, rough fabric wrap-around skirts, and their chests were draped with necklaces formed of shells and sea creatures.

The people chanted in a sing-song fashion. One stoked the fire until the flames roared. The woman screamed, and Tarian, horrified, watched as the men thrust her into the fire. The group quickly joined hands, forming a circle around the flame, as they chanted and hummed. Tarian pulled on her power, trying to gather water so fast it gave her a headache, to thrust it at the flames. It didn't answer her call. No water energy burst forth, and the fire didn't die, the people didn't stop their chant, and the woman continued to burn.

They're killing her!

The need to *do* something overpowered Tarian. She raced forward, and without thinking reached toward the fire to pull the woman from the flames. As she leaned in, she tripped on something and stumbled, falling face-first in the fire with a scream, her arms up to shield her eyes.

When she landed, sand kicked up around her, scraping her arms and legs. She rolled with it, hoping to put out the flames, before coming to a stop with the realization that she felt no heat, no pain, and smelled no charred flesh.

Tarian opened her eyes to a vast, star filled sky. The cave had vanished. In its place, a quarter moon shed a gentle glow on the beach. To her right, the ocean moved slowly in and crawled back out, a gentle caress on the soft white sand. Tarian scrambled to her feet.

Walk, Keeper.

She turned quickly, hoping to catch the woman in white. But all she got was the scent of jasmine. "Who *are* you? What is this place?"

Next to her, the remnants of a huge bonfire smoldered and crackled. It put out a gentle warmth, but nothing threatening. The sound of voices beyond it beckoned her, and she moved around the bonfire. On the other side, sitting on low, rough stones, were a pair, man and woman, deep in conversation in a language she couldn't understand. The woman leaned toward the man, her eyes dancing in the starlight, a soft smile on her lips. Her body, an open invitation. She blinked at him and laughed, a warm, husky sound. The man caressed her face, and leaned in for a kiss so tender it made Tarian's eyes water.

They can't see me. Nobody can see me.

Feeling like an intruder, Tarian stepped closer to the pair. The woman with dark brown skin and deep brown hair cascading down her back, wore a tight leather tank top and rough brown fabric wrapped around her waist. The two had stopped speaking. They gazed into each other's eyes in a look so intimate that Tarian averted her own, looking out into the forest beyond them, embarrassed to be eavesdropping on so private a moment.

The forest was mostly a dark mass formed with lumps of tall bits of gray, trees in the starlight. But within the deepest black, two vivid points of light stared out. They swirled from red to orange, as though they were flames, candles perhaps set to light a path through the trees.

They blinked.

Tarian squinted. They blinked again. Closer. *Fire, in the forest, that moves?* She stepped past the two lovers, closer to the trees. The flames remained in the dense part of the foliage, but they hovered above the ground at the exact height suggesting they were eyes, not fires. They blinked again, and blazed.

Angry? No. Jealous.

Tarian turned back to see the couple had moved from the stone to the sand, and lay together, the woman on top, moving as lovers do. Their passion and joy was obvious.

She looked back at the jealous fire in the night and found it staring at her, instead. Fear raced up her spine. "What are you?" She whispered.

The eyes blinked, fire extinguished. As though it never existed.

Walk, Keeper.

Tarian spun. "Who the hell are you? Walk where?"

The scent of jasmine tickled her nose. The couple rolled in the sand, oblivious to her or the fiery eyes or anything else but their passion.

Feeling spooked, Tarian backed away from the forest, her toes gripping the sand as she backpedalled away from whatever lurked there, to the ocean.

Walk. Remember.

"Remember what?" She turned to the ocean. No dolphins greeted her. Just the gentle roll of ocean waves, the enticement and serenity of the water. She longed for a swim. The desire felt so strong that before she could stop herself, she'd stepped knee-deep into the water. The tide lifted her off her toes, and she let it take her, body spilling forward into the next wave.

29

The warmth of the ocean embraced her, made her feel whole in a way nothing else did. She dove deep, rejoicing in the freedom of movement unique to her favorite element. Connected with nature, she gave her body and soul to it. She swam with the current, moving further and further out to the deepest part of the ocean. Around her, the endless serenity of the sea.

Tarian swam until, her arms weary, she had to stop to rest. It was easy to rest here. Just drift. Relax. No worries. No cares. No world destroyed by madness. No baby.

She frowned at the thought. *Why did I think that?*

Keeper, Walk. The voice sounded insistent, and a bit frantic. Urgent. Worried.

As the words entered her mind she remembered hearing them before, and it sparked something else. The vague thought that nothing was as it should be. She looked around, wondering what was wrong.

No fish.

She'd never, ever swam in an ocean without being surrounded by various sea life. Nothing moved in this ocean but her. And then something else struck her as very odd.

No smells.

She hadn't smelled the fire on the beach. Nor the sea air. Nor the fire in that cave…her home…

Realization slapped her, her heart racing with the knowledge. *I'm trapped. I'm nowhere. This isn't real. Am I dead?*

She tried to say the words out loud but only bubbles emerged. Frantic, she gathered focus to make a travel portal home. Her power ignored her. No portal opened.

Spooked, Tarian paddled for the surface. She'd destroyed the Stulos. All but one.

Fire. Chaos.

As she swam, she thought about what that meant. The world was stretched to the breaking point. If she didn't break the last one soon, they'd all be lost. Destroyed. Or maybe tossed forever, like this, on the Wind. And the baby...

I'm lost in the Cosaerie! That's why you keep telling me to walk. I have to walk the Wind. But I don't know how.

She searched her memory, but it was hazy, fuddled, and a mix of things she'd seen and done, some of which she knew weren't real. *Or are they?*

Her home, just a cave where people threw one another into a fire? That couldn't be real. It couldn't be. They didn't do that sort of thing. But she remembered Macari complaining bitterly about a scene she'd witnessed on the Wind, the murder of people on a white sand beach.

All that has been is written on the Wind.

Tarian stopped swimming. The surface was no closer than it had been. She was getting nowhere, and her body was past exhaustion. *How do I walk the Wind when I'm stuck in water?*

All that has been is written on the Wind. Walk, Keeper. Find your child.

My child is dead. They're all dead. I can't feel them. I can't find them. I don't know how to Walk the Wind.

Find your child.

She's dead. She's dead. She's dead. Tarian couldn't stop the words from tumbling over and over and over, spinning her around, shredding her heart into a thousand tiny pieces that scattered in the water. Hair floated into her face and she tore at it, and the dress. Memory flooded her, of the birth, the Stulos, her sister, the baby, Macari, Lasair, First Mother, the baby. The baby.

I never gave her a name.

Regret, for the lost opportunity. Yet another thing to add to the long list of things she should have done. Wished she'd done. Misery stole into the empty place where her heart had been. Despair, and longing, coupled with a need so intense it frightened her. All she wanted now was to forget it all. The memories hurt, seared themselves into every pore. Her palm itched and burned, her chest throbbed, her soul ached.

Walk, Keeper.

She shook her head. *Walk.* Stupid suggestion. How could she? She drifted in an endless sea, where even the Ancients had forsaken her. Where her power meant nothing. Where her daughter had lived, if only for a moment. There was no way to walk here. Only drift with the tide, the whim of the sea.

But I've never been one to drift. And this isn't my sea.

The lack of dolphins disturbed the deep anguish, stirred a spark of hope. This wasn't a real ocean. She didn't need power to breathe. There were no fish. No dolphins. This wasn't real.

It's not real.

It's a memory.

Thinking back she realized that's what all the scenes had been, memories. Sitting at PJ's, the black sand beach, the odd receiving hall, the white sand beach, the ocean. *All that has been is written on the Wind.* But it wasn't obvious exactly when those things had happened. She'd seen all levels of the past. Not just seen, *witnessed.*

And there in the forest, connected with someone with bright, glowing, fiery eyes.

Lasair.

He'd been there, spying on the couple. And he'd seen her. *How?*

Tarian scratched at an itch in the center of her palm, trying to wrap her mind around the problem. She faced a puzzle, the pieces spread so far and wide that she couldn't see the straight edges. Couldn't put the pieces into place. Something was missing. A corner piece, or maybe the center. It was like she drifted in the middle of a storm, with chaos all around.

Chaos.

She closed her eyes, realizing at last why she should walk, and not drift. *I'm on the Wind, and I'm trapped in the scenes. I need to get out of the scenes.*

But Wind Walking wasn't one of her talents.

Her palm burned and she dug at it with her fingernails, irritated. When she looked she saw the mark for Air still there, and it throbbed, an angry red welt. Ruarc's mark, which he'd given her before she entered the Wind the first time. Could she use it?

The artifact was gone. Surely the mark had no use anymore. Still. It throbbed, and itched. Hope flared. If she could…

She closed her eyes, and held out her hand, palm up. She pictured the key as she'd seen it in the Wind, every inch of it. The white glow. The translucent color, the shape that seemed to shift as she watched. The way it drifted suspended in the Wind, surrounded by chaos but somehow not moving with it. It had been in the center of the Wind, outside of the stream and outside of any scenes. That's where she needed to go. She tried to picture every last detail, even the blurred colors.

The image she created grew, expanded and filled the space around her, pushing back the ocean. A long, white-hot filament burst forward from her palm into the sea, chasing away the darkness, filling her closed eyes with light that threatened to burn the retinas. She winced, but kept the trace going. She'd never tried to travel and track at the same time. It might not work. She pushed harder, willing the trail of magic to pull her along to the wherever the artifact was now.

The track tightened, solidified. She kept a tight hold on it, even as she spun in circles so fast she wanted to throw up. Suddenly, the spinning stopped, though her head continued on the revolutions.

Disoriented, she opened her eyes. In front of her, an endless black sky dotted with millions of points of light. The darkest, starry night she'd ever seen. Her feet moved as though walking on pavement, but touched nothing solid. The trace she'd been trying to execute drifted in front of her, a lazy white light that wavered on the Wind.

The urge to follow that line powered her forward. She needed to *see*.

Remember your child. Remember your promise. Remember your destination. Remember your journey.

The sweet smell of jasmine carried the words. Tarian breathed it in, let it out with a sigh and the words "I remember."

But she's dead. Does the destination even matter anymore? I've failed her.

No answer came to her on the Wind. This answer, it seemed, she'd have to find for herself.

30

Reluctantly, Tarian dropped her trace. She'd managed to get out of the endless scenes of history, but not out of the Cosaerie itself. She hovered just on the edge, in the center of the black night, and tried desperately to figure out what to do next. Nobody to ask for help or guidance. No way to connect with Water or call on the dolphins for aid.

Alone.

The stars winked, as though at a private joke.

Wind roared, leaving her untouched in the center. The calm in the storm. She watched the stream whirl around, mixing colors from scenes here and there.

She held out a hand to let her fingers trace a path in the Wind. Power rippled, sending tingles up her arms. Something brushed her fingertips. She ignored it. If she spread her fingers, it created different patterns. Fascinated, she watched eddies of color form around the space between her fingers. If she pushed her fingers together, it popped a bubble. She did this a few times, experimenting.

Fire. Waits.

The words, forced into her brain through her contact with the Wind, made her wince. They brought with them a reminder that she'd made a promise. An Agreement. One more Stulos remained to be broken. And while it waited, Lasair held the weight of the world on his shoulders. He couldn't leave the Between as long as the split remained intact. He'd been trapped there for thousands of years. Waiting. Guarding. She couldn't imagine that expanse of time, alone. She'd felt his longing, and his hope, with each step of her journey. If she didn't finish, he'd never be free. Guilt stirred within her as she considered the burden and strain he must be under.

Realization slapped her in the face. The world hasn't collapsed. Yet.

She could still keep her Agreement. Her baby died in the destruction of Air. Would that death be in vain?

No.

Tarian gathered her thoughts and pain like a blanket. She'd honor the child by completing the Agreement. The world would continue, because of her. Tarian knew in the private spaces of her mind that she'd never have been able to break Air without the baby and her amazing, powerful, unusual gift. She'd amplified the magic around her and returned it, tenfold. *That,* more than anything, was why the Stulos exploded. First Mother had no idea. The baby couldn't be used to create. She was built to destroy.

Destruction is creation. Isn't that what Lasair said?

One more. Just one more and the planes would unite. Magic would return to the human world.

So will the daemon and every other magical creature that's been hidden.

But we can deal with that. We'll have magic.

Shoving her grief into a corner of the empty space that used to be her heart, she walled it off. She'd deal with it, after. For now, she had a promise to keep.

Decision made, Tarian felt a renewed sense of purpose, which was instantly confounded by an insurmountable problem. She had no idea how to get out of the Wind, in order to get to the Fire Stulos. And once there, she'd no idea how to break it on her own.

One thing at a time. First things first. How the hell do I get out of here?

The blast of destruction had forced her into the Wind. That, and she had a feeling perhaps the Shee had helped her find the way here. She'd seen the girl in white just before everything turned chaotic. Whatever the reason, she'd have to somehow reverse the trip.

Walk through scenes? She intently rejected the idea. She'd been lost, with only vague memories of why she was there. It would do her no good to get lost again and forget where she'd been going.

Remember your destination. That's what the girl had said. The Shee had been sending her hints, she just hadn't understood them. And for some reason, they didn't sit still long enough to hold a conversation.

A tickle at the back of her neck alerted her to a presence she knew. When she held a trace on someone, she usually felt this tingle when they were close. She kept loose traces on everyone in her immediate circle. Alex, Daric, Calliope. Though she hadn't felt them since she'd crossed into the Between, they remained active. And still out of reach. It wasn't any of them.

Who's there? She sent the thought out, not expecting an answer. Focused on the tingle, the feeling of *familiar*, and tried to identify it that way. No signature scent reached her but after a moment she knew who it had to be. It felt light as spring sunshine.

Macari.

Tarian turned in place, searching for the daemon. All she found were winking pinpoints of starry light in an endless black void, and the roar of the Wind around it. She closed her eyes to shut it all out and focus on a trace.

The ping returned to her so strong, it was as though the daemon stood right on top of her. Tarian opened her eyes to find Macari staring back at her, inches away from her face.

Macari grinned. She touched Tarian's hand with her own. *Miss me?*

Tarian opened her mouth to reply, then realized she didn't need to. *The baby! What happened to the baby?*

Macari's grin faltered. *I'm not sure. She was pulled from my arms in the chaos. I took us to the Wind as the Stulos released, but the backlash was incredible and I only just now found the center. She could be drifting.*

Tarian bit her lip and shook her head. *She's not here. I can't feel her. She...* The shield around her heart and despair at the loss of her child threatened to break.

Macari squeezed her hand. *I'm sure she's alive. She wasn't caught in the blast. She WAS the blast. I've never seen anything like it. She just took and took and took and then as I stepped into the Wind, she released. She didn't...it wasn't an explosion. Not like you think. Whatever it was, she caused it. The force knocked us back into the chaotic portion of the Wind, that's all. I'm sure she made it, Tarian. I'm sure of it.*

The confidence in the daemon's mind tone eased Tarian's fear to a manageable level. Even if it weren't true, she could hold onto it as hope. If the baby were here on the Wind, she could find her.

Macari shook her head. *We have a problem. The pressure...I've seen it through windows I opened as I worked my way to the center. The world is in chaos.*

Macari squeezed her hand again and sent image after image into Tarian's mind. Waterspouts in the desert. Earthquakes on both sides of the magical divide. Some of the Erckling crossed over to the human plane. People screaming. Buildings crumbling. Tarian winced, wishing the images would stop.

It won't last much longer. I can feel him. Lasair's trying to keep everything together, using the Between to soften the blows, but he's losing the battle. Macari patted the artifact lodged in her naval.

Tarian nodded. *Time to keep my promise. How do I get out of here? Can you take me?*

Macari considered, her head tilted to one side as they drifted in their black void. *No. There's no way to tether to another. Each walker must forge their way alone.*

Tarian's stomach sank.

Macari smiled encouragingly. *But I can teach you how. You are Air as much as water. You can do this. You must move with intention, each step deliberate, concentrating on your goal. The end destination. Let go of yourself and your need to control anything else. That's why I dance. To let go of myself and fully connect with the Wind. You must become one with the past in order to move to the future. Let it flow through you. You can't live in the past. You can't change it, but it can change you. And you can use it to step forward. Does this make sense?*

Tarian frowned. *No. This doesn't make any sense. All this talk of past and future. What's that got to do with getting out of here?*

Macari stomped a foot on non-existent ground. *All that has been is written on the Wind. Look around, Tari. See it. Everything that has ever happened, since the dawn of the world, since the first Ancients arrived, it's all here. It forms the Wind. Air is the element of communication. Don't you see? All of this history, it forms a link to the present and future. To get out, tap into the link. Focus on your destination. If you've seen it, you can go there. Choose somewhere you know.*

Tarian bit her lip. *I don't need to go somewhere I know. I need to go to the Fire Stulos.*

Macari stared into her eyes, as if she could force understanding through her pupils. *Have you seen it?*

Tarian thought about it. The First Stulos, in the center of a sunken caldera, surrounded by lava. *Yes. Sort of.*

Macari squeezed her hand. *Then go there. Link to it. Focus on it. That's how we travel, Keeper. That's how air flows. Join the stream, focus on the destination, let the journey form around you and through you. If you keep it in mind, ignore everything else, you'll get there. I'll try to follow, but I can't lead you and I can't pull you out. This is a path everyone must forge on their own. The Shee have been released. I'll ask them to help me find the baby. She's so strong. They'll be able to find her.*

Tarian swallowed a sudden lump in her throat. *I'm not a dancer.*

Macari grinned. *No. You're a fighter. You have your way, I have mine. Use it. Good luck. I'll see you on the outside.*

Macari let go of Tarian's hand, raised her arms, and danced away into the roaring stream around them.

I'm a fighter. Tarian thought about that. Fighting wouldn't help, here. She couldn't use her body to muscle her way through the Wind, even if she weren't still heavy from pregnancy. Wind was impossible to fight, physically.

But before a fight, I always meditate. It was how she connected to her own power in a deep way, and how she initiated traces on people. She closed her eyes, and took steadying breaths. Tried desperately to calm her mind and racing thoughts. To forget she was trapped, that her baby might be dead, might be alive, that she had no idea what had happened to the others she loved, that the world hung suspended on the brink of collapse while she drifted here on the Wind.

Breathe.
Empty thoughts.
Breathe.
Let it go.
Breathe.

Everything swirled around her, making it difficult to focus. Realizing complete calm was probably not possible, instead she substituted focus and purpose. She pictured Fire in her mind. A flame that she let grow into the Stulos, then supplied the surrounding landscape. The lava. The spurts of fire. The Stulos. She focused on it, and let go of her power, sending it out into the void as she would a trace. Felt it get swept aside by the Wind. Focused harder.

Breathe.
In.
Out.

She slowed the breath, taking long beats of pause in between. Placed herself in the scene. She stood, in her mind, facing the Stulos. Her destination. She noticed the spurts of flame dancing around it and realized they were Ancients. They fed this Stulos as surely as the dolphins fed the water, with power and chaos.

She saw them, then. Really *saw* them. Unlike the other Ancients, these fed off the Stulos, and dispersed the power back into it. They pulled, then pushed. They took, then gave. A steady in and out, pressure, release. Fanning the flame. A living, breathing thing. Not a column of power, a personification of something that existed all around them and through them.

Creation.

Tarian let her power drift to them, join with them. Wrapped around the fire, she used her Air energy to fan the flame. She let go of herself then, and joined the Wind.

31

Tarian stepped out of the Wind onto a small black rock in the middle of a pool of molten lava. Heat engulfed her, drawing sweat out of every pore. It rolled down her forehead and the sides of her face, dripping onto the hot rock. The black robe Ruarc had given her clung to her skin, and she felt her hair hanging limp down her back as though she'd just stepped out of the ocean. It struck her that this place felt oddly familiar. The rocks were black porous stones, like sponges. Like those of her home.

In front of her, the last remaining Stulos burned with the energy of a thousand suns. It was Fire, in every sense of the word. It was a giant column of liquid lava reaching toward the sky with hungry fingers.

Around the Stulos, flames flared up from pools of lava to feed it. As she watched them she realized they weren't flames at all. *Ancients.* Odd creatures, with more fire than body. They leapt from pool to pool, forming, dissolving, reforming. Their bodies didn't have structure. They didn't look human, or like anything she'd ever seen before. At best, they appeared to be what Water and Fire would look like if they procreated. No eyes. No hands. Like the flame on a candle but more solid. She wondered if she touched them, would she hear voices like she did the Caraigg? *Or would they simply burn me to a crisp before I had a chance to find out?*

The small part of her that controlled fire found joy in these surroundings. But it was a fraction of where her main talents lay, and next to the Stulos it was nothing but a lump of coal.

She touched the medallion, and heard a dolphin cry in response. Reassured in her own power, Tarian turned slowly, surveying the rest of the area. Pools and tendrils of lava wrapped around black lumpy rocks. All of it was encased in a giant bowl with sides that extended so far up they'd be impossible to climb.

An active volcano.

She sniffed, and caught the scent of sulfur and acrid smoke, and the slightest trace of salt. *The ocean is nearby.*

No vegetation survived the heat of this area, but she hadn't expected any.

No sign of Macari.

Why hadn't the daemon made it out of the Corsaerie? She was far more experienced.

Tarian turned a bit more, looking for the daemon girl. Flames continued to dance from pool to pool, aimed in her general direction. They teased the rock she perched on, as if saying hello. On instinct she bowed to them.

"Lasair sent me." She felt foolish saying the words out loud, but it seemed to excite the flames. Some flared higher, others twisted and leapt faster.

Those closest to her paused a fraction of a second, then leapt away. She watched them go, turning in place to trace their path.

Her gaze stopped when it found another shape balanced on a small rock in the distance. She expected to see Macari, but the shape wasn't right. She squinted, then sucked in a breath and hissed. *First Mother!*

Once again First Mother held a baby in her arms. Excitement and relief flared in her. *She lived! She made it! Macari was right.* Tarian started to move, halting at the edge of the rock. Lava surrounded her. There was no path to walk, no rock to hop to. She'd have to travel, if she wanted to get close to the woman. And any travel portal used Air as its basis. The daemon could trap her in the Wind or do something worse.

First Mother shouted over the roar of flames. "Did you think it so easy, to use my own element against me? You think I'm like a human, weak?"

Tarian shook her head, eyes fixated on the baby. She looked alive, whole, unharmed. The Air Artifact was no longer lying on her chest. The baby slept, seemingly unaware of the heat.

"If you've harmed her..."

First Mother took a step and appeared on another rock closer to the Stulos. "What I do, I do for all. You, with all your abilities, originated with the Mayfanta. You wouldn't understand. It's not within you to see the right path. And this," she glanced down at the baby. "Her essence screams Mayfanata. And fire. *Fire.* She connects with the Ancients. They accept her, so they accept me. She's meant to be here, and meant to feed the Stulos. It is her destiny. I am saving her, from you. From your inability to see her true purpose. From a selfish world."

"You're insane. Twisted beyond belief, if you think killing an innocent child will do *anything* good."

First Mother took another step, carrying the baby two rocks closer to the Stulos. The Stulos raged at their approach. Blue in the center, red and orange around the edges. "Surely you noticed, Keeper, that the Dulra agreed with me. Balance has been disrupted. And by now you must realize what it means. Chaos rains down, taking both sides with it. They must have told you. Tell me, *Keeper*, did they offer you an Agreement?"

Tarian started at the words, surprised. "Were you eavesdropping?"

"And what did they offer you, to destroy the world? Immortality? A chance to remake it as you see fit? What was your price?" First Mother took another step closer to the Stulos.

Tarian winced, sucking in a breath at the thought of her child being so near the Stulos. Only a few steps remained separating them. Though her daughter showed no signs of stress, First Mother's robes hung limp and damp around her from sweat. Her hair, usually in a neat bun, lay in a tangled heap, with strands escaping their confines. Tarian watched the sweat pour down the sides of the woman's face. Her Agreement with the Balance Court was to save the world, not break it. They wanted her to ease the pressure, to release magic so that the world could continue forward.

But First Mother saw that as a death sentence. *Why?*

"I asked for nothing. Don't you get it? If I don't break this Stulos, the world will collapse. We're all gone. Everything is gone. You. Your daughter. My daughter. Everyone. Why can't you see *that?*" Tarian looked around for a path closer to the woman, and found a rock a few feet away that might work. It would barely hold her, but if she were steady on her feet she could leap to it.

She didn't dare portal. Couldn't use Air. Heat pressed in on her. She swayed, trying to keep her balance when all she wanted was to let her knees buckle. It felt like an oven, and she was a loaf of bread.

"Of course, the selfish always think the ends justify their means. They always think they do what is right. But I know the truth. If the Stulos aren't renewed, then the planes collapse and destroy everything. There'll be nothing left but chaos. But that's what you want, isn't it? You like chaos. All humans thrive on it." First Mother spit the words, one lip bent upward in disgust. "This child is just the beginning. Can't you feel it? Can't you feel *her?*"

Tarian nodded, knowing the woman skirted a fine line between reality and insanity. She did feel her daughter, every wonderful piece of her signature. She was amazing, unique, and wholly new. A blend of Air, Water, Fire, and Earth. All four elements. And a powerful talent that Tarian didn't even begin to understand, one she'd exhibited in the womb. The ability to draw energy from everyone around her, to pull it inside, and then send it out in ever increasing strength. And her scent, a combination of burning wood, turned earth, and fresh salt air.

If...*when*...the girl reached her true potential, she'd be an unstoppable force.

"She's a baby. Just a baby." Tarian whispered, thinking fast. *Get to the child, get her out of this crazy woman's arms.* Options flashed through her mind. She could call Water, a natural counter to Air. But how? It wouldn't be enough to simply throw a jet of water at the woman, with all the heat in the area it would probably erupt as steam. And it would hurt the baby. If she rushed her, tackled the woman physically, most likely she'd run into the invisible trap the woman surely held around her. And First Mother might drop the baby in the process.

Any move she took would hurt the baby.

Desperate, Tarian searched for some answer. Some way through.

Break the Stulos.

If she completed her task, her promise to break all of them, releasing magic to the world…it would be too late for the First Mother to use the baby to rebuild them. She needed a Stulos to grow another. Without it, she'd be undone. But she still held the child in her arms. Would she relinquish her hold on the baby if there was no further use for her?

Seriously doubt it. No, she'll kill her. Just because. The unknown scares her to death, and the baby is the embodiment of the unknown.

I need to stall her. Think, Tari. How to break this Stulos?

It was down to her. Alone. Just her, and the Water Artifact. *How can I do this alone, when the others took so much? It's not possible. It can't be done.*

But it has to be. I can't fail her. Or them.

Tarian licked her lips, wishing she had more moisture in her mouth. Everything had gone dry. Even her sweat had stopped pouring. Time was running out. If she didn't act soon, she'd die of dehydration before she got the chance.

First Mother took another step closer to the Stulos, a manic look in her eyes.

"Stop!" Frantic, Tarian jumped forward. She landed on the rock next to her and nearly toppled over into the lava. Around her, two of the Fire Ancients twirled and danced as though anxious to get a taste of her. "Don't go any closer. I'll…."

"You'll what, *Keeper*? Stop me from saving the world? I don't think so. I would give anything to save it. Would you do the same?" First Mother panted. Her crazed eyes looked from Tarian, to the baby, to the Stulos, back to the baby. "Your sacrifice is a child. One child, to save the world. Is that so great a price? Mine has been so much more."

"What have you sacrificed?" Tarian shouted. "You use someone else's child. What have you given up for the good of all, First Mother? Show me what makes you worthy of the title *Mother*." Her voice poured every ounce of derision and frustration and scorn for this woman who couldn't, wouldn't *see*.

"More than you can possibly fathom. You who have lived so little. You *do not see*."

"Don't you throw those words at me. You don't get to use those words. You're *blind!*" Tarian screamed. "Blind, if you think using a baby on an impossible mission will change or save anything. You can't do it, *Mother*. It can't be done. You know it can't be done. The only hope now is to end this. Break this Stulos so we can all move forward. All of us." Tarian stared at her baby, heart in her throat. "This world isn't just for us. It's for her."

First Mother stood straighter. With one hand she smoothed her impossibly matted hair. The other gripped the baby tightly, who whimpered and wiggled in protest. The baby opened her eyes, staring around.

Tarian gasped and looked for another rock to move to. In front of her, flames danced and sparked, and lava melted away to reveal a stone. She stepped to it, then to another, and another. First Mother's eyes widened as Tarian moved closer. Tarian felt the force of Air she gathered around her like a cloak. She pulled it tight, weaving it into something Tarian couldn't even begin to follow.

The baby began to cry, her tiny hands wriggling free of the blanket. Tarian screamed in frustration. "You're scaring her!"

First Mother smiled, an expression that did not meet her eyes. "No, Keeper, you are. I will soothe her pain. In a moment, it will end, and she will join the elements. She will be so much more than she is now. I grant her eternal life, and the chance to ensure our survival. She will be remembered for her sacrifice. Which is more than I can say for you." First Mother turned away, toward the Stulos. Tarian couldn't see the baby any longer but she could hear her. *Feel* her.

The child had grasped the energy from the Stulos, and the two were pulling on one another. It was a cosmic tug of war, fought by Fire and child. Pressure built around them, filling the caldera with so much power that rocks began to lift, dripping lava. The rock Tarian stood on rose a few feet, and she nearly fell. Struggling to keep her balance, she lost sight of First Mother for a moment. Fire Ancients danced around her, forming a circle.

"Help me. Help me save her. Help me break this thing. I can't do this on my own." Her voice shook as she said the words. She had no tears to cry.

The Ancients flickered and flared higher, moving into each other until they formed a tall fiery pillar about two feet in diameter. It waved in front of her, then formed a platform close enough for her to jump to. Tarian leapt onto it, crouched low as it started to move toward the Stulos. As it moved, a clear, familiar vision passed through her mind. Of a woman, stepping into the flames. She shook her head to dispel it.

As she drew closer she saw First Mother stood on a platform of Air directly next to the Stulos. Her face glowed in the blue orange of the power column. She held the baby in both hands, outstretched, as though offering a sacrifice to a fiery god. *Just like the people in the cave.*

"Faster. Hurry!" She shouted as she gathered focus in Water. Hoping a blast would at least distract First Mother long enough for her to get close. To maybe grab the baby. Or to stop the energy weaving. Another second and First Mother would complete her task. Tarian saw a web forming around the baby. It shone an odd white-gold light, encasing her in a cocoon. The baby wiggled and cried. The Stulos bulged and grew, flaming higher into the sky, dark red thunderclouds forming over it. *If there's a hell, it looks like this.*

"Let the renewal begin." First Mother cried out, and with a shove of power, lifted the baby on a cushion of air.

Tarian watched, stricken, as the baby moved closer and closer to the Stulos. As the flames engulfed the child, a sob wrenched her throat and tore her heart. With a scream she threw herself off the platform, at the First Mother. They landed in a heap on the rocks below, rolling toward the lava with frightening speed.

First Mother created a field of air around the edge of the rock which stopped their momentum. They both crashed into it and lay, panting on the hot stone. Tarian kicked at her. First Mother laughed, a maniacal sound. "You're too late. It's done."

Tarian rose to her feet and turned to see the Stulos had doubled in size and continued to expand. In her heart, she knew two things. The Stulos was about to explode, and her child would be destroyed with it if she wasn't already. This wouldn't be a gentle shove into the Wind guarded by a friendly daemon. The child went alone into Fire, and it would explode into nothing but ash. Nobody could survive this heat. This chaos. Nobody.

But what if she did? She was wrapped in a net of Air.

The ember of hope was enough. Tarian turned to the First Mother, who still lay on the ground. "Tell me, First *Mother*. What would you personally do for the sake of the world? For your child? Think of Macari. Would you walk through fire for her?" First Mother's gaze faltered and fell. "So maybe it's not the Mayfanata who are selfish, after all."

Tarian turned to the platform created by the Fire Ancients. She stepped on it, facing the Stulos. She willed it to move forward, to take her inside. As she neared the edge of the Stulos, she felt it siphon every bit of energy and power she possessed. It took, and took, and took, and she gave. The dolphins cried, and she gave. The medallion burned, singeing her skin, and she gave. The smell of burnt hair, of flesh, filled her nose. She focused on her daughter, on the signature she knew had to be there somewhere. Hoped was there. She steeled her nerves.

Held her breath.
Let go.
And stepped into the Stulos.

32

Fire closed around Tarian and embraced her. Pain forged a path through every atom of her being. She struggled to maintain her focus, keeping need foremost in her mind.

Break the Stulos. Save the baby. Break the Stulos.

As her flesh melted, a bolt of pure light seared her chest. Dolphins cried in the distance. Her thin hold on sanity stretched to a breaking point.

Deep inside, she knew she wasn't going to make it. She'd die here, burned by the flames and chaos. How could she disperse the energy this last Stulos held? Now she was part of it, and it consumed her. To disperse it meant to destroy herself with it. And her daughter.

A spark flared white in the sea of red, orange and blue. She sensed it, even if she couldn't focus on the source. White. The absence of all colors.

Or the combination.

Instinctively, she turned. Drifted closer to it. In front of her, flames leapt and twisted, forming a figure that resolved itself into human form. Tarian gaped. *Lasair.*

His eyes flashed as he bowed his head in greeting. She floated before him, flesh melting, not understanding why he was there. She'd failed. Hadn't she? He should still be trapped in the Between. She hadn't done enough. Hadn't been enough. Her daughter was lost. The world was lost.

She shuddered as a wracking sob wrenched her heart out of her throat.

Lasair looked up, extending his arms toward her. He offered a bundle of light.

Keeper.

The light beckoned, and she obeyed. It spoke to her, drew her, *needed* her.

Fire seared her bones but she answered the call. Her hands reached out to touch the light, to take it into her arms. As she took it from Lasair, he dissolved into flames.

Release. He sighed, and evaporated.

Tarian cradled the light he'd offered, stunned as it slowly morphed into a small infant with eyes like the sea after a storm. She stared at every beautiful inch of her.

My baby.

Tears fell and evaporated in the intense heat. It didn't matter. Nothing mattered now but this. Her child, in her arms, at last.

The baby giggled, stretched her fingers out toward Tarian's face, and blasted her with power beyond anything she'd even experienced or imagined. White light seared her eyes and mind, and she lost her fragile hold on reality. The world exploded in a shower of white, red, orange, blue, and gold.

33

Cold gulped Tarian down a long throat to a pit enveloping her in white frost.

For a while, she felt nothing else. Not even pain. Just numbing, eternal, cold. She drifted on an iceberg of it, naked. It pressed in on all sides, but it failed to impact the ache in her heart. She had to be dead. The baby, too. This must be the Beyond, and the Beyond was terrifyingly cold. If she could feel her teeth, she was sure they'd be chattering. No child could live here. No child could survive that fire and explosion of magic, no matter how powerful she might be, no matter how special, no matter how much Tarian wished it otherwise. She'd failed. Failed to save society, failed to save magic, and failed to save her baby. Despair held her in the palm of its hand and squeezed.

After a few moments the iceberg morphed into something hard and cool. She ran her hand along it without opening her eyes. It felt smooth, like marble. Cold, but not frigid like ice. She was in the Beyond and it was made of marble.

"Keeper Tarian A'Marie Maitea Xannon, your side of the Agreement is fulfilled."

The words drifted past, disjointed. They should mean something. They did mean something. Keeper. She was Keeper. Keeper of the Dolphin Throne and the House of Xannon. The title circled around her head. It meant something, to be Keeper.

Agreement. Fulfilled?

Tarian shifted her head, aware of the sharp stabs in her sides, her shoulders. Her knees were on fire. Odd, given the cold. The skin on her chest burned. Her breasts stuck to the marble surface. She pried them off with shaking hands, trying hard to ignore the way the tender skin stretched and then snapped away.

She lifted her head and opened her eyes. Better to face whatever it was than grovel on the floor, naked. She found two Balance Court members staring at her. No emotion. No judgment. They simply waited, their hair a riot of colors and their faces an exact mirror of each other. Next to them one of the Caraigg bounced, his wide eyes blinking at her.

The sense that something *waited* filled her. Her thoughts refused to register anything beyond the two words, and the notion that her baby had died. Agreement, fulfilled. Baby, dead. The words grabbed her heart and squeezed.

Fulfilled.

She'd done it. She'd broken the last Stulos.

Not me. The baby. Oh, the baby.

She gulped down the lump in her throat. She needed to realize. Accept. The baby was gone. She'd died in that flame as First Mother had intended, though the outcome certainly wasn't what First Mother had wanted. Not if the Agreement was fulfilled. Her heart hardened and a spark of anguish deep inside her chest fed a pearl of hate. Hate for the woman who dared to use the title *Mother*.

"Keeper. Are you ready?" The gentle voices asked in unison, high and low pitches blending into perfect harmony. Neither kind nor hostile. Balanced.

"For what?" Tarian tried to get to her knees, but instantly regretted it. They were bruised and scraped raw. Her entire body felt sunburned. She looked down. She was naked. Completely, bare-assed naked, with boobs and a stomach still too big for her body drooping toward the floor and red, raw skin. The dolphin medallion remained embedded in her chest like some sort of three-dimensional tattoo. Her first instinct was to cover herself.

Shame filtered through the grief, but didn't disturb it much.

It didn't matter. Her soul lay stripped bare by the loss of her child. It just didn't matter what they did to her anymore. Standing naked in front of the Court wouldn't change the worst moment of her life. She pushed with her hands and got to a standing position, wincing a bit as different body parts protested.

When she stood fully erect, she glanced around. What she saw astounded her.

Daric. Alex. Macari. All stood to one side, waiting, with a mixture of expressions ranging from concern and worry to, of all things, pride. None stepped forward to help her, though the look of longing on Daric's face told her he'd like to. Macari held a bundle of towels in her arms but didn't offer them. Her expression was worried, hesitant. Nothing like the confident girl Tarian had met on the beach.

First Mother, her face a mixture of defiance, anger, and defeat. She stood closer to the flame in the center, back stiff, hands clasped in front, lips pressed tightly together. A pace away, Ruarc, a half smile lifting his lips as his eyes took in her naked body.

Tarian tried to breathe. A sob forced its way out in a guttural sort of growl. She'd survived, but the baby hadn't. And now they were all here to witness her failure. She hadn't been able to protect her own child. What kind of mother failed her child like that? She should never have been Scion. Never have been Keeper. She'd warned them. She was only good at silly things. Tracking. Fighting. Swimming in the ocean. Avoiding responsibility. Not this. Not motherhood. Not leadership. Not anything useful.

"Is Keeper ready?" The voices echoed around the nearly empty hall.

Tarian sobbed. Punishment was surely coming. And she deserved it. She nodded.

"Keeper Tarian A'Marie Maitea Xannon, House of Xannon, balance has been questioned by First Mother of Benata Court. First Mother contends that the Scion was conceived using daemon energy and that such conception disrupts the balance of the Court system.

"The Balance Court declares that balance has, indeed, been disrupted, but not as claimed. The building of four Stulos, though agreed upon and faithfully bargained for by all Ancients and daemon, set in motion events that resulted in the current imbalance of the natural order. Only by their destruction would balance be restored, and magic be returned to the rightful place. Such was agreed upon, and has been accomplished."

The two Balance Court members turned toward First Mother. "Scion of the House of Xannon is a mixture of all planes and all elements and as such, in perfect harmony. Balance upset by the Court of Benata has been restored by the House of Xannon. A debt has been incurred. To such, the House of Xannon shall henceforth form a third Court, in order to stand for the thus far unrepresented Humans."

They turned back to Tarian as one unit, each with one arm outstretched. "Keeper Tarian A'Marie Maitea Xannon, do you accept the charge of Holder of the Human Court?"

Tarian gaped. Her mind worked furiously to process the words. She'd stopped listening at the words "Scion…perfect harmony." But the baby was dead. She had to be dead.

"Keeper, do you accept the charge?" They repeated, their tone neutral.

Daric tried to reach her but stopped as though some invisible force held him in place. His voice, deep with concern, reached her instead. "Tarian, they're asking if you'll lead the world. It's a pretty fair deal. You should probably say yes now."

"The baby…" she choked on the words.

"She's fine, Tarian. She's sleeping." Macari rocked the bundle in her arms, and shifted the cloth to reveal the sweet face of her baby girl. "She has quite the ability. She magnifies the power of those around her, sort of like an amplifier for sound. Or, that's what Alex says." Macari glanced sideways at Alex, who grinned and nodded. "She takes all the signals, boosts them, and then sends them out.

When you broke the last Stulos, everyone who was present for your Agreement was pulled here, to the Balance Court."

"She's…" Tarian couldn't stop the tears. She couldn't stop the sobs. Relief, pure relief, flooded her with every emotion she could name and many she couldn't. She stood there, naked, in front of friend and enemy, and marveled at how much it meant to simply know her daughter was safe at last.

"Keeper Tarian, do you accept the charge?"

Tarian looked at the faces. Daric, full of concern and love. Alex, the same expression with a mixture of something she couldn't put a name to. Macari, her eyes glinting with expectation and excitement. First Mother, angry, ashamed, or perhaps just frustrated. Ruarc, quite obviously pleased.

Tarian stood naked before them, stripped bare of all she had been before. Pretense washed away. Her old life, gone. A new one stretched in front of her, with her daughter and the faces she loved at the center of it. That, and a world infused with power they would not understand and would need a lot of help mastering. She'd done more than she ever would have imagined. And it wasn't over yet. She had a promise to make, and a promise to keep. She glanced at her daughter, nestled in Macari's arms, and knew she'd do anything if it meant a chance at life for her.

"Yes," she whispered.

"Such is decreed by the Balance Court."

Power rushed from the Dulra toward her, a blue wall of fire that washed over her and into her. It buried itself into the Water Artifact embedded in her skin. This time, it didn't burn. This time, it sang.

34

Several days later, Tarian lounged in an armchair next to her mother's bed, in her mother's suite of rooms, and stared with adoration at the girl in her arms. The infant suckled at Tarian's breast while one tiny hand flailed. Tarian caught it, tenderly stroking the fingers with fascination.

"I still can't believe it." She kept her voice low and soft. One thing she'd learned in the past few days was that the baby was easily distracted.

From the other side of the room, Daric looked away from a monitor broadcasting the news. "What?"

"We made this. She was just a thing invading my body and now…she's a person. I'll never get over it."

"You will. When she hits her teens and you argue over everything from hair to how long she swims in the ocean, you'll be over it."

Tarian grinned. "I don't think so. Wonder who's more stubborn?"

"You. Hands down." Daric flashed a wicked grin at her. "I can already tell she has a bit of Calli in her. She has you wrapped around her fingers."

"And toes." Tarian glanced at the monitor. "Anything new?"

Daric shook his head. "Not in the last few hours, no. I think the media is having a hard time keeping up."

She frowned, the innocent moment shattered by reality. "I've made a real mess, haven't I?"

Daric shrugged. "Change is always messy."

"I don't know how you do it."

"What?"

"Stay so optimistic. Look at that." She pointed at the newscast. A worried reporter spoke rapidly while behind her, thick angry red clouds boiled. "Magic is falling everywhere. They have no idea what it is or what it'll do. It's complete chaos, and it's my fault."

"Wouldn't say all your fault. You were asked to do it."

"I agreed."

Daric crossed the room to kneel in front of her. "Relax, Tari. You're scaring her."

The baby had begun to protest Tarian's tightening grip. *Shit. I didn't even notice. Some mom I am.* She took a deep breath and relaxed. The baby gulped and burbled, then went back to suckling. The baby's gaze rested on Tarian's face as though she knew exactly what was going on, and exactly why her mother was tense.

"It's spooky how wise her eyes are." Tarian shifted to ease the pressure on her arms.

"Well, she's seen a lot in her life." Daric's eyes twinkled.

"Too much." Tarian agreed. She looked back at the monitor. "I have to get out there. Those poor people."

"There's not a lot we can do right now, Tari. We talked about this. All of us agreed we had to let the magic fall before we could do anything. Right now, it's just a vicious thunderstorm."

"And earthquakes. And tidal waves. And…"

"Point is, we don't have the manpower to do anything about it right now. Two worlds are joining. That's bigger than all of us, human, daemon, or Ancient. But we can put plans in place to mop up after. Fact is, there's no way to keep it from happening even if we wanted to. Which I still say, we don't." Daric squeezed her knees. "You wanted the world to know magic. Now it does."

"Yeah, but at what cost?" She started to rock, but whether it was to soothe the baby or herself she wasn't sure.

"No good thing comes free, Tari. We'll get through this. *They* will get through this. And you have a lot of people in place to guide them. Tomorrow, we'll make plans for the transition. Next week, Calli has scheduled meetings every day to coordinate education resources and an outreach to the human government."

"Former human, you mean."

"We're all human. We just all have magic, now. It's a good thing, Tari. A very good thing. Sometimes good things are a little scary at first, but it doesn't change the good part."

Daric looked significantly at the baby, then flicked a hand at the monitor to turn it off. Tarian protested but he shook his head. "No more news for you. Time to focus on us."

Tarian groaned. "I don't think my body is ready for that, Daric."

Daric patted her thigh. "I meant, all of us as a family. Specifically, how all of your family is waiting for you to do something. There's a contingent of women upstairs who might riot if you don't. Your sister is leading it. She's scary."

Tarian wrinkled her lips in mock confusion. "I don't know what you mean."

"The baby needs a name, Tari."

"Now?"

Daric kissed her on the cheek. "I'm going for coffee. When I get back, have a name ready. No more stalling."

Daric winked and left, closing the door softly behind him. She grinned in spite of her worried mood. It was moments like these that made her realize just how much she loved that man.

She continued to rock the baby as she surveyed their new surroundings. She'd moved into her mother's suite of rooms, below the House of Xannon, after she'd returned from the Balance Court. She couldn't think of any safer place to keep the baby. Surrounded by rock, imbued with the power of thousands of years and countless women who'd lived here. The emergency escape tunnel to the ocean available steps away, just in case.

She glanced at the window. Outside, the Old Woman hovered, her old eyes winking as she surveyed mother and child. After a head bob, the Ancient moved slowly out of sight, having checked in on the baby as she now did every evening. The rest of the pod drifted by as well, nodding their own greetings. At least two were always present, now, just outside the window. Watching. Protecting. Tarian's bond to them strengthened and renewed every time she communicated with them. She smiled at her guardians, grateful to have their steady presence.

In the corner, a snuffling sound announced the arrival of one of the Caraigg. It crossed the room to touch her hand with solid, rock paws. *Perimeter is secure. We boost safety. No daemon may pass through stone of House without permission. Keeper, rest well.*

He jumped and dissolved down into the stone floor. It looked like rock melting into rock, and always fascinated her. Her information network took their promise seriously, and gave her daily updates on the status of the House, or any other information they thought useful for the Keeper to know. She smiled. *They are so happy to be free. At least I did one thing right.*

Tarian glanced down at the baby. *Maybe more than one thing.* She squeezed the baby's hand lightly, taking in the fresh powder scent that didn't quite mask the baby's personal signature. *Every day I smell something a bit different. But mostly she smells like a cozy fire on a rainy night.* Pleased with the description, she voiced it out loud. "Is that what you are? A cozy fire?"

The baby hiccupped her response but didn't stop feeding. "Hungry little thing."

Fire made her think of Lasair. She knew he'd been released when the last Stulos collapsed. The Between no longer existed. But she hadn't seen any evidence of him. She had a feeling he was out there, watching from the trees somewhere. She'd asked the Caraigg to be on the lookout for him, but so far they hadn't reported any sign of the Ancient. He was bound to turn up, sooner or later. Somehow, she felt a connection to him she didn't quite under-stand. Maybe later she'd track him, to ask about it. Maybe.

A small fire burned in a pit, casting a warm glow throughout the room. Her mother's things around her helped her feel better about the whole motherhood thing. Somehow, it seemed as though her mother were still guiding her. Except now she'd listen. Her lips twitched at the thought. *No I wouldn't. At least, not to her face.*

She was still staring at the fire when Daric returned.

"She's still eating?" Daric chuckled.

"I'm not sure." Tarian frowned at the baby. Her lips had fallen slack. "She fell asleep *while* eating. I've never done that."

"You sure about that?" Daric set two cups of coffee on the table next to Tarian and held out his hands. Tarian handed the sleeping infant to him and felt her body melt at the way he tenderly held the child in his arms and rocked her.

"So, Mama, time's up. Have you named her?"

"I already did. I just haven't said it out loud. It's such an important thing, isn't it? A name is everything. She'll be stuck with it, have to carry it and all that goes with it. Seems an awful lot to stick on a baby."

"I think I've said this before. It's just a name. No matter what you call her, she's going to be herself. You can call her 'baby' for the rest of her life, or Beth, or Hilda, or Dirtblossom, it won't change who she is."

Tarian raised an eyebrow. "Dirtblossom?"

Daric laughed. "Point is, it doesn't matter. Just give her a name already."

He was right, of course. Silly to worry about it, but she did. She worried about a lot of things that never used to bother her before. Just one more thing in a long list of things that had changed over the past year. Before, she'd felt powerful and confident. Now, her heart existed on the outside of her body, and most of her power did as well. The overload she'd carried around during the pregnancy vanished with the last Stulos. She'd returned to normal levels, which felt weak in comparison to that contained in an infant who now gripped her heart in a tiny balled fist. It was a lot to think about.

It would take planning and patience, to teach the girl to control her energy, to focus her strength, and to be ready for when the time inevitably came for her to use it. As magic settled on the world and two planes of existence became one, someone would have to lead the way. Teach those who'd never held magic to use it. Help those who were lost. Protect those who couldn't pull enough magic to protect themselves. Someone would have to show the way to balance it all, spark the flame of a new generation and new world.

Daric sat down on the edge of the bed, the baby cradled in his arms. "Dirtblossom it is then?"

Tarian laughed. "No. Ember. Her name is Ember."

Curious what happens next? Sign up for the newsletter at http://melindavan.com, which provides sneak peeks, behind the scenes looks and images that inspired the stories, plus advance notice of new releases.

I hope Promise of Magic took you away, if only for a short while, from the day to day stuff life heaps on us. The best way to ensure that authors continue to provide fun escapes is by leaving honest reviews at your vendors of choice. Your opinions matter to others who are trying to decide what to read. And they make authors do happy dances.

If you'd like to connect, you can find me at these places on the interwebs:

Website: http://melindavan.com
Facebook: https://www.facebook.com/MelindaVanLone
Twitter: @MelindaVan
Instagram: http://instagram.com/mvanlone

More in The House of Xannon

STRONGER THAN MAGIC
Tarian Xannon fights demons like the rest of us.
This time, the demon just happens to be real.

FINDING FLAME
All that has been is written on the wind. But
will the past save the future or destroy it?

PROMISE OF MAGIC
Some promises are deadly to keep.

TAKING EARTH
The whole world can change in 24 hours.

ELEMENTS OF MAGIC
Balance is hard, and sometimes deadly.

www.ingramcontent.com/pod-product-compliance
Lightning Source LLC
Chambersburg PA
CBHW061143170626
46809CB00003B/965